www.11-9.co.uk

Blue Poppies
Jonathan Falla

First published by

303a The Pentagon Centre
36 Washington Street
GLASGOW
G3 8AZ

Tel: 0141 204 1109
Fax: 0141 221 5363

E-mail: info@nwp.sol.co.uk
www.11-9.co.uk

11:9 is funded by the Scottish Arts
Council National Lottery Fund

ISBN 1 903238 37 4

Typeset in Utopia
11:9 series designed by Mark Blackadder

Printed in Finland by WS Bookwell

Cover image: Drolma from the Chumbi Valley, Western Tibet
© Pietro Francesco Mele/Tibet Images

For my parents,
who sent me out into the world

Part one

Before the Chinese burned Jyeko village, a tax-official from Lhasa stayed there. For years no revenue had reached the capital from that remote corner of Tibet's eastern province of Kham. So, in 1948, Lhasa sent its own collector. It was a four-month journey into ever-more resentful districts. But the zealous young man brought his wife and baby daughter, declared his intention to stay for as many years as it took – and was generally hated.

The Lhasan family rented a large but gloomy house in an alley off the village square. They had no true friends: the family was not welcome in the better houses, and the husband was too proud to consort with anyone else. So they lived in isolation. The tax official rode about on business with his nose in the air, intruding and questioning, making demands and enemies of the Khampa people. His young wife cared for her baby, the only living thing that returned her natural warmth. She did her best to spin out barely civil conversations with the market traders, and grew sad and quiet at home.

In their second autumn, they heard from Lhasa that her parents had died. Her husband announced that they should make a pilgrimage to a lamasery several days' travel to the north-west, near Chamdo. They took two yaks to carry the baggage, while husband and wife travelled on smartly tacked ponies. Their daughter, now a timorous toddler, rode in front of her mother.

Their departure from Jyeko was observed by a number of people who bore the tax-official no love. The little caravan left the village on the Lhasa trail, out past three votive shrines and then through a scattering of small vegetable gardens. Beyond these were stone animal pens. Here stood clumps of squat wind-twisted firs and larches, picketed in sparse pockets of soil and thrusting their roots under boulders for purchase against the gales. Beyond this point, no trees grew, only sorry little barley fields on terraces from which tons of rock had been lifted over centuries.

They moved steadily upstream towards the stark snowfields,

travelling alone. Turning north-west, they passed through the shadow of the Grey Ghost, the peak that reared like an enormous hook above Jyeko. On they went, following the steadily narrowing valley floored with smudges of dark green moss among the rounded pebbles.

On the second day, they came to a gorge in which the trail flirted with a precipice above a river. Where the dirt track reached the entrance to the gorge, baulks of timber had been laid in rudimentary steps to a narrow rock shelf. This ledge, halfway up the perpendicular cliff, was the only possible means of passing onward above the seething river. It had been used for generations, and the rock face was scratched with imploring prayers. The grey-green surface was damp, greasy with perpetual spray and centuries-old lichens. The ledge was so narrow that the ponies and yaks had barely sufficient room to place their hoofs, and the loads snagged on the wet stone.

The woman had no liking of heights. When she saw where she was expected to ride, her nerve failed and she began to get down from the saddle, the child inside her coat. Her husband turned to see what she was doing, and shouted a curt order to remount immediately, to keep her eyes out of the depths and to follow him. He called that the ponies were used to it; they were more sure-footed than she, and should be allowed to find their own way. So she climbed back up, her strength diminishing as rapidly as her nerve. The pony moved ahead, and she managed to raise her eyes and fix them on her husband's back as he rode proud and silent before her. But she could not help seeing ahead of him, to where the ledge gave out. There, for twenty yards, the way consisted of nothing more than slippery tree trunks laid on stakes driven into the rock. She felt sick with fear, a clammy sweat adding to the cold river spray as she fought to keep her eyes up and her hand tight on the rein. They passed beyond the timbers, back onto the rock ledge, and her heart began to steady.

Then she heard, over the boom and hiss of the gorge, a deep scraping sound among the rocks overhead. Before she could comprehend it, her husband and his pony were smashed off the ledge by a clattering swarm of black boulders. He disappeared instantly into the cold billows to their right. A second later, she was struck on the head and the leg, and thought that she, too, was dead, but the blow knocked her in against the rock wall. Her pony, in a spasm of terror, launched itself backwards and vanished, legs flailing, over the edge after her husband.

When her wits returned, she heard her little girl screaming. She tried to stand upright on the slippery ledge to find her child but collapsed. Her leg was broken in two places, crushed by boulders.

She reached Jyeko two days later, draped over one of her yaks. She had somehow contrived to tie her daughter on with ropes so tight that they cut her flesh. The little girl was mute with shock, the woman barely conscious. For once, the villagers were merciful and brought her to the monks. Many weeks later, as the first winter storms were gathering, she and her daughter were back in their house, alone with each other.

*

The young widow's name was Puton. It was acknowledged privately in the village that she was as good-looking as any woman from Lhasa could hope to be. The Jyeko people, however, had remarked that her brows joined in the middle, a dark smudge of soft down meeting above the bridge of her nose. Before the accident, they had not been sure of the significance of this. Now though, they were certain: she was marked out as dangerously ill-fortuned.

They took Puton to the physician-lama at the monastery. The monk saw the barely suppressed disdain in the villagers' faces and protective pity ran freely in him. His name was Khenpo Nima. He was in his early middle age, a tall, powerfully built man with a shaven head. With gentle ease, he lifted her from the animal while bellowing at the novices to prepare a room in the outbuildings.

For two months he cared for her. The leg was smashed: it would never be good again. Splinters of bone spiked into the nerves of her right thigh, so that, at its slightest movement, her face contorted in agony. Khenpo Nima bound and stretched the limb with wooden splints, laying it on a thick, oily sheepskin. He prepared for her quantities of his best cures, principally an infusion of a rare blue poppy that caused bone quickly to set firm. It was a remedy he alone in Jyeko used: that species of poppy was only known to grow in one near-inaccessible valley beyond Moro-La, so it was expensive to make. But he did not stint its use for Puton.

For several days she was delirious. In the cold, sucking marshes of pain, she surfaced and sank again, terrified of her helplessness. Often, as she came to, she saw the open smile of Khenpo Nima looking down at her. She knew that she was defenceless and dependent; sometimes her hand fastened on his deep red robe. He brought two village women to tend and clean her when she fouled herself. He saw to it that the little girl was cared for, and brought her each day for Puton to clasp tightly. So they came to trust Khenpo Nima, and when he said it was time for them to return home, Puton went without a murmur of protest. He sent food each day, and told her to rely on him.

Slowly, she recovered her strength, but her spirits seemed gone for good. The old house hardly enlivened her. It was tall and teetering, three storeys of wooden rooms clustered like barnacles to a mud-brick core, with steep ladders everywhere, their timbers rotten. Puton could never keep the storeroom clean enough to discourage hordes of crisp brown cockroaches. They rustled across the floors and the sacks of grain, and climbed the walls and ladders to the living room where she would find them running over her daughter's cot. In the byre, flies bred in the animal dung, and swirled up to the family rooms above.

Puton did her best, sweeping clumsily with one hand, opening windows, rubbing at the iron kettles and brass jugs on the shelves. But her leg hurt dreadfully, and she had little courage for cleaning. There was a crude mural of the Lord Buddha daubed on the whitewash behind the fire, and she stared at it while the barleymeal simmered.

The house was at the back of town against the

mountainside. Her upper rooms were dark, their windows small, the panorama restricted to the neatly framed summit of the Grey Ghost. In summer these rooms were sweltering as the sun beat down on the flat roof through the thin air. In winter they were cold, with only rough boards to close the windows, and keen draughts everywhere. So the young widow who was unwelcome in the village hardly knew where to sit in her own house.

Only when the monk Khenpo Nima came to visit did she relax and smile. He would sit with her in the upper chamber, admiring the view of the Grey Ghost's beaked summit. She listened to his advice and laughter, his news and stories of the world from which she hid. But when he left her – alone except for her little girl, in almost constant pain – she brooded helplessly and became the prey of fear.

*

When she had first come from the capital, Puton had thought Jyeko a miserable little hole. She had not expected a city, of course. In all the turbulent province of Kham there was only one town of any size: Chamdo. Poor little Jyeko had a small, scruffy monastery jammed onto the hillside, no more than two hundred citizens and a few dozen houses. The homes of the poor were dens of stone rendered with mud, the roof of one storey leading to the door of the next, with notched tree trunks for ladders that resembled saws from a giant's toolbox. The better houses were wooden and gloomy. No one had any furniture, except perhaps a crudely squared log near the fire for a table. The village lanes were stony and narrow, steep and twisting, full of rubbish and excrement. By mid-afternoon, when the sun was strong, an odour of urine and burnt juniper hung in the air. There was no order in the place, no controlling hand. The Khampas were too wild, too horse-crazy, too brigand-blooded to ever make a civilised town. That, anyway, was what Puton had grown up hearing in Lhasa.

She had told herself to be patient. But when she saw the sorry little market square, its handful of traders in tea, tinware,

radishes and mutton outnumbered by the dogs, she sighed for
Lhasa.

Jyeko had one small claim to importance. The village stood
on the banks of the Wi-chua river and it had a bridge, made of iron
chains slung from two stocky towers of timber packed with stone.
It was narrow, and swayed alarmingly in the autumn gales.
Beneath it, the water ran rapid and deadly cold. Minuscule ice
crystals, washed from the glaciers, gave it a milky opacity. Jyeko
parents warned their small children, 'If you fall in, we shan't see
you again.' Though Jyeko was ill-kempt and the houses
dilapidated, the villagers took care of their bridge. The cords and
boards were scrutinised by everyone who crossed, and promptly
repaired. This was a trade route, albeit a minor one. On the far side
lay Sikhang – and the infinity of China.

There was just one building on the far bank. It was as large
as the largest house in Jyeko, but squat and forbidding. The four-
square outer walls were of smoothed mud, the small windows
strongly barred; the double doors were reinforced with iron. Above
the main block a flag hung, blue and red with a white sun. On
rough wooden benches under the outer walls, soldiers of the
Nationalist Chinese Army sat smoking. Unless there were passing
tea merchants for them to pester, they had nothing to do. Trade
had slowed to a trickle, near-throttled by China's civil war.

The people of Jyeko regarded the soldiers with contempt.
They were miserable conscripts a thousand miles from their
homes and were reputed to be opium addicts. None could sit
straight on a pony, and none appeared to know which end of a
sword to hold. Puton was wary of them, but felt curiosity and pity
too. She heard whispers of terrible beatings in the barracks. She
wondered what their homes were like. She recalled her uncle's
unfashionable opinion: that the Chinese were capable of
remarkable things and had vast cities full of green ceramic
dragons.

Then the talk of war grew. It was not Tibet's war, thank
goodness. The Chinese were tearing each other's eyes out, the
infrequent traders reported, unimaginably vast armies swept back

and forth across plains of smoking towns and rotting crops, of ditches filled with the corpses of animals, of roads choked with panic-stricken refugees. Few in Jyeko had much idea who was fighting whom. Puton's husband said that the more wars they fought in China, the more secure Tibet would be. But to Puton it seemed that the soldiers across the river grew more sullen daily. When she overheard the talk in the market, she turned cold. She wished in her soul that she was safe in Lhasa.

After her husband's death, she grew more fearful still. Sometimes she would wake in the night thinking she heard gunfire, or dragons swooping, or barbarian cavalry roaring through the town. But it was only the cracking of ice or the slither and crash of a rockfall in the gorges. It was not a Chinese military assassin creeping through the bedroom that had startled her, but a pair of cockroaches scuttling. She would sit up in bed and stare across the room at her daughter. The child slept undisturbed, and Puton told herself not to be so spineless. Still, she woke every night in the cold sweat of fear.

Khenpo Nima made her crutches of wood and leather. She attempted to walk unsupported across the upper room, and Nima beamed encouragement at her, but her balance was poor. She fell repeatedly with a resonant thump onto the gritty wooden boards. The pain shot through her thigh, and she sobbed. Her little girl cried in sympathy. Nima would frown, and pick up Puton easily with one powerful hand. He held her by the back of her tunic, as though it was the scruff of a kitten's neck, and she tried again.

When she could move without tumbling, Puton ventured to the market. The stocks of barleymeal bought in by her husband and stored on the first floor were enough for many months, but she longed to eat something fresh and green, she ached to see something bright, something coloured: a twist of carmine silk, a roll of indigo cotton, a jar of pickled radishes, a bright copper lamp. She wanted to smell the pungency of an incense stall scenting the wind, or to see wooden boxes of sulphur and rock salt brought by nomads from the Chang Tang, or a tall stack of brick tea, and all the oddments that found their way to Jyeko market:

Bangalore padlocks, Bengali elephants' milk for a cure-all, Mongol boots and bundles of soft Russian leather, a few Japanese photographs of cherry blossom and battleships, hand-tinted.

Puton went to her husband's chest and took out a little money. After a moment of hesitation, she applied a touch of rose madder to her cheeks from a Chinese tin labelled Three Goat Beauty Cream.

Her girl, Dechen, was now three years old. Puton had given her a Khampa nickname, perhaps hoping that the child might find the friends her mother lacked. But Dechen had never gone far from her side. Today, as Puton went out into the lane, Dechen stayed close by.

Progress was slow. Puton moved with one crutch, her leg still weak. She saw the half-bricks protruding from the dirt, the dark green slime of the ditch, the scraps and bones on which she might slip, and she passed carefully round them. Dechen clutched her skirts, and she felt unsteady. With a pang, she prised off the little girl's hand.

The market was busy, and for a moment Puton was not noticed. When two traders at last saw her and stared, she moved on through the crowd. But a hostile susurrus began. For some minutes Puton gazed round at the stalls, trying to convince herself that she was glad to be there. Then she heard a malicious snort behind her, and felt Dechen tug nervously at her free hand. She stopped in front of a haberdasher's table, trying to still her nerves as she peered at buttons and braids. The trader, a woman with a hare lip that gave her a permanent snarl, stood hand-on-hip and glared at her. And then took a brown-black oilcloth from under the stall and laid it over all the goods.

Puton looked up at her.

'I want to sell my goods,' sneered the hare-lipped woman. 'I don't want them tainted with your sort of luck.'

Around Puton, the market voices fell silent. She looked at the peering, grinning faces. She felt the terrified press of Dechen's hand in her own. Then she turned and lurched back to the lane and her dark house.

Khenpo Nima visited that afternoon. He called to Puton up the steep stairwell but she didn't reply. At first he smiled to himself, thinking that she was enjoying her liberation. But then he saw, in the gloom above him, the soft, frightened shine of Dechen's eyes at the ladder's head. Alarmed, Khenpo Nima climbed up, calling again, 'Miss Puton?'

She was sitting on a stool by a barred window on the far side of the room. Khenpo Nima said, 'Miss Puton?' but she didn't move. She gazed out of the window fixedly. When Nima came closer, he saw the wet streaks and smeared rose madder on her face.

'I shall not go out again,' she said, almost inaudibly.

'You shall go out in my company,' he retorted, 'and anyone who speaks ill of you shall answer to me.'

He stood over her, tall and vigorous, and looked again at the mountain in the distance. He remembered that her husband had died in its shadow. He felt momentarily dizzied with pity for her and with anger at his uncharitable people.

As he thought all of this, Nima heard the sound of a mule's tread in the lane and he looked down. At once, he smiled with indulgent amusement. Below, the curious figure of a 'Ying-gi-li' sat stiffly on a hard Tibetan saddle, followed by his house servant, prodding the mule with a stick to move it along, but furtively, to save the foreigner's pride. Inadvertently, Nima chuckled, then remembered where he was. The young widow was gazing up at him, puzzled.

'I shall see to it that you are never without protection,' he said sternly. Puton lowered her face. To divert her, Khenpo Nima told Puton about the peculiar coming of the Ying-gi-li, who was now also in the care of the Jyeko lamas.

*

two

The lamasery at Jyeko was modest: three dozen monks, no more, lived in its flat-roofed halls. The walls were of stone crudely rendered with clay, the lower part ochre and the upper third a blistered and faded raspberry red. A chill stream frisked down the mountainside behind the village and tumbled over rocky steps by the gate, where it powered a little waterwheel. This ground no corn; the leather paddles turned an arrangement of prayer flags that should have kept a constant *om mani padme hom* twirling heavenward, but the device was in poor repair and prone to jamming.

Though the lamasery was small, it was reputedly ancient. The main gates were suitably massive, bristling with iron nails. But within the walls, everything was on a modest scale, a muddle of arcades and oratories with praying machines of every size: little wheels that rattled and tinkled in the windows, wheels driven by leather cups to catch the wind, inscribed prayer tables you could spin with a finger, great drums packed with paper prayers surrounded by butter lamps like throngs of gleaming admirers. From one window, steam billowed night and day. In this chamber, a cauldron the size of a barrel was kept simmering for the provision of limitless buttered tea.

The physician Khenpo Nima was by no means senior in Jyeko. Though the establishment was humble, they had a Venerable Abbot, a humorous old gentleman. It was the Abbot who, against all precedent, had banished the ferocious mastiff guard dogs from the monastery. He disliked their slavering malice, he said; it was not the thing for a place of peace, and he feared they'd bite a child one day. The holy compound was guarded instead by four dead dogs, crudely stuffed with straw and propped up on sticks in the front court. Their decaying muzzles hung open in a desiccated snarl, their teeth brown and dusty, their eye sockets empty and dry. They were, said the Abbot, quite sufficiently terrifying to keep out evil spirits.

The Abbot had no interest in administration or affairs of state: all official post from Lhasa was Khenpo Nima's concern. When Lhasa informed Jyeko that they were sending a transmitter to establish a radio station, it was Khenpo Nima who opened the letter and read out the announcement in the refectory.

'Reverend One, what is radio?' enquired a novice.

'I have seen this at Chamdo,' said Nima. 'It is a box of iron from which voices fly through the upper air.'

'It is a prayer wheel, then, Reverend One?'

'It is not. These voices are letters, not prayers. They fly to Lhasa, or wherever they are directed.'

'Are they extremely loud, that they may be heard in Lhasa? Are the spirits of the upper air disturbed?'

'Not at all,' said Nima.

The novices looked at one another, some bewildered, some frankly incredulous.

'Don't look like that!' snapped Nima. 'I repeat, I have seen this happen at Chamdo. A foreigner worked it. I saw the Governor speak a greeting to Lhasa. I heard Lhasa send greetings back again!'

The novices nodded respectfully, silenced by Khenpo Nima's irritation. He was not above cuffing their ears.

'Why are we to have this box, Reverend One?' another asked.

Nima hesitated – and a novice interposed: 'So that Lhasa may hear of trade caravans from China.'

'But there aren't any, not since their war began.'

'So Lhasa will be anxious for news – '

'Enough!' bellowed Khenpo Nima. 'Too much gossip and speculation. A Ying-gi-li will come here; we are to prepare a house for him.'

When their 'English' arrived in Jyeko three months later, the house was ready. Khenpo Nima walked to meet the official caravan of ponies and pack animals at the pass two miles from the village. He looked at the slim young man who sat on a pony regarding him a little apprehensively. Nima saw blue eyes puffy with chill and sleepless nights, crisp sandy hair and a chin covered in pale stubble.

He was a former soldier called James Wilson.

'Your journey is over,' Khenpo Nima smiled up at the traveller. The young man looked down at the monk, his shaven head and shabby robe of purplish red.

'I can't wait for a hot soak,' he said. It was a curious phrase, and Nima puzzled over it a moment, surprised that the newcomer spoke Tibetan at all. He took the pony firmly by the bridle and marched it down the hill to a house at the edge of the village. Lhasa's orders were coldly clear: the Ying-gi-li was to be made very comfortable, so that he stayed.

The house had been built for a Chinese trader: it was a clutch of bare rooms surrounding a courtyard, which was enclosed by mud-brick walls topped with flat stones against erosion by the rain. It was entered through a timber-arched gateway with a rough double gate. There were stables and stores, good outhouses for the radio, even a bathroom with a stone floor, crude duckboards and a hole in the wall through which the water drained into the lane outside. For the winter, there was a *kang*, a stone sleeping platform with a fire beneath. Khenpo Nima had installed, on a chain, a huge and savage mastiff with bloodshot eyes that snarled at anyone in the gateway. As housekeeper, he had recruited a grim old Khampa who owed him many favours, a reformed but impoverished bandit with a snuff-stained moustache called Karjen. He'd ordered Karjen to sweep the goat-droppings out of the bedroom. Then they could only wait to see what the foreigner might require to keep him contented in Jyeko.

When they arrived at the courtyard gate, the mastiff bayed in outrage. Khenpo Nima watched anxiously for Wilson's reaction. The young man merely smiled at the dog, which fell silent and followed his movements with curled lips and a rumbling in its throat. As the pack animals were led in and the boxes unstrapped, the Ying-gi-li stood in the middle of the yard looking round. Then, in his curiously accented Tibetan, he called to Khenpo Nima: 'Whose is the house, then?'

'It is your house, sir,' replied Nima.

'Well, it's just grand. And you're to call me Jamie.'

He gave Khenpo Nima a broad grin. Hugely relieved, Nima beamed back at him.

'I've been in Lhasa nearly a year,' said Jamie Wilson. 'It's great to move.'

He spun on his heel and went off gaily to poke his nose into every room, and to direct the unloading of his packs and cases.

When Khenpo Nima returned next morning, he was surprised to find the great mastiff dozing peaceably in the sun. The house fires were blazing to drive out damp, the rooms were chaos, and a clump of gawping children blocked the gateway. In the kitchen, Karjen fussed noisily with pans and fuel. In the yard, two youths had taken it upon themselves to groom the pony and pack mules. But Nima could not see Wilson.

'Up here!'

The Ying-gi-li was waving and grinning from the flat roof of the outhouses. A tree-trunk ladder stood against the wall; Khenpo Nima climbed. The roof was neatly stacked with the usual fuel reserves of dried dung but in the centre there was a bizarre new structure: a tall metal pole from which four strong cords stretched out and were lashed around large stones. A coil of coated wire lay nearby at which the young man was tugging with some sort of tool.

'Antenna!' said Wilson.

'Ah, yes,' replied Nima, unenlightened.

'Terrific place for it. Reception should be excellent.'

'Reception, yes!' said Nima, happy to join in his pleasure, whatever the cause.

'I'm putting the set in the room directly below. Come and see.'

Wilson scampered down the ladder like an outsize squirrel. Khenpo Nima followed more restrainedly, oddly conscious of his clerical dignity.

In a small storeroom, the radio transmitter sat on a table improvised from planks and mud bricks. It was not imposing, nothing more than a grey box with small round glass windows and black knobs on the front. It hardly seemed adequate for speaking with Lhasa – indecently small, even, for such a momentous task.

When it was turned on, said Wilson, little lamps would shine inside the windows. Two cords came out of the front, one attached to a chunky black object on a stand, topped with mesh, the other to a small contrivance with a metal lever. Wilson prodded this with his finger, making a merry rhythmic clicking. He said it was like writing in the air, and he would be teaching some local men how to do it. He handled the parts of the radio with care, but no special reverence.

'It's an American model. There's three now, one in Lhasa and another in Chamdo. We've trained Indian operators there. Can you get me a couple of stools?'

'Anything you require,' said Nima. 'What makes it go?'

'Oh, there's a petrol generator. It can stay in the shed by the gate.'

'Ah, yes, generator!' Nima knew the word and felt pleased. He had come across generators at Chamdo where the government office had one, causing lanterns that hung like giant water drops from the ceiling to shine brilliantly. They did without butter-oil lamps altogether. On his visit there, Nima had found the smell most peculiar. Then he'd realised that there was no smell.

'I can run a cable over the arch,' said Wilson.

'Cable?'

'For the power. From the generator to the radio.'

Nima looked at the arch of the gateway, and the rooms on either side. 'Please, put the generator in this room with the radio,' he said.

Wilson stared at him.

'No chance. The noise, the fumes.'

'Oh,' said Nima, regarding the arch unhappily.

'It'll do just fine over there,' said the Ying-gi-li.

'It might not be so wise,' murmured Nima. He was wondering what the effect on the spirits – or, indeed, on the Abbot – might be. Neither spirits nor abbots were used to passing beneath an electric force. It seemed to him a foolhardy proposal.

'Not wise?' Wilson bristled. 'And why would that be?'

A few yards away, the mastiff opened its eyes. Wilson was

looking at Khenpo Nima with his chin up. The monk thought, he is stubborn, and I am instantly disputing with him, which is the last thing I should do. 'You are certain that this is best?' he asked.

'Quite certain,' said Wilson.

'Then, of course, it is a wonderful arrangement.'

'Great stuff,' said Wilson. 'You ever played ping-pong? I could teach you that too.'

Two days later, Wilson told Khenpo Nima that he would make his first test transmission that evening.

'Mr Jemmy, you will wait till tomorrow morning? The Abbot will come. He has seen the equipment at Chamdo, and he must bless this. Please, this is important.'

Wilson nodded. 'Bring him along first thing.' He smiled cheerfully. Nima was filled with relief and a sudden liking for the foreigner.

'Ah, first thing!' he concurred.

*

When the sun came over the shoulder of the Grey Ghost, the dust of snow on the pastures vanished in moments. Even so late in summer the rays could burn through the thin veil of high-altitude air. But in the shadows, the water in the pails was ice-capped. The ponies' breath plumed out of Jamie Wilson's stable where they stood wearing embroidered blankets of thick yak-hair cloth. Karjen pushed past the animals into the fuel store to bring in kindling and dried dung for the stoves. The Ying-gi-li demanded hot water for his morning wash, and for the evening too. Karjen couldn't see how the fuel stocks would last more than a month. He foresaw his winter spent collecting freeze-dried dung on the pastures, and clicked his tongue in annoyance.

But the young foreigner certainly kept busy. Soon after dawn, Karjen was pottering about the kitchen preparing breakfast: butter-tea, Chinese biscuits and a tin of the sticky orange jelly the Ying-gi-li had brought with him. Karjen moved slowly: he was not a young man and was swaddled in ragged grey sheepskins against the cold. He had reckoned he had a good while before the young man would be up and wanting anything, so he was put out to see Wilson standing in the doorway clapping his arms round his sides and grinning. 'Karjen, morning! Does it get much colder than this? I'm ready for a cup, if you can manage.'

Karjen stared at him in astonishment. Before he could speak, however, sounds came to them: bright ringing harness, hoofs and voices. Karjen was about to cry, 'The Abbot!' but the Abbot got in first.

Every monk in Jyeko came through the courtyard gate, a bustle of maroon milling about the Venerable ancient beaming down from his pony. They grinned, they chattered, they looked about them in excitement. Khenpo Nima stood with the bridle in his hand. He glanced up at the cable beneath which they had passed without mishap, and laughed aloud. 'First thing, Jemmy, first thing!'

'That's great!' beamed Jamie Wilson. 'Karjen, the generator, please.' Overawed by the occasion, the decrepit bandit stood dumbstruck. Jamie pointed to the shed and repeated patiently: 'Generator, Karjen.'

The engine raced, then settled to a modest puttering. The old Abbot settled comfortably on a stool by the radio table; the door was jammed with monks, and the lamps and valves glowed warmly. Jamie stood aside, waiting. The Abbot picked at his gold tooth pensively as he regarded the Morse key and the microphone. He touched both gently, pulled his robe tighter across his front. Then he began to speak in a mellifluous singsong voice and antique intonations that Jamie could not follow.

'He says, he wishes to bless this radio,' Khenpo Nima murmured in Jamie's ear. 'He says it will be a wonder to listen to Lhasa, and he begs forgiveness of the spirits of the upper air and trusts they will not be unduly disturbed by flying messages. He gives thanks to you, Jemmy, for your important contribution to Tibet's safety at this difficult time.'

'O, it's not my doing ...' blushed Wilson, but Nima's hand stilled him. The Abbot had taken a scarf of creamy white silk from within his robe, and now laid it around the microphone.

'He asks,' continued Nima, 'are we ready to begin?'

The Abbot glanced slowly round the room, the furrows on his ancient face flexing into a broad grin as he leaned towards the microphone and said, 'Over!'

Jamie smiled, leaned forward and said, 'Come in, Lhasa, over,' then motioned the Abbot to release a switch in time to catch the accents of the Indian operator in the capital: '*... ing you, Jyeko, go ahead, over.*'

'Khenpo Nima, please tell the Abbot that he can now make his report to Lhasa.'

Nima murmured in the Abbot's ear. The Abbot looked at Jamie Wilson, then spoke quietly to Nima.

'He says that he has nothing to report,' explained Nima.

'But ... nothing to say to Lhasa?'

Nima shrugged.

'The Chinese are still here. No one comes, no one goes. Nothing to say.'

*

The house was a shambles: wooden boxes spewed out books, clothes and tools. Nothing was put away because there was nowhere to put anything. Jamie turned a tea chest upside down and began to stack technical manuals on top of it.

'Is this like a Ying-gi-li house, Jemmy?' asked Khenpo Nima.

'Not very.'

Nima sat down with surprising gracefulness, and watched Jamie pottering and sorting his belongings. He frowned awkwardly. 'You have many things. I myself have nothing. We shall find you a cupboard. I think we can find you a table also.'

'I'll make do. I'm not here forever.'

'You want to go home?' cried Nima anxiously.

'Home? To Inverkeithing? No chance. That's war, you see. You escape, get to move, to see things. That's what I like.'

'Oh. You have been in a war? Which war is it?'

'*The* war – how many do you need? I was in Malaya, a radio instructor.'

'You maybe fought the Chinese?'

'We were allies.'

'Oh ... '

Nima stared at him, and shifted awkwardly on the rammed earth floor. 'Jemmy, do you think I am very ignorant?'

'For pity's sake.'

'But I know nothing ... '

'Oh, come on!' Jamie felt his face reddening. Delving into a chest, he drew out a flat oval of coloured wood with a short handle. 'Ah, now, here's something.' He rummaged again and produced a small box, opened it and took out a gleaming white ball. 'There we go!' he exclaimed. And he dropped the ball onto the oval. It bounced lightly, crisply up into his fingers with a sharp and hollow *tock*. 'Remember I said? You have to make a table. I'm going to teach you lads ping-pong.'

*

three

On Khenpo Nima's orders, Karjen painted *T4JW Tibet* in white letters over the outhouse door. The monk had written out the callsign very carefully on a scrap of ruled paper, but Karjen's rendition was somewhat approximate.

At nine each morning, Khenpo Nima would bring a brief report to go to Lhasa in ciphered Morse. Each evening, Jamie would take down any directives in return. Apart from Lhasa, there was a gaggle of hams in Australia to greet, and a pundit in Hyderabad who was disconcertingly good at chess. But there couldn't be much idle chat. He had to conserve his tins of petrol, brought from India at absurd cost. He had a pedal dynamo for emergencies.

Only the Chinese preoccupied him. Lhasa did the official monitoring of Radio Peking's foreign-language broadcasts but Jamie tuned in too, well aware that China was the reason for his presence. The Tibetan government had three radios: one in the capital, two on the frontier with China. Khenpo Nima's daily reports were made up of trivial routine business that for centuries had gone overland and taken months about it with no harm done. What Lhasa wanted now was rumour, scraps, hints regarding the chaos and slaughter of China's civil strife – and whether it was coming closer to Tibet. But there was precious little of substance.

Otherwise, the day was Jamie's own, his spirit was free and his curiosity without limit. And he lived in *Tibet*, of all places! The Royal Corps of Signals had spirited him from Inverkeithing, from a suburb of tight-lipped Episcopalian tradesmen to barely-imagined places: the desiccated tracts of Palestine, then the dank rubber groves of Malaya. After that, he'd wanted to know what more there was. The day in New Delhi that he'd signed a contract to work in Tibet, his young head had throbbed with some sort of ecstasy. War had set him loose in the world, and he loved it.

He felt it all the more when he saw the grandeur of this country. Khenpo Nima took him into the summer hills, secretly surprised that Jamie could manage a pony without a Tibetan hand on the bridle. The house mastiff came with them. Jamie had christened this majestic dog Hector; he lolloped easily alongside the riders. They would climb to the low pass on the Lhasa trail half an hour from the village, and look back eastward. Jyeko leaned against the mountain flank, gigantic heaps of crumbled greenish mica-schist hard up behind it, the yellow and red of the monastery walls bright among the dirt and dark timbering of the houses. The young man thought it glorious, and began to paint it in delicate watercolours.

They'd traverse the lower slopes of the Grey Ghost range, over rocky tracts smudged with thin grass. They would trot above the indignant faces of the little pica, half mouse half rabbit, that burrowed in thousands in the tufted topsoil. The pica left the ground like worm-eaten board, its tunnels a risk for the ponies. Hector would pounce, snout down into the holes, and dig with officious fury. He never caught a pica, but sprayed gravel and dirt in bold arcs as he wrecked their homes. Then he'd look up at Jamie with a pleased see-what-I've-done expression, and trot after the ponies once more.

On they'd go, starting the high-horned antelopes and the wild ass, watching the Jyeko goatherds, and the sheep and yaks gorging while the summer permitted. They'd see blotches of black on the southern plain where the nomads had set their big felt tents whose poled-up guy lines looked like spiders' legs. The geese went sailing overhead in threes; black-bearded lammergeyers streaked across the cliffs.

Where the snows had melted off the sharp grey stones, primulas and blue poppies sparkled in the scree. In the tremendous rains they hung their heads so that they were not washed clean of their pollen. The saussurea, like bearded jellyfish, huddled in protective white down, while the trumpet gentians shut up tight at the first cold touch, to gape wide again the moment the sun reappeared. The poppies' intense blue scintillated through the droplets, a brooch of tiny sapphires.

Khenpo Nima showed Jamie the furry edelweiss and

saxifrages that split the rocks, the cobalt borage, crimson and yellow scrophulas. He pointed out the strong herbs strewn across the meadows that made the air rich, and told of the cures that each one worked. He waved to the far south-east where the river sank into gorges with alder woods and a promise of warmer, lower valleys. And he pointed to the score of glittering peaks around them, naming each one. Jamie laid his head against a rock and gazed, entranced.

'And so you love our Khampa country?' said Nima, pleased.

The young man frowned. 'Well ... it's grand as anything, isn't it? The air is so light. Nothing weighs down.'

But the sharp, blasting rains made him duck his head; in moments there'd be rills bubbling down the hillsides; the ponies skidded and trembled on the slippery turf, the reins were sodden and Jamie's hands numb. He loved it, once in a while. Afterwards, the direct blaze of the sun had their coats steaming in a minute.

Sometimes Karjen would show Jamie how he stalked the *na*, the wild sheep, and killed them with his musket. It was a weapon from another time, a black powder matchlock with a spindly bipod of antelope horns. It took a long minute to prepare and fire, in which the agile *na* might easily escape. But Karjen's hunting dogs cornered them among the crags and barked to signal. Nima cried, 'They're here, the *na* is trapped!' and waved excitedly. Karjen brought Jamie to the gully's edge, gestured him to brace the musket on its stand, to light the matchcord with flint sparks and blow on it till it glowed, then to tug it down into the powder bowl. There came a startling, hissing flash, Jamie jerked aside and the ball smacked off a rock beside Hector. Alarmed, the mastiff yelped and skulked behind a boulder as Jamie stumbled and fell. The opportunist *na* jumped past them all, hurtled to the crannies and ledges above – and was gone. Karjen flapped his arms in despair while Khenpo Nima howled with laughter. 'Sorry, Jemmy, so sorry! Rotten lousy Tibet gun! Ha!'

Jamie picked himself off the ground, rubbing the side of his head, grazed on a rock. He looked with annoyance at the ramshackle musket lying with its antelope horns twisted under it.

Karjen picked up and tenderly straightened the contraption. He spat – then remembered his manners. 'My old thing ... sorry, Mr Jemmy. You bring us a good British gun and teach us all proper shooting. That'll scare the wits out of the Chinese, Reverend – Tibetan shooting and British guns!'

'Ah, Jemmy,' laughed Nima, 'you see how we cannot do without you now.'

Jamie smiled.

Everything was new to him, the manners, clothes, accents, houses, the drinking of barley beer. Though he'd been in Lhasa almost a year, the province of Kham was utterly different. The women were fiercely opinionated pragmatists, who would marry four brothers at once *and* rule the house. The men were tall, often very tall indeed, well over six feet. Their faces were sunburned and aquiline, and their hands clanked with crude silver rings. Their hair was tied in thick tails wound on top of their heads, and in anything short of a blizzard they walked with their rough robes off one naked shoulder. They wore sheepskin in winter, felt in summer. Their reputation was for shameless brigandage, for appalling ferocity. They would wait for weeks in the rocky hills, then little bands of twenty Khampa men would swoop on the tail of caravans of two hundred or more and rush off with animals and silver, silks, guns and ammunition. In the market at Jyeko, one did not enquire too closely as to the provenance of horses or trade goods.

Fascinated, Jamie would sit gazing and sketching. He examined the triumphant bandit-cavaliers who strutted through the lanes, long swords at their waists; or the farmer-serfs, their spines sore from labour and their hands like charred wood; the pilgrims in rags and knee pads who measured their prostrated length every yard from monastery to remote monastery; the huntsmen come to buy gunpowder, and their precious dogs with curled red-grey lips; criminals in shreds of sackcloth with their feet chained and their hands cut off, condemned to a short life of shuffling and whining for food; the merchants – Khampa, Tibetan, Chinese, even Indian or Mongol – bustling about their business to make the most of the summer caravans, their money sewn into their robes and a wary eye on the horsemen. Jamie watched, drew their portraits and made them laugh, sitting in the late-summer warmth.

A month later, on the high pastures an hour from the village, the scent of the plants was gone. In September, the grass withered and the temperature fell a degree lower each night. In October, the ice took hold.

Storms came, presaged by yellow and violet clouds. For days at a time the village went into hiding. High winds scoured the lanes with small snow crystals like grit. The gales banged and buffeted hour after hour, leaving the ears dulled and aching. After losing the antenna twice over the parapet, Jamie learned to lower it on his roof at the first hint of changing light.

Travellers from Sikhang spoke of a turn in the Chinese wars, of colossal armies breaking apart and fleeing. Over the chain bridge, the forlorn garrison of Nationalists seemed frozen in fear. Jamie sat on the flat roof of his house, and made a watercolour sketch of the bridge and the grim little barracks. He could see the glinting bayonet of the solitary guard who stamped despondently at the far side, longing for the fire within.

'Now they are unhappy, and have insulted ladies in the market,' said Khenpo Nima.

'If I was them I'd pack up and go home,' said Jamie.

Nima replied, 'Where to go? Their homes are all burned now.'

The two men sat quiet for a moment, the paintbrush tinkling in a cup of water.

'Jemmy? I have a letter come from Lhasa.'

'Oh, yes?'

'Lhasa says, your old contract will finish soon. They send a new one.'

'That right?'

'So now, I must ask you to sign.'

Jamie stopped washing-in the eastern peaks. 'What makes them think I want to stay?'

'Oh, but you do want to! In Khampa country!'

'Well, though. With a Chinese war and all?' He began painting again, little flicks of his finest brush doing the grey chain bridge.

Nima watched him with dismay. 'Do you want to go home now, Jamie?'

'Oh, heavens, no. But I might like to move about.'

'You have someone special at home?'

'Nima! No chance.' He was blushing; his rendition of the bridge was spiky, the perspective nonsensical.

'So why will you not sign your new contract?'

'Nima, I'm just thinking, all right? I might want to move on, I don't know. I've done the best part of two years in Tibet. There's other places I'd like to see.'

Nima held his tongue for a minute. Then suddenly he smiled broadly. 'Hey, Jamie, that table? We have done it.'

*

He rode to the monastery that afternoon, passed through the gates and crossed the courtyard. Beyond this was the prayer hall, full of columns, dark red paint and gilding, shadows, smoky flickering and the rancid reek of burnt butter-oil. A stern, elderly lama sat cross-legged on a carpeted dais with a desk; arrayed before him were a dozen young monks seated on mats with wooden stands for the scriptures. Their master intoned the verses: they replied, then sipped from copper beakers of buttered tea – and looked round in mid-chant as Khenpo Nima led Jamie through.

Beyond the scripture hall was a large chamber with splendid painted beams. In the centre stood a table of raw, rough new wood, to which Jamie attached a little green net. Then from his knapsack came the hard white ball and bats. Jamie curled Khenpo Nima's fingers around the handle.

A resonant clicking reached the prayer hall. A moment later, the double doors sprang open, banging back hard. A dozen monks jammed the opening to gaze into the chamber. The little celluloid ball bounced in quick, gentle arcs across the table, which was not terribly flat and sometimes sent it off on wild trajectories. Khenpo Nima dabbed valiantly at the ball, Jamie calmly caught and sent it back, and the big monk leaped up and down, his voluminous purples swaying. The closer Nima peered at his target, the less often he hit it true. More often it flew across the big chamber with a shrieking novice in pursuit.

*

'I will accompany you to your house, Jemmy, and you shall read this new contract.'

They walked together, Jamie leading his pony past the sellers of butter, trinkets and brass implements. In the centre of the market, two Nationalist soldiers stood arguing with a tobacco trader. He was refusing them credit; as they turned away, the soldiers shouted obscenities at him.

'The Chinese would not have spoken like that a year ago,' said Khenpo Nima. 'They are frightened and quick to anger now.'

They moved into the lanes – and again heard shouting.

It came from the double doors of a sizeable house, gloomy and uninviting. There stood a young woman. Her heavy black hair, hastily pushed back, framed a finely made face now twisted with anxiety. A little girl stood beside her, clinging to her mother and snivelling with fright. The woman supported herself with a stick in her left hand; her leg seemed misformed. In front of her stood three men, who spat imprecations at her while they pointed into the house and leered maliciously.

Khenpo Nima stopped and stared at the dispute.

'What is it, Nima? What's happening?'

Jamie had not seen the woman before. She pushed her hair back once more and lifted her face to answer the jeering men. Though she looked hunted and at the mercy of her tormentors, though she was injured and weak, though she had a child to shelter, though she was pleading, still she had pride. Jamie saw the fear that gripped the woman. Her body wanted to curl into a ball, but she held herself upright by willpower: the mouse that defies the cat. She lifted her stick to block the door to the three men. They laughed at her and turned away.

Then they saw Khenpo Nima, and their faces changed at once. They stepped aside with a hint of a bow, and departed.

Khenpo Nima hurried forward. Jamie stood still and watched. Steadying herself against the doorframe, the woman reached down for her daughter. The child buried her face in the folds of her skirt. Her mother spoke quickly but quietly to Nima, gesturing with her look after the three men. Her eyes, dark and narrow, tilted downwards at the inner corner, were awash with tears. Jamie felt a desire to touch her, to say something comforting though he had no idea of her trouble. He realised that he was staring. Nima was listening closely, leaning forward and frowning. The woman glanced at Jamie, who felt awkward suddenly. 'Nima, I'll get on home,' he called out. 'I'll see you shortly.'

'Yes, yes,' agreed the monk, distracted, and turned his attention back to the woman.

Jamie mounted his pony and rode on through the village, more disturbed than he could account for.

*

four

When Khenpo Nima rejoined Jamie at his house, both men were subdued. Karjen cranked the generator; they listened to commands from Lhasa concerning trade passes to Assam. There was nothing relating to China. Jamie shouted at Karjen to stop the generator, and the yard fell silent.

The house had improved little since Jamie's arrival. He was no home maker. Paints and brushes, radio valves in tatty cardboard boxes, clothes, harness and books still littered the corners. The upturned packing case still did for a table. On this Karjen placed wooden bowls of dark tea with globes of butterfat rotating on the surface.

'What is this one?' asked Khenpo Nima, picking up a flat tin and tugging at the tight-fitting lid.

'Moffat toffee. My mother sends it from Scotland. Go ahead.'

Nima placed a toffee in his mouth and sucked thoughtfully. Jamie puffed across the surface of his cup, blowing the greenish globules aside so that he could avoid them.

'What was all that with the girl?' he asked.

'You *see* these men?' Nima sighed. 'They tell her to leave. The landlord is a rich man: he says he cannot risk having her there. He says his animals abort, that he gets no milk, this is wrong, that is wrong, and it is all the woman's fault.'

'How come?'

'She is bad luck. You see that she cannot walk so well? Now his property has her bad luck and he wants her out.'

'Where can she go?'

'Nowhere. No one in this village wants her. Tomorrow I shall go and speak with that man again. He will do as I say. He will leave her alone.' He paused, frowning, then fished in his long robes. 'Now, more important, Jemmy.'

He brought out a flat, grubby packet of oiled cloth: a government envelope. Jamie regarded it without enthusiasm.

'Jemmy, Lhasa must know if you are staying. You must give

an answer.'

'How long?'

'Five years.'

'No chance!'

'This can be your home.'

'Who says I want a home? Maybe I've other plans.'

'You are courting? Bring that person to Jyeko.'

'Nima, there's no one. I'm not ready for all that.'

Khenpo Nima surveyed Jamie's shambles, the kit and clothing cast anyhow, the poor comfort. 'Your house is not so nice, Jemmy. This Karjen is hopeless, I shall find someone better.'

'Karjen's fine. Look, Nima, a year. Maybe I'll stay another year.'

A pause came between them. Through the window Jamie could see the dour Karjen grooming the pony, retying a string of red beads in her mane. The villain had his charms. Jamie said: 'Anyway, Nima, the Chinese might do something.'

'China is no concern of ours.'

'Oh, Nima, really!'

Khenpo Nima peered at Jamie and tacked about. 'You know, your Ying-gi-li sugar piece is good.'

'That's Moffat toffee.'

'We can make things sweet for you, Jemmy. We can look after everything for you in Jyeko, and no worries.'

But shortly after this, the monk took the contract back to the monastery, still unsigned.

*

Two days later, three Chinese soldiers came to market to buy barleymeal. Spotting a mule, they demanded a loan of it to carry the heavy sack over the bridge. The animal's owner asked for payment. The Chinese laughed at him, called him a grasping barbarian and loaded the sack on to the mule anyway, saying that he'd have it back soon enough. The Khampa insisted on two rupees. The Chinese sergeant barked, 'Stand aside!' and began to drag the reluctant beast across the square. A murmurous crowd blocked their exit. The Khampa merchant grabbed at the sack and pulled so that it fell and thudded into a black puddle of crushed ice. In an instant there was jostling, Tibetans cursing, soldiers bringing rifles off their shoulders, until they were separated by Khenpo Nima and other monks.

Enraged, the sergeant spat on the ground in front of Khenpo Nima.

'Who the hell do these scum think they are? China gives orders, Tibet jumps. Understood?' The soldiers looked nervous; their sergeant had pushed his luck. Voices to the rear flung lurid Khampa insults.

'All right, that's enough,' said Nima. 'I see that the real problem is that this old-fashioned mule won't move without instructions in Tibetan. Now, if you gentlemen would grant a small sum for its *master's* services, you may leave the barley in his safekeeping, return to quarters at your leisure and I will personally ensure that the grain is delivered when the market closes this afternoon. How's that?'

The sergeant stared at Khenpo Nima in disbelief, looked round at the growing mob, hesitated a second, then snapped, 'That'll do fine.' He tossed a rupee at the merchant. Khenpo Nima gave the man a threatening scowl and he picked up the coin in silence. The soldiers pushed out through the crowd and marched off.

Nima sighed. He had other problems. He was on his way to speak with Jamyang Sangay, Puton's landlord and a notorious old cuss.

*

That afternoon, a little procession moved through the back lanes towards Jamie's house. A first pony, led by the tall figure of Khenpo Nima, was laden with household goods, bags and small boxes. Among these was wedged a little girl. Next came two mules, each carrying sacks of grain and trade bricks of tea bound in rawhide. Last in line walked another pony on which Puton rode side-saddle, her stick resting across the wooden pommel and her twisted leg draped awkwardly. The animals moved lethargically through the streets. Khenpo Nima heaved on the leading rope, not in good humour.

As Puton rode quietly at the rear, absorbed in her thoughts, a small stone landed on the ground just in front of her pony. A little puff of dust flew up and the pony stopped dead, staring and pricking its ears. Immediately a pebble struck Puton on the shoulder.

A knot of four or five children skulked behind the corner of a compound wall. Their faces bobbed in and out, leering, until the bravest reached for another stone and flung it. The missile struck the dirt behind Puton; her pony shifted nervously. For a moment, the young woman felt a surge of fear, until she saw that not one of the children was more than six or seven years old. Her eyes pricked with sadness.

One child, older perhaps, bolder and more cruel, stepped swaggering into the open. He began hopping and dragging one leg in the dirt, pulling a grotesque face and uttering strangled groans. His companions shrilled with mockery. The boy began again, dragging his leg behind him, groaning loudly until he fell on the dirt, shrieking with mirth. Puton turned her face away. She slapped the pony's rump and tried to catch Khenpo Nima seventy yards ahead.

Jamie was building a stone plinth for the generator when the caravan came through his gate. He heard Hector snarl, and looked out. Puton sat motionless on her pony. Khenpo Nima stepped forward. 'I have found you a housekeeper, Jamie.'

Jamie scowled. 'I'm really not needing ... '

'Yes, her name is Puton and now she has no home, and there is her little girl, Dechen. Please, Jemmy? You know, soon it is New Year – a new friend for good luck.'

Jamie looked at Karjen, who glared at the newcomers and spat, 'Don't I cook? Don't I clean? Why does Mr Jemmy need a bad-luck cripple woman in the house?'

'Old criminal, you are not beautiful, so mind your tongue,' said Nima curtly. 'Jemmy, you saw what happens at her house. You felt pity, I think.'

'Well, that's not like taking her in.'

'She can work, you see. She does not move so fast, but she can work.'

Without risking a reply, Khenpo Nima went quickly to the ponies. He lifted Dechen down and set her on her feet. Small and forlorn, she gazed without expectation at the Ying-gi-li. Nima's making me responsible, thought Jamie, I don't want this. Khenpo Nima lifted Puton from her saddle. As she came down hard onto the ground, Jamie saw that she winced. For a moment, she stood quite still, white-faced, holding her breath. Nima stood close, with a friendly hand on her arm. He looked round at Jamie, his face pleading.

'Oh, God, they can have the back room over there,' said Jamie, defeated. 'I think it's empty.'

Nima beamed at him. 'This is very wise, Jemmy. And little Dechen; they will be a family for you.'

'Nima!'

'Yes, Jemmy, I know, it is just for now.'

The monk left them, leading the ponies away. The woman stood helpless by her sacks and bundles. Jamie regarded her, until he remembered himself, and called: 'Karjen? Give her a hand, won't you?' He turned to go inside.

*

Karjen gave Puton a broom; he made no move to sweep the earth floor of the storeroom himself. He dragged the packs to the door, left them there and went away.

Some minutes later, Puton stood leaning on her stick as the dust clouds she had created swirled and resettled. She contemplated her change: from a huge and gloomy house that she hated, to a single cold room in a house where they appeared to hate her.

She made up a nest for her little girl with blankets and a heavy sheepskin coat. Dechen went and sat there in silence. There was no furniture. Puton arrayed her own belongings as best she could on her boxes. She had a few fine items from Lhasa still. The best of these, a chased silver charm case tasselled with yellow and purple silk, she placed on the pack-saddle under the small shuttered window. It did for a shrine.

She lowered herself heavily down to the sheepskins on the floor, Dechen moving in under her arm. For several minutes she sat staring at the silver casket, waiting for whatever came next. Until Dechen touched her arm, looking up behind her.

Jamie stood in the door, awkward and embarrassed. 'There's nothing here. I didn't realise,' he blurted out. 'I mean, we can find you things. Heavens, I'm sorry.'

Puton regarded him with her direct eyes.

'I just wasn't expecting … ' mumbled Jamie. He looked round the bleak chamber.

'It's cold. There's no fire. We'll get you a fire. Karjen!' Jamie bellowed with mortified anger. 'Karjen will bring you a brazier and some fuel. We have plenty, use all you need.'

She bowed her head a little.

'My name's Jamie,' he said, 'Jamie Wilson. I'm sure you knew that. That's what you must call me: Jamie, or Wilson, Mr Wilson, whatever you like. And you are Puton, so Khenpo Nima says, anyway. He doesn't get much wrong, does he?'

She stirred, reaching for her stick. With an ungainly scrape she pushed herself upright. Jamie made an involuntary move to help, as he would have done at home. But he stopped himself.

She stood before him, half crippled, homeless and hated, and she was still proud. One moment she had seemed a sad heap on the floor, needing his protection. Now he found that she was tall for a Tibetan woman, and was standing upright as best she could. Her eyes were quite black and dramatically sculpted. He saw that her brows came together darkly over the bridge of her nose. He realised that she was perhaps a year or two older than himself, and he remembered that she had seen her husband killed. He saw that she was nervous, struggling for the remnants of her dignity.

She said, 'I give you my heart's thanks. I will work for you.'

'Really, you don't need to worry about that. It's no trouble having you here.'

'But when it becomes a trouble you could send me from

this house,' she said. He was silenced. She continued, 'I will earn my keep.'

The next morning, Jamie stood half clothed by the heated sleeping platform in his bedroom. He was letting the warm radiance from the stone soak into him for a last minute before dressing. He held a pair of green fatigue trousers and was examining the grime on them morosely.

As he stood in his long winter underpants, trying to be interested in the problem, the door of the room clattered open. If Puton felt any hesitation, she did not let Jamie see it. She marched across the room, her stick thudding into the thick rug. Without ceremony she put out a hand and took the filthy clothes from him. Then she turned and departed, leaving Jamie to search his boxes for more trousers.

*

five

When the Reverend Khenpo Nima first asked Puton to come to the house of Jemmy the Ying-gi-li, she had protested. They were sitting in the upper room of her wooden house. Dechen played on the floor with a small heap of bright woollen braids. She laid them out in rows, arranging them by colour or length, then began to make patterns, stripes, circles and fans, humming softly to herself.

But they had to move. Khenpo Nima had been to the landlord and had remonstrated: how could he expel a defenceless woman and a harmless child? The merchant had remarked 'with the deepest respect, Your Reverence' that the family's problems were not his. Nima had warned him of the spiritual consequences: such a lack of charity was a short cut to being reincarnated as a goat. But the merchant riposted that bad spirits worried him more. Puton seemed to have some unsavoury ones in attendance on her, and he wanted them off his premises. Khenpo Nima came as near to pleading as his clerical dignity would permit, but he saw that the man was immovable. So, where were Puton and Dechen to go?

Returning infuriated through the market, Nima saw Jamie peering at the trinkets and trade goods. The women smirked and teased, throwing obscene but genial banter at the young man who grinned back at them cheerfully. All at once the monk believed he saw the solution not just to a housing problem but to other difficulties also.

'Jemmy, do not marry a market woman,' cried out Nima. 'They smell of rancid butter.'

'How would you know, Reverence?' squawked an offended harridan with gobs of mutton fat up her arms. 'Been sniffing up close, have you?' Cackles went round the stalls.

The monk gave a politic laugh and called to Jamie: 'Where are you going just now?'

'Oh, upriver to do a couple of sketches.'

'You coming back this way soon, Jemmy?'

'I should think so, with this bitter wind.'

'Very soon?'

'Well, half an hour, maybe. Why, what's urgent?'

'Nothing urgent! You make me some nice pictures, and I will like to see them.'

Khenpo Nima smiled disarmingly. Jamie dithered, nodded and moved away across the square, then out beyond the bridge. Nima hurried at once in the direction of Puton's house.

Puton, however, merely bit her lip when Nima told her his idea. She sat on the bed listening in respectful silence as he spoke. Her look went towards the window and its prospect of the Grey Ghost. Nima saw pain fill her eyes.

'But it's a splendid idea!' he urged again. Puton lowered her eyes; Nima could hardly catch her words.

'Reverence, he will think me malformed.'

'Rubbish! He will meet an exceptionally beautiful young woman who happens to walk with a stick '

'I do not know this man. Dechen and I will be defenceless in his house.'

'But Mr Jemmy will *protect* you. He's a kind young person.'

'Reverence, the villagers will think that I am his whore. My husband received no proper burial, he was lost in the gorge, and now I am to be the whore ... '

'Oh, please!'

'Forgive me, but already they say ... '

Khenpo Nima had positioned himself by the window and he glanced repeatedly down to the far corner of the lane.

'Miss Puton, you will not be alone in Jemmy's house. His servant Karjen is there: he'll be watching closely, believe me. Karjen will tell the world what's what, have no doubt. I tell you, it's the very safest place for you.'

'How is it possible for a foreigner to protect me?'

'You will see. Mr Jemmy is considered exceedingly important by Lhasa. He is *all* our protection from the Chinese.'

Puton peered up at Khenpo Nima as though trying to look through some evil darkness. The monk saw it. 'Ah, it's the Chinese that really worry you.'

'I cannot sleep,' cried Puton, 'for thinking of the Chinese. There is my little girl also – '

'Come here. Now you shall see.' Khenpo Nima interrupted her so abruptly that she was startled. She fumbled for her stick. He called impatiently, 'Come to the window. Let me help ... Quick, now!'

He reached out, seized her, and lifted her bodily.

'Look! There, you see?' said Nima. 'That is our hope.'

As he carried Puton to the small window, a rider came into full view in the lane. Jamie rode with a light touch, letting the pony find its own pace, picking its way through the rubbish and the bones. He wore a small knapsack on his shoulder, with his hat off to catch the last sun. The breeze tousled his hair, he was fit and gentle, nodding and smiling to walkers in the lane.

Held up to her own window by the monk, Puton watched him. Khenpo Nima called out: 'Jemmy! Hello, have you drawn wonderful things?'

'Oh, just fine. Hello, up there!'

Jamie smiled up at them, his face open and glad. Puton drank in his look, saying not a word. The pony passed on by.

'There's an end to your danger,' laughed Khenpo Nima. At his words, Puton's heart bounded. 'There now, be easy,' said the monk. 'We shall move your goods this afternoon. I shall come with ponies myself.'

He returned her to the bed in one effortless lift. For a moment, Puton felt herself flying.

*

She would work, she would keep out of Jamie's way, she would give no one grounds for gossip. She felt Karjen's resentful, suspicious eyes on her and she minded her manners. As the days passed, Puton observed the curious habits of the Ying-gi-li. She thought many of his ways absurd. But soon she saw Jamie for what he was: a young man not terribly adept about the house.

And so she took care of him. Karjen stayed outside: he

managed the heavy work, groomed the horses and doctored them with powdered dry meat and brick-tea, went to the market, found the fuel and saw to the building maintenance. Indoors, Puton took over. She washed and cooked for Jamie and made him a home as best she could. She cleared and tidied, and began to arrange a few items more decoratively. She found in store a heavy roll of rugs, blue and burgundy red, from Baluchistan. She beat the rugs free of ancient dust, laid some on the living-room floor, and draped others over seats and boxes. Karjen grumbled but Jamie smiled and nodded his approval: 'That's an improvement.' At last, and rather timidly, Puton brought one or two sacred items from among her own goods: a *tanka* painting of the Heavens, and a beautiful copper lamp of her husband's, which she placed on a box beneath the painting.

'Lovely,' said Jamie, who, after all, had a painter's eye. He stood in the centre of the room, regarding the small display with his head cocked on one side. Puton felt warmed by his gratitude.

She watched Jamie closely: she must, in her own interests, know him as well as she could. She noted his dislike of rancid butter in his tea. She watched what food he ate readily and which dishes he was merely polite with, and she did her best to please his tastes. She saw him look revolted at pans licked clean by Hector the mastiff, so she cautiously prodded the huge dog out from the kitchen with her stick. Each evening, when Karjen heated a mere half-pan of water for Jamie's wash, she filled it full, braving the old brigand's wrath. The basin would be carried into the bathroom and Karjen would go to inform Mr Jemmy. Shortly thereafter, merry splashings and hideously tuneless incantations would begin. Puton, in the kitchen next door, would listen attentively, trying to visualise exactly how a Ying-gi-li washed. And she warmed his bed, stoking the fire under the sleeping platform.

Every morning, Jamie went to the radio room at the same time, calling Karjen to start the generator. Puton contrived to have tea ready in a bowl on the radio table. Afterwards, Jamie and Karjen would often go out riding. Left in the house with Dechen, Puton began going into Jamie's bedroom simply to linger. She touched nothing: she merely sat on the bench at his writing table, her stick leaning against it, gazing round the room at his possessions, at his clothes, his bed, his books and letters. She wondered what he smelt like close to.

On the wall above the table, a number of watercolour sketches were fixed. Puton peered at these, puzzled. Tints and washes, hints of sky blue seeping through the heavy paper, coppice, cattle and shoreline reduced to pale bands of colour: these were so far from Tibetan notions of painting as to be almost indecipherable to her at first. But with time she saw that they were distant landscapes, bled from Jamie's memory into the cartridge. She realised that it was his home speaking to him. She said to herself that a man who makes pictures of his home must want to be there. With a pang, she told herself that to depend on this person would be foolish.

When, however, she saw Dechen touching a book of pencil drawings, she cried out anxiously, 'Stop that!' She hardly ever used such a tone to her little girl, and Dechen's face puckered in fright. Puton checked herself and considered: folly or no, Jamie had become a precious part of her defences, on no account to be jeopardised. He had begun to replace Khenpo Nima.

*

six

The ping-pong went splendidly. Even senior lamas allowed themselves a seemly knock. The novices played so eagerly that the Abbot expressed concern: they were here to pray, to recite and learn, not to whack little balls and shriek. Khenpo Nima apologised hastily and asked Wangdu the Disciplinarian to impose limits. But Wangdu, a stern giant, revealed a boyish liking for the sport himself. One or two of the monks could soon give Jamie a passable game. Sometimes they played 'Round the Table', with a dozen shaven lads in swathes of maroon careering after each other to seize the bat in turn.

Even as they played, traders from China brought word of war, but as the winter deepened into December and the shadows froze, Jyeko felt itself safe. The exhausted, shambolic armies of China would surely not risk the Kham wilderness in winter. Radio Peking gave no clue. But the merchants brought rumours.

Each morning, Khenpo Nima came and sat with Jamie at the radio table, and sent these rumours flying on to Lhasa. Each day, also, he observed the woman and her girl. Puton worked in the kitchen and pounded Jamie's clothes on the stone floor of the bathroom. Karjen never spoke to her. Nor did Jamie converse with her much. Still, Nima thought that the Ying-gi-li followed Puton with his eye. Or perhaps Nima just hoped he did.

The contract was still unsigned.

*

Karjen dressed like a nomad, with an oily sheepskin coat, fleece to the inside. Even indoors, he hardly ever removed it. He preferred to slip both arms free and tie the sleeves in a cumbersome bulk around his middle. Winter sun on snow could burn the eyes through the high, thin air of Kham. Karjen wore goggles of leather with a narrow horizontal slit, which gave him the look of a malicious troll. He was a squat, muscular figure with a flat head and a short bristly moustache.

He was the last survivor of a dynasty of brigands. It was a profession that might have earned him amputated hands, but in the rebellion of 1931, Karjen, his father and brothers had been in the first ranks that stormed the castle at Nyarong, screeching their hatred of all things Chinese. When the gates were forced, a Chinese colonel raised his pistol to shoot Karjen's father through the head. But the Khampa swung his sword to take off the colonel's pistol hand, then twirled the blade over and down to remove the other arm as the officer stood in speechless surprise. Finally, with a reverse slice, the warrior decapitated him. The effect of this spectacle on the colonel's men was that the defence collapsed, and the Lion Standard of Tibet was raised over the castle.

The Chinese had come back; Lhasa and Peking had settled the matter between them, leaving Kham embittered. The rest of the family had been slaughtered in the defeat. Karjen the brigand, anointed locally as the son of a hero, had been persuaded into more peaceful ways as a factor for the Jyeko monastery. He was hopeless at it, and his duties contracted progressively. Which was how the old patriot now found himself as 'houseboy' to a Scottish radio operator.

He was a most entertaining riding companion. His voice was a wet scrape, like a blunt knife taking the last flesh off a bloody sheepskin. He gobbed and hacked, but his yarns were inexhaustible.

'See that gully beyond the stream, Mr Jemmy? We trapped a platoon of Chinese there in thirty-one. My brother Agon climbed up the rocks above. The rest of us blocked their escape and shouted: 'Chinks! We're going to feed your bollocks to the lammergeyers! We're going to string your eyeballs on wire!' They were so scared they retreated right underneath Agon who set off a nice little rock slide and buried the bastards.'

Karjen's notions of the religious life were similarly scabrous: 'My sainted mother wanted me to be a lama. Can you imagine me as a lama, Mr Jemmy? I'll tell you why I said no. I was a rather pretty young lad at the time – it's true! – and I didn't fancy being buggered to Nirvana, beg pardon.'

They had paused by a stream with ice-scalloped margins. 'Lovely spot in summer, this,' growled Karjen through his greasy moustache. 'Covered in flowers and herbs. You'll see that Reverend Khenpo Nima out here grubbing around for his cures. Not an ache in your body he can't put a petal to.'

In the sun, a small group of grunting yaks sought the last soft grazing. The outside of each grass tussock was frost-blasted, brittle and yellow, so they thrust their noses into the heart. As Jamie watched the huge bulls, he became aware of a soft, coppery ringing in the air behind him, faint but clear.

'Mr Jemmy! From Lhasa!'

Over the low brow of the pass came a procession of ponies, mules and baggage yaks in single file.

'See the red tassels? Official messengers,' said Karjen.

They heaved the ponies round and pelted across the stony tract into the village. Small children chased after them through the lanes squealing, 'Jemmy! Jemmy!'

The State courier, his bridle bedecked with red braids, had paused at Jamie's gateway.

'Mr Jemmy? Your radio oil and some letters. Lhasa's regards, and where's your contract? Reverend Khenpo Nima! Humblest greetings to the Abbot ... '

As Jamie received the oilcloth packet of mail, Puton was watching from the porch. There were no messages for the widow of Lhasa's tax collector. Jamie felt her black eyes on him as he came across the yard. He gave her a quick smile, and stepped past into his room.

*

Khenpo Nima's letters had not cheered him at all. The instructions regarding Jyeko town he gave out at once. Then he went to inspect his other problem. Jamie was stomping about his house with a cheery brusqueness that, to Khenpo Nima, rang hollow. 'What splendid news from your home, Jemmy?'

'It's all months out of date.'

'Oh,' said Khenpo Nima, thoughtfully. 'I am sorry. There is heavy snow in the southern passes, so ... What is in these old letters?'

'Family guff, Nima, hatch, match and dispatch.'

'Something special?'

'They want me home, actually.' The monk stared at him, fearing the worst. 'Dad says I've a place secure on the electrical salvage but it won't wait for ever. And Catriona next door all grown up and asking after me.'

That afternoon, he went out and distributed half a tin of Moffat toffee to the urchins in the street, like a free man.

Two days later, the afternoon of 1 January 1950, when Khenpo Nima entered the little radio room, Jamie flagged him to silence. The radio glowed soft orange, and hissed. As Jamie touched dials, the hiss swayed deeper, then lighter – but there were no voices. At last he sat back and turned off the apparatus.

'It's official. Jesus ... '

'What has happened?'

'Radio Peking. They want Tibet.'

'What have they said?'

'A New Year announcement. "Tasks for the People's Liberation Army for 1950: the liberation of Taiwan and Tibet." That was it.'

Together, they sat in silence for a moment, staring at the instruments that gleamed in the shaded room like malevolent eyes.

'Well, come on, Nima – they propose to invade.'

'Jemmy, they will not come through Jyeko. We are out of the way, we are nothing. Only some safety precautions are necessary,' said Khenpo Nima, in a decided tone.

'Oh, that's good.'

'In fact, we have already started in Jyeko. No need to fear. Come upstairs and see.'

They climbed the tree trunk ladder to the roof of the radio room. Jamie peered about, wondering if perhaps he'd missed the construction of gun emplacements overlooking the bridge.

'There,' said Nima, pointing, 'and on the hillside.'

All Jamie could see were small plumes of smoke.

'What am I looking at?'

'So many prayers. You can see the fires.'

'Prayers?'

'So many. You know, I had letters yesterday also. Lhasa has ordered a redoubling of our burnt offerings.'

Jamie stared at the twists of juniper smoke coming from the distant rocks. Dismayed and embarrassed, he could not look at Khenpo Nima. The monk said, 'You think we should do something more?'

'Perhaps you need some rifles. Or to set charges on the bridge. Things like that.'

'You see, Lord Buddha has taught us ... '

'Nima, it's all right. If you want to defend Tibet with incense, that's your affair.'

*

He rode out of Jyeko by himself. Though the village laughed at his curious posture, Jamie rode well: he'd been the signals officer with a cavalry regiment in Palestine. If there was a constraint now on his bravado, it was one thought: if he should fall and break bones, the nearest decent surgeon was in Calcutta.

He rode west, making for a rocky spur a mile outside Jyeko. The wind was sharp, unhindered by any forest; the Jyeko valley was bare, at fourteen thousand feet too bleak and blasted for anything to stand tall. He left the pony and scrambled up heaps of frost-split schist to a votive cairn: a squat stack of rock that would endure storms. A broad yellow cloth had been newly tied round the flanks. Twenty feet off rose an old, weathered pole, almost white with sun and the scourings of snow and sand. Between this staff and the cairn a cord was stretched from which hung scores of small white flags block-printed with prayers – 'wind horses' – that moved gently in the chill breath of the glaciers. A few yards away, a stone ring enclosed the incense pyre. A steady stream of richly pungent juniper smoke billowed upwards into the freezing blue.

In the thin air he could see more clearly than hear. Beyond the pass lay an expanse of plains, broken by domed reddish hills, snow-dusted now. There, in summer, the yak and wild ass came for pasture, with griffon vultures on watch on ten-foot wings.

Then the mountains steadily closed ranks and rose higher, until there was hardly a flat pasture in two hundred miles. The grand massif of central Tibet looked to Jamie like mountains in Heaven, a wall of ice-blue poised lightly above the clouds. A score of peaks draped with steep fans of snow, a thousand white spearheads pointing skyward. The sun gleamed within the ice like a shining edge on a sharp blade. A throng of air currents drew plumes of ice crystals up the flanks into the clear blue. He saw a russet-breasted lammergeyer glide over the gullies.

Jamie felt himself extended by the sight, his spirit broadened.

He looked down at the village, the chain bridge, the barracks in Chinese Sikhang on the far side. Jyeko's children scampered through the twisting, muddy lanes. There was the monastery, there were the homes where they delighted to call him in, to give him their best meals in their best bowls, to offer him warm furs and to nudge their daughters towards him with outrageously smutty asides, hooting with laughter. He could see houses where they'd taken money from him in *migmag*, 'the war of many eyes', then fondly let him win some back. Always, they smiled for him. If they laughed, it was never in malice.

He'd never been so welcome – but he was *other*: the warmth he'd found did not altogether relax him. Here, he was never quite calm. He thought of a Khampa child he'd seen the previous evening, asleep with its head on its father's lap. Such sweet capitulation, oblivious of care, would be denied him in Jyeko. He would be watched, allowed for, set aside. Every day there was an undercurrent of anxiety that made him long for that sleep.

Yet, as he recalled the similar sleep of his own childhood, he frowned. He'd grown up like that: lovingly circumscribed, tenderly constricted. And he'd escaped.

It was no duty of his to defend Tibet: he was quite clear about that. He'd be out. Not home: somewhere new. And the more he moved on, the lonelier he'd be. He gazed down at Jyeko, longing to embrace it, longing to leave. He took a deep breath and a grip on himself, and rode home.

*

seven

A sky-blue pavilion stands in a field outside Jyeko. The monks are busy. They carry yak-wool rugs, brassware chased with curlicue dragons, hangings of red silk crowded with black script, braziers and a tea-kettle, cushions and a dais of cypress wood. The fires are lit and the tent fills with the sweet scent of burning juniper.

The Jyeko people and their prairie neighbours stream out of the village. Rough herders come with matted hair cut in a fringe above their eyes and nothing but a greasy sheepskin gown and rawhide boots. Townsmen in turbans stride about in noisy geniality, with tobacco pipes and leather snuff pouches, baggy trousers tumbling over their boots. The girls are in their best aprons, red, blue and green, with bright twists of braid about their heads. Market women, out to make a killing, bring baskets of sweetmeats and cakes. Travelling hawkers have dried fruits for the picnic: sweetly acid Nepali apricots and figs from Si-ning-fu, raisins from India and sun-blackened Bhutanese peaches. Children run and shriek among the vendors while babies peep from their parents' massive coats, their faces puckering against the cold.

The village grandees ride sedately in gowns of Indian silk over their furs with high red collars and rupees for buttons. Their servants have spread rugs and cushions on the frozen ground. Mounted on mules, well-to-do women are swathed in rainbow tunics, their hands hidden until they blow their noses on their fingers. At their belts hang châtelaines of silver and prettily embroidered cases for their eye shades.

But all attention is on the young men riding Jyeko's best ponies. They're the stars of today's serious matter: the New Year racing.

Nothing can happen without the Abbot, and the crowd mills aimlessly in anticipation. Then, at the village margin by Jamie's house, the procession appears. Khenpo Nima, on foot, leads a piebald Yarkand pony bearing the Abbot in a yellow silk robe and a crescent-shaped mitre. Around him flock his novices spinning prayer wheels, and lamas bearing the long copper trumpet that booms its single rumbling note as they march across the stony open ground towards the tent, the village cheering the Abbot to his seat.

Two figures emerge unnoticed from Jamie's gate and come hesitantly towards the games field. The woman pushes herself along with a stick in her right hand. Her left hand holds onto a timid little girl, who stays firmly in her shadow.

Puton has hardly set foot in public since her venture to the market – but the procession, the trumpet and the bells had passed by in the lane. Puton had seen her little girl watching from the open gate, and it was too heartbreaking. Now they have come out, they will see the New Year sports. For her daughter she'll risk it.

She moves slowly towards the games field, keeping to the rear of the crowd and behind the Abbot's tent. The rough ground falls away in front of the pavilion; here the people cluster, chattering, guzzling and expectant. A small space of honour has been cleared for Jamie Wilson who sits on a sheepskin, sketching. A gang of whispering, elbowing urchins stand behind him, peering over his shoulder.

A bullseye target is suspended in a square frame, with another nearby. A dozen young men on ponies follow a monk who stops them fifty yards away. Each rider carries a short, stiff bow and a quiver of arrows, with a long musket resting across the pommel. The ponies, quick-eyed and rough-haired, wear blankets embroidered in scallops of red and black, with reins of twisted red and white cord and their tails bound in coloured tassels. Across the chest hangs a strap of bells. As the ponies trot, a silver ringing fills the icy valley.

Dechen can see nothing over the heads, so her mother brings her to the left flank of the gathering. Now people notice them and murmur. Puton tenses, avoiding the eyes that scowl at her and her daughter. But her look defies the crowd: *So, here I stand: what of it?*

Then a horn blows.

A single rider kicks his pony into a gallop. They career

straight at the two targets, the rider hefting his cumbersome musket. Just twenty feet from the first bullseye, he shoots and hits the white outer ring. A puff of chalky dust spurts out. He slings the gun frantically over his shoulder, grabs at his bow and quiver, is past the second target, then swings round in his saddle and looses an arrow backwards. There is a thrilled scream from the crowd – but the rider canters away in mortification. He's missed.

*

Jamie Wilson sits with a pad of cartridge paper on his knee, watercolours on the ground by him, his pencil moving excitedly over his paper.

'It is very difficult, do you see, Jemmy?' says Khenpo Nima, crouching by his side. 'He must hit both targets.'

As he speaks, there's a shriek and a cheer from the crowd: an arrow has almost impaled a spectator.

'It's just wonderful.' Jamie smiles. 'What's the prize?'

'Oh, nothing but honour.' Nima looks round. 'I must speak with someone,' he says. Jamie sees Puton toss back her braided hair and there is a flash of silver at her throat: the little charm case she carries on a cord. Jamie asks himself how it is that he's been looking at her throat so closely. He returns to his drawing.

Puton sees Khenpo Nima approach and she relaxes.

'Excellent,' he smiles, 'you've come. Just the thing.'

'For Dechen's sake,' says Puton. 'But it was a mistake.'

A knot of small boys smirk nearby, while youths whisper together, glancing over their shoulders. Khenpo Nima tries to be boisterously encouraging. 'Ah, it was the wisest thing! What can you be thinking?'

'That I am despised here,' says Puton quietly, 'that my daughter is small, that the Chinese are coming.'

Horsemen rush the targets, their muskets smoke, arrows strike true or patter on the dirt, while one rider simply falls off in dismay. Elsewhere, the best huntsmen are squinting along their matchlocks at a quartz target, while others shoot arrows with hollow heads that fly whistling like frightened birds.

Nima's sleeve is tugged: Karjen nods towards some young men by the ponies, pointing at Jamie and at a monk who is just now placing a red silk scarf on a post – the goal of a race.

'Jemmy,' says Nima, 'they are saying, will you ride in the horse-race with them?'

'No, thanks,' answers the artist.

'Because,' continues Nima, undeterred, 'they say that they want an easy victory.'

Jamie pauses in his brushwork, looks up at Nima and then at the waiting ponies. They are so smothered in decoration that he wonders how they can see past the rosettes.

Khenpo Nima shrugs. 'The boys have seen you riding about town but, of course, Ying-gi-li don't know the horse's tail from its ears.'

'Arse from its elbow,' retorts Jamie, icily.

'What?'

'Don't know its arse from its elbow. They say that, do they?'

'So I hear ... ' begins the monk.

'Well, they're about to bloody learn otherwise.'

In a moment, Jamie is striding towards the ponies and the crowd sees, whistling with delight.

*

A musket cracks a blue wisp into the air. A dozen ponies start, eyes bulging and ears back as the riders kick. The hard ground clacks beneath the hoofs, the children screech: *Jemmy! Jemmy!* Jyeko jumps up, laughing, as the ponies career round the marker rocks; even the Abbot, beaming, gets stiffly to his feet. The young Khampa men press hard on their ponies' flanks, thrash as hard as they can in their soft boots, pushing at the turn, bawling in Jamie's ear, yelling obscenities, laughter and splendid curses.

Then into the last straight, smack in front of the village crowd, almost trampling the children, pelting towards the red silk scarf on its post. (Heaven knows how Jamie won: maybe his pony was so alarmed at the bizarre foreign rider that it sped frantically, or perhaps his arm was a fraction longer at the grab. Maybe they let him win for the fun of it.) With a splendid lunge he seizes the scarf. And before he himself quite realises, Jamie is parading on his skipping pony before the wild village, flourishing the red scarf over his head.

'Pretty girl!' roars Jyeko. 'Jemmy's pretty girl!'

'Jemmy!' yells Khenpo Nima. 'You must choose, you must give it to your pretty girl!'

'I haven't got one,' laughs Jamie, as the pony circles.

'Yes, of course, in your house,' Nima bellows back. 'There she is!'

Jamie sees Puton standing apart as always at the crowd's end. Careless and delirious, he neither wonders nor hesitates. He hoiks on the braided neck-rein, pushing the pony along in front of the crowd. Then, in a swift movement, he drapes the scarf across Puton's shoulder as he passes.

For an instant, the noise falters and almost dies to silence. Until someone bursts out clapping and laughing:

'Yes, bravo, Mr Jemmy! Bravo the rider!'

It is the old Abbot. A trifle wobbly and supported by two monks, he stands in the shelter of his white and blue pavilion, smiling and applauding. The astonished crowd dutifully declares its approval. In front of them, Jamie circles again on his pony, beaming with triumph. Puton clutches at the red scarf, bewildered, thrilled, surprised in every corner of her heart.

*

eight

At the end of March, flights of geese were seen. Then, after months of cold that made lips bleed, of blocked mountain passes and wearying storms, the spring came to Jyeko. Puton began each day with a new flush of hope and gratitude. She devoted herself to giving her little girl any scraps of joy she could – and to caring for Jemmy the Ying-gi-li.

In her room, the folded red scarf was placed under the silver charm box. In the night, Puton would recall the young rider who had laid it on her neck. She would touch a finger to the fringe of the scarf with a sensation that she had felt – but faintly – in the early days of her marriage. She could not name it but she marvelled at it. She was in the grip of a pretty imp that swarmed on her breast, frightening and delighting her all at once.

But when this happy imp approached her heart, three dragons with spiny green tails, bloodshot eyes and toxic breath barred the door. The first was Malice, which would do her good name to death. The second was Desertion, the day she might find her protectors gone. The third was Reproach, which stirred each night: in a vision of a gorge, a storm of black rocks, a horse and a man falling with his cry lost in the roar of water. She would wake under her sheepskins, sweating, suffocating. She would light a lamp for comfort and lie motionless, listening to Dechen's easy breathing. And she would wonder how she could tell her husband that she honoured him still, to give him rest.

*

The Chinese Nationalists were still there across the river. Some garrisons on the Tibetan border had declared for the Communists and gone home, leaving their dismal barracks empty. Some had murdered their officers, cast off their uniforms and become traders. Some had fled south through Sichuan and Yunnan to join the Kuomintang army in exile in Siam. A few, as at Jyeko, listened to KMT broadcasts and tried to believe that victory was assured. They sat tight, their morale and their stores dwindling together.

One morning in April 1950, Jamie Wilson went as usual to the radio room where he was joined by Khenpo Nima. The monk smiled at Puton, put out a hand to Dechen, but was preoccupied. He followed Jamie inside. Puton observed them: since arriving in Jyeko she had become acutely sensitive to mood changes around her. The slightest hint of anxiety or menace and Puton's skin began to prickle, her flight reflexes springing to the alert. Now the generator began its slow *tug-tug* behind her. She returned to her work, hanging Jamie's laundry on a sagging cord across the yard.

Khenpo Nima had his bulletin ready in an exercise book. As Jamie applied the cipher (of schoolboy simplicity), he glimpsed Dechen skip across the yard, dodging the new-melted puddles. The clothes-line was twitching slightly. In his mind's eye, he saw Puton's hands raised to the cord. At that moment Nima cleared his throat portentously: 'The final item will be for Cabinet attention only.'

More interested, Jamie waited for Khenpo Nima to dictate. The monk turned back a page in his exercise book.

'Word has come,' said Nima slowly, 'of Chinese military preparations in Chengdu. Merchants tell us ... ' He spoke in a tense monotone reporting the arrival of high-ranking officers in Sichuan, of survey teams on the dusty roads, of matériel stock-pilings. He concluded: 'Our prayers will be redoubled. Tibet need have no fear.'

Jamie encrypted the text and tapped it out. The monk sat back on his stool glaring at the transmitter. Jamie had not seen Nima on edge like this before. Out in the yard, the washing hung still. Puton had either gone indoors or was there listening.

'So, I am finished,' said the monk. 'Shall you come for ping-pong tonight? You have not been all week and Wangdu declares he shall beat you today.'

'He'll beat me soon enough,' said Jamie.

'Then come, for humility.'

Khenpo Nima stood, pushed the exercise book into his

woven shoulder bag, strode through the gate and was gone.

Jamie sat quietly, his finger toying with the dull brass of the Morse key. He felt the unhappy ignorance of isolation: cataclysms might take place of which he would know nothing until it was too late.

Karjen appeared in the doorway and grunted, 'Finished?'

The generator tocked in the background, sipping away at the petrol store.

'Two minutes.'

Jamie reached forward and spun the dials a moment, not knowing what, if anything, he sought. He found only a babble of Morse, squealing Chinese music, atmospherics, and what might have been Soviet football results or the news in Greek for all he could tell. Nothing else.

A shadow fell, just a slight change in the light from the doorway. Jamie glanced up at Puton and smiled. He reached for the main power switch.

'...*Fox 5 Sugar Dog calling Tare 4 Jig William. Do you read? Over.'*

'Who the hell's that,' muttered Jamie, 'at this hour?'

Scottish accents. Coming from where? His hand moved to the tuner and the ill-focused, fuzzy voice slipped away, then returned.

'*This is Fox 5 Sugar Dog, position Rosyth, Great Britain, calling Tare 4 Jig William, Tibet. Do you read me? Over.'*

For a moment, Jamie stared at the radio, frozen in astonishment. Then he was tapping frantically at the Morse key. The voice replied: *'Aha! Good day to you, Tibet! That's fine to have got you at last. How do you read Rosyth? Over.'*

A most peculiar sensation swept through Jamie, a compound of adrenaline, intoxication and disbelief. 'That's ... Rosyth!' he stammered. 'Just over from Inverkeithing, you see.'

He could receive voice from anywhere, but at long range, his little transmitter had only the power to send Morse in reply. He tapped and glanced again at Puton as though she must witness this. She watched, not stirring.

'Excellent, Tibet! We've been trying for two weeks, you know. My name's Dinsmore, it's my radio. Stand by, please.'

Jamie whispered, 'Bloody Rosyth!' His eyes, dilated in the half-dark, latched onto the loudspeaker. Then came another voice, Scottish again, politely female, painstakingly clear: *'Hello, James. Can you hear me?'*

Jamie whispered: 'Mum ...?'

'Can you hear me, dearest?'

He grabbed at the microphone and shouted, 'Mother, it's Jamie, can you hear me? Can you hear me, over?'

' ... still there, dearest? Over.'

'Damn,' he yelped. 'Just bloody damn!'

He began tapping again as fast as he could. The reply came: *'James, that's fine, we're getting your message. It's wonderful to know you're well. We've been worried, dearest, with all the news. Here's Father.'*

A solid, man's voice: *'Hello there, son.'*

Jamie turned once again to Puton. Emotion swelled within him, choking his words, springing from his eyes.

'That's my father.'

It was all he could say. Puton regarded his streaming face thoughtfully, slowly nodding.

*

She swept the house with one hand, the other on her stick. Dust and dirt billowed out of the door into the spring sunlight. The sound of the brush filled the morning as the generator slowed and stumbled to a standstill. Then Jamie appeared at the door of the radio room. He took a few steps and halted, as though confused or blinded by spring. Again he moved, uncertainly, across the compound towards her.

'It's Mum and Dad,' he began. 'They've found a man with a transmitter. They've tried before.'

Puton peered at his face: he seemed neither happy, nor ... what? She felt her heart shrivel in fear.

'They want me back in Inverkeithing,' said Jamie. The dragon of Desertion thrashed his green tail.

*

Jamie was quiet all day, keeping to his room.

In the afternoon he took out his paints, adding a pale colour-wash to some of his sketches of the market. He would frequently stop in his work and stare at the pictures on the wall in front of him, frowning.

Puton continued with her tasks, taking quick checks through Jamie's door. At last she came and stood there silently. It was a moment before Jamie looked round.

'Hello,' he said, faintly surprised. 'Are you wanting to come in and clean?'

She didn't reply at once. When she spoke, it was both deferential and insistent. 'Mr Jemmy, you have spoken with your family today.'

'That's right.'

'In Tibet, our country, we have holy lamas who can speak through the air like this.'

Jamie felt secretly impatient, the tensions of the morning still with him. But her seriousness charged her face, made her handsome. He agreed: 'That's right, something similar.'

'I wish to speak to my husband, as you do.'

She nodded towards the radio room.

'Oh, yes?' said Jamie. 'Can he speak to us?'

Puton replied, 'He is dead now. We were attacked.'

Jamie kicked himself. 'Yes, I see,' he responded lamely.

'He is come again. My husband is a yak now,' she remarked matter-of-factly, 'because he has had no proper funeral.'

'A yak?' queried Jamie.

'It is the big animal with much hair ...'

'Oh, yes, I know.'

'Near Lhasa. He is eating grass there. If we speak in the air as you do, he can hear.'

Jamie gazed at her. Puton met his eyes. He had been about to laugh, but was now astonished by her dignity.

'It is more than a year,' said the widow. 'I have only Dechen.'

There was, at last, a note of pleading. The dragon of Reproach had sent her to him.

*

Khenpo Nima came later, listened to the bulletin from Lhasa, then commanded Jamie to appear at the monastery that night and be whipped at ping-pong. As the monk left, Karjen moved towards the generator shed but Jamie signalled him to leave it running awhile. Puton was standing on the porch holding Dechen by the hand. He beckoned to her, went into the radio room, and Puton followed.

The young woman sat upright, calm and confident, holding a white ceremonial scarf. The radio still glowed live.

Jamie adjusted a dial or two. He said, 'Where exactly is your husband?'

'At Nagche,' replied Puton. 'His name is Gonpo Namgyal.'

Jamie pulled the black microphone close, removing all expression from his voice: 'Calling YAK Namgyal,' he said. 'Calling YAK Namgyal, I have Puton for you. Stand by, please, over.'

He slid the microphone across the table to Puton. She spoke at once, slowly and respectfully, asking her husband's blessing in her new life and saying that she prayed for him. Meanwhile, she took the white scarf from her lap and laid it around the microphone as the Abbot had once done.

Jamie sat quiet, taking a toffee from his pocket and observing her. She spoke on, calm and steady, and with gentle satisfaction as though a long injustice was being put to rights.

At last she stopped, folded her hands in her lap and sat still. The faint yellow light of the main dial was reflected in the corner of her deep black eye. He had never seen her so beautifully tranquil. One dragon had departed from her heart. She looked up

and smiled at him with the joy of release for which she had no
words and sought none.

*

nine

Her expression stayed with him and disturbed him. It said to him that she was freed and ready. But for what, he did not understand.

Jamie observed her going about her work or playing with Dechen. He made mental catalogues: that she was in pain but never mentioned it; that she was almost invisibly discreet but noticed everything; that she worked continuously but never forgot her daughter; that she was a cripple but that it strangely enhanced her beauty. Sometimes there would be an instant's stillness, an alert poise, and then she'd work on. She had felt his look, and a moment or two later she would lift her face with the beginnings of an embarrassed smile.

Increasingly unsettled, Jamie would stomp off to the monastery for gossip and ping-pong.

In the village, the prayer flags were doubled and redoubled, with cords looped across the narrow lanes and wind horses streaming. Every house had an incense brazier relit each dawn. Every *chorten* was newly bound in yellow. Every herdsman, merchant or housewife in the street seemed to be carrying a little prayer wheel and spinning it urgently. In the monastery hall, the huge prayer drums turned without cease until late in the evening.

But when Wangdu finally beat Jamie two sets to one, the monastery reverberated with mirth.

'See how we learn your ways when we wish,' Khenpo Nima teased.

Jamie riposted sharply: 'So where are the radio apprentices you were going to find me, Nima?' The Tibetans seemed to think that by avoiding learning radio work themselves they'd oblige him to stay and do it.

'Come, Jemmy,' said Nima, with a hand on his shoulder. 'The day when you are sick, I shall heal you with the skills of a thousand years. Tibet changes slowly, but only for the best.'

They were drinking tea in the scripture library. In front of the door in the evening light, Khenpo Nima sat with crossed legs over which was spread a sheet of fine, soft leather. A heap of dried and discoloured flowers filled his lap; through these he was sorting minutely, head bowed. Stalks and rubbish were dropped to his left, stiff brown leaves into a jar to his right, and what Jamie supposed must be the petals – darkly diaphanous, like old brown butterfly wings – fell onto a wooden board before him.

'When our abbot was younger, we journeyed to Kantu-Dzong and he showed me these growing wild: my best poppies, blue when they were fresh. They are for healing bone. We don't have them growing here.'

'But the meadows are smothered in blue poppies.'

'You have not looked closely. Some have little spines on the stalks, some on the leaves. Some grow tall and spindly on the open meadow, some hide in the scree. Some are not blue at all, you see, but yellow or golden, even. So many. This one is the rarest, the dearest to a physician's heart.'

He waved airily towards high shelves. 'A thousand years of physic, Jemmy. There's not a plant in the Himalaya that I can't use.' He studied Jamie's face, but saw no response. Nima folded the thin sheet of leather over the dried flowers that remained unsorted, and stood up. 'Now you must see how our waterwheel is working today.'

Outside the monastery gate, the stream bubbled in its channel, the wood and leather prayer wheel spun briskly and a clapper knocked loudly to announce the departure of prayers to the skies. Two monks worked with rough wooden trowels, cementing the outside of the water-race with a mix of clays.

'Automatic!' beamed Khenpo Nima. 'So many prayers to keep out the foreign dragons. This man too.'

A young man sat on the wall, poorly dressed in old sheepskins and rotten felt boots bound with twine. He leaned and dipped a carved wooden block, into the water again and again.

'He is printing Buddhas in the stream,' said Nima, and Jamie smiled indulgently.

But when they reached his house, Jamie's good humour vanished. Even as they passed through the gateway, he stopped and bellowed: 'No, Karjen! Get those down right now!'

The old man was on the roof. The radio antenna was festooned with fluttering prayer flags and Karjen was tying more to the guy lines. He looked down in surprise. Khenpo Nima put a hand to Jamie's shoulder but Jamie pulled free and strode into the yard, livid with anger. 'Get them off, Karjen! Do I have to come and do it?'

Karjen looked at Nima, uncertain.

'Jemmy,' said Nima, 'Lhasa has asked for all possible efforts at prayer ... '

'That's an antenna, not a bloody wind horse stable. It's modern equipment, understand? I'll have it treated with respect, Nima, not arsed about with!'

'It is respect ... ' began Nima.

'Serious respect!' snapped Jamie. 'You have to get serious, Nima! You think your waterwheel is going to keep one Communist out of Tibet? Is that what you think?'

He stepped smartly to the ladder. Khenpo Nima watched him climb.

'We deal with China in our way, Jemmy. That is for us.'

'Oh? Hasn't stopped them before, has it? Still, if you can do it with prayers, you've no need of me and the radio. I'll take this down and be off home to Inverkeithing, if you'll excuse me.'

He had taken out a pocket knife and was busily sawing off Karjen's flags. Karjen stood back scowling.

'Jemmy!' shouted Nima, climbing after him. 'Jemmy, please, listen to me, stop this.'

Jamie paused a second, looking into Khenpo Nima's eyes. He said: 'I came here under contract, I've a job to do, but that's it. I'm happy that I came, but I'm not a Tibetan.'

The breeze picked up the little flags from where Jamie had dropped them on the flat roof, and whisked them over the parapet. Khenpo Nima regarded Jamie with sadness. 'You are family to us now, Jemmy. We thought you would like to be a part of our prayers.'

There was a movement in the doorway of the house. Dechen crept out to see who was speaking so loudly. Behind her,

Puton came awkwardly and looked up towards the roof. Jamie saw her. 'Nima, I'm not ungrateful,' he said, more quietly, 'don't think that. But I'll not be caught up where it's not of my choosing.'

'Of course, Jemmy,' said the monk, sensing reconciliation, 'We are so thankful to you here, do you know? Please, come down, and let us leave this matter.'

Jamie relented. A moment later he followed Nima down the ladder. Karjen picked up the remaining flags and furtively retied several before descending also.

*

At nightfall, Jamie withdrew into his room once more, painting. The evenings were cold already and the *kang* stove-bed was alight. It was far from ideal, of course, attempting delicate colour washes by the light of a smoking butter-oil lamp. But he knew what he was about – which was a studied dreaming.

The village outside fell quiet behind heavy wooden shutters, but breezes moved among the little prayer bells mounted on springs that had proliferated in every courtyard. Their tinkling seeped throughout Jyeko. If you tuned a sharp ear to the darkness, you'd catch a sound like a feather passing among glass chimes. Jamie, though, was too absorbed – so he did not hear Puton's stick move across the floor of the outer room.

She tapped twice. Surprised, he froze with the watercolour brush in his hand. She tapped again, and he rose instantly to open the door. She stood in the doorway regarding him, with the light from a lamp behind her making an aureole in the margins of her hair. Her face was shadowed, until Jamie moved slightly to his left and the table lamp found her. She pushed a loose lock away from her cheek, lifting her face.

She said, 'If you permit, I have something for you.'

He thought, her voice often has this tinge to it, half pride, half apprehension. He remembered his manners. 'Heavens, come in!' he said.

She hesitated. 'No, I only ... '

But he had already backed aside from the door and waved her in: 'Please, take a seat. The *kang* is warm. Please.'

So she came forward, glancing at him, and sat on the fur covers, placing her stick beside her. Jamie went back to his stool at the table.

'I am sorry to disturb your work,' said Puton.

'Just sketches.' He smiled, wondering what she made of his ever-so-British watercolours, so unlike the heavy gouaches of Tibet.

Puton looked down. She held in her hand the red scarf from the games. Was she going to give it back? Had he offended propriety somehow? She said: 'I have tried to make this beautiful for you, though it is not beautiful like your painting.'

She held it out, folded. It was certainly the same scarf. Puzzled, Jamie put out a hand. As he did so, she let the scarf fall open towards him.

At both ends, some eight or nine inches of the red silk were covered in embroidery. The individual stitches were minuscule, barely visible in the quivering lamplight. The threads were indigo and green, cobalt blue and white with, here and there, fine gold traces. The patterns swarmed exquisitely over the silk surface: miniature dragons and mountain ranges, tiny geese in flight, all twined into a square frame. In the centre of each design, in coiled blue and white, were the letters of the radio call-sign: *T4JW.*

He lifted the scarf close to his face to peer at the work, and whispered, 'Good grief.'

'It is the "call-sign", yes?'

'Yes!' replied Jamie. 'It's ... it's really astonishing.'

She watched him closely, a hint of anxiety discernible in her face. Then she relaxed a little, realising that he found the gift acceptable. 'I have made this for you,' she began, 'because you have honoured me with friendship.' Jamie looked up at her face which lamplight caressed. He saw that the downy hair that joined her brows was not so much black as a dark honey. 'And because you have given us a home, which Jyeko would not.'

Jamie thought: What was my life like before she came? He could barely remember.

'It's been my pleasure,' he hazarded. He felt awkward, caught out. The woman and her child had permeated every corner of his rooms, bringing a civilising warmth. A quality had come into the house like the rich, sweet scent of a herb that had perfumed his world so subtly that he'd not noted its coming.

Puton reached for her stick.

'Don't go just yet,' he said quickly. 'Please, be comfortable for a moment.'

She regarded him, then slowly put down the stick. She looked towards the pictures fixed to the wall above his table. 'You have painted your home,' she said levelly, 'because you are wishing to go there.'

'My home?'

She examined the paintings: an idyll of heather, lochs and foreshores. She said: 'Is it somewhere that I could live?'

'You? Yes, I suppose. Good heavens, why?'

'I have to live somewhere also, with Dechen.'

He saw concentration in her gaze, he thought that he saw her nostrils flare with some emotion he could not read. Even as he saw it, a notion came to him: that this woman might live anywhere and make a home of it – just as he himself could not.

'Well,' he grinned, 'let's go to India, I say. You come and keep house for me there. Life could be pretty civilised, I should think. We must do it!'

It was said with all the light sincerity of a young man's moment. Puton remained motionless, save for a slight rise and fall of her breast. He heard her breathing; behind that, wisps of the brittle prayer bells out in the lanes. He moved to sit alongside her on the warm covers of the *kang*, twisting to gaze at her profile and the pores of her skin. They remained complicit in stillness for half a minute more.

Then she picked up the embroidered scarf from the tumbled furs between them. She turned to Jamie, saying: 'This you can wear when the wind creeps about your throat.'

She lifted it, her every movement slow and steady as though not to startle an animal. She raised it, passing the end behind his neck while he stayed still. Then she tied a single turn in the scarf in front of Jamie's throat.

'Call-sign T4JW,' she said, smiling full upon him for the first time. His mind reeled as though struck a blow, all his loneliness screeching with desire.

At that moment, a clumsy wooden banging came from the yard: Karjen on his way to the latrine. Puton caught her breath, tensing. 'He will see that my room is open.'

'So what?' said Jamie, surprised.

'But it is Karjen!'

'And it's my house,' said Jamie, thinking that he should perhaps assert some authority.

'He will tell the village.' She grabbed her stick and stabbed it downwards at the very moment that she tried to stand. The stick caught awkwardly in the rug. Puton had not gained her balance; she staggered clumsily against the side of the bed, twisting her foot. She gave a small cry of grief, of fright. Jamie's hands went out to her sides, catching her.

'Easy!' he said, setting her down. 'No harm ... '

'Oh yes!' she cried, breathless from the pain flashing through her leg. She grasped the stick with whitened knuckles, rose and was gone through the open door.

*

If Karjen was spreading rumour, there were no echoes; Khenpo Nima said nothing. But for Jamie it was enough that Puton was alarmed. A silent net of searching looks fell over the house. Puton stayed clear of him.

Only at meal times did she approach him. Jamie would take his seat and wait; Puton would enter with a bowl of hot buttered barleymeal in her free hand. She would make her way towards Jamie, and Karjen would stand directly behind her in the doorway. She would feel the old man's look on her back like a whip teasing naked skin before it strikes. She would raise her eyes to Jamie, filled with questioning. Jamie, able to see Karjen's stare across her shoulder, tried to smile blandly. It all made his scalp crawl.

Khenpo Nima was there twice daily: he sensed the mood that encrusted everything like salt drying on skin. He observed Puton bringing food and refreshment to Jamie, how she laid clean clothing on his bed with a particular slowness. He observed how Karjen hovered and glowered, how the bandit's temper decayed, how he cursed the ponies for nothing. Nima was there one day when Karjen pursued little Dechen from the living room with murderous snarls. He had seen the little girl pick up a small box of blue lacquered wood, and had roared, 'Theft! Theft!' so that the child ran weeping to her mother. Nima heard Jamie cry out, 'Karjen, that's not necessary, she can have it, I'd like her to have it ...'

And when the old man stamped away to the fuel shed, Nima glimpsed the looks that Jamie and Puton exchanged. In those eyes, he saw youth boiling and burning. In the poised stillness, he saw two spirits hurtling towards each other. It alarmed Khenpo Nima, but delighted him more.

Over tea that evening Jamie was edgy and taciturn. As they ate the last of the Moffat toffee, Khenpo Nima said: 'Jemmy, I think that Karjen is a problem for you?'

Jamie did not look at him. 'A problem?' he queried evasively.

'Perhaps he is sometimes in the way.'

Khenpo Nima was smiling gently at him. Oh, what was the use in pretending anything? Nima continued, 'It is no part of our deal that you must have Karjen in your house.'

The moment he said this, Khenpo Nima kicked himself hard. But it could not be unsaid.

Jamie frowned, as though recalling a difficulty. 'Our deal? You mean that contract you were flourishing a while back? The old one must have expired, surely. Wasn't it due?'

Jamie stood and went through the door of his bedroom. He hoiked open a box under his table and pulled out a long brown envelope, saying, 'It was for some silly period like twenty-one months, wasn't it? No, just twenty. So that's ... May, June, July. It expired in July. For Heaven's sake, am I still meant to be here?' He looked askance at Khenpo Nima. 'Why didn't you tell me?'

The monk shrugged. 'What could I say?'

'So, you just hoped I'd forget all about it?'

At that moment, Dechen appeared timidly in the doorway and an instant later Puton's hand was on the child to restrain her. As she pulled Dechen back, Jamie's eyes clung to her.

'I would like to stay, Nima,' murmured Jamie, and the monk knew that no contract was required. He smiled slightly at Jamie's inability to look him in the eye.

'And Karjen?'

Jamie blushed violently, quite out of his depth, whispering: 'He never leaves us.'

Khenpo Nima regarded him with avuncular fondness. 'In two days is our festival,' he remarked, 'because our farmers gather their barley. We have mask dances to drive away ancient demons – and, you know, we face some demons now.'

'Oh?' said Jamie, half-heartedly. 'That must be entertaining.'

'Our villagers find it wonderful and Karjen will certainly be attending. He will be there all night. Jemmy, I'm afraid you must be absent from the monastery, because we shall be addressing foreign devils.'

'Oh. Then I will stay at home.'

'I am so sorry. Also, Jemmy, I think Miss Puton should not come to the ceremonies. You are aware that there are some problems among the villagers about her.'

Jamie looked up curiously at Khenpo Nima.

'It is best that she remain here that night,' said the monk. 'I shall inform her. May I take one last English toffee? They are almost finished now.'

*

Singing comes from the bathroom; the woman croons, her silken lilt broken by splashes of water. The tune trickles past the doorjamb, winds out on to the dark porch along with lamplight, a little girl's laughter and curlicues of vapour. Puton bathes Dechen and herself together. Both are naked, Dechen standing on the duckboards, Puton seated on a small stool. She takes scoops from a steaming wooden tub to rinse the borax off her girl, and Dechen stamps her feet on the wet boards, delighted. Then her mother fills the tin scoop again and pours it over herself, the warm water rolling down her brown breast to pool between her thighs. There the short black hair waves like waterweed in a deep pond. Dechen dips one curious digit among her mother's softened pubic curls, toying. The next deluge goes over the child's head. The lamplight bends and waves about them, illuminating a haze of a billion water droplets looping and twining towards the crack in the doorway. On a slight draught, the vapour goes in paisley curls out into the night.

Karjen is with every other villager up at the monastery. But Jamie waits motionless in the darkness. He stands a yard from the door, listening to the splashes, giggles and crooning from within, watching the golden glimmer through the cracks. He sees the shadows lurch as the woman rinses soap off her child and her own breast. His head feels swollen and heavy on his shoulders, bursting with blood that swills and rushes. He has not announced his presence to Puton bathing, but she understands that he is there.

*

Grander, wilder shadows, bulging and swaying under the wooden colonnades. Huge grim masks lurch towards the villagers so that children cower, warriors pull back a fraction. There are stags' heads and demons, appalling gods, gilt and crimson heroes. All the inhabitants of the upper air are here, lurching in terrific conflict. Shawms and breathy flutes wail, and rough hide fiddles scrape, faster, faster, as the gongs crash and the cymbals smash together. The heroes loom out of the smoking torchlight, the demons stagger, flourishing charms and battle-axes: the fight is on!

It is late now. The open yard of the monastery is jammed with people, nomads pushing for a view between prim merchants' wives. Karjen is grinning with satisfaction at the sight of battle. The market women ogle the pop-eyed devils that will rape them all before disembowelling them with white tusks. Children between their parents' feet pull a fold of their father's gown around them as a shield.

But not every monk in Jyeko is out in the courtyard. In a side hall, something fearful has begun. An aged lama with the gift of prophecy is subsiding onto the hammered earth. Khenpo Nima and three monks hold him, for the headdress that he wears is massive, a crushing weight. The oracle sweats and pants and stares into an abyss that has opened in his brain. The monks shiver at the old man's words.

*

Jamie whispers, 'I'm so sorry, what shall we do?'

Puton gasps again, the bone splinters in her thigh jagging into some long nerve. She sits up on the bed, wincing, motionless for a second. Jamie tenderly places a fold of fur across her bare back and shoulder, for the room is icy although the fire beneath the *kang* is lit. He feels the draught touch his own naked flank, and he slips an arm round her waist for warmth.

At last she relaxes and breathes more easily. She turns and looks at the clumsy young man. 'We shall do this,' she murmurs, and carefully turns her full nakedness towards him, pushing him flat on his back on the warm stone bed. With her hands she cautiously lifts the hurting thigh across his young body, laying it down without any pain. Then she sinks onto his chest and her face finds his cheek and neck. Her body is weightless.

'There, Jemmy Ying-gi-li,' she says, as the flood tide rises within her. 'Now you won't hurt me.'

*

Near midnight he climbed onto his roof swaddled in fur. Even with the heavy coat, tremors ran through him, an electric flicker in every muscle. They were not the shivers of cold, but a body reverberating. His head seethed, charged far beyond its normal capacity. He made a mirror of his mind, and saw the woman lying quietly on the warm *kang* in the room below. He had stared at her as she slept, printing her inwardly, shape and texture. The skin of her cheek a hint red and roughened, after the years of battering wind. The dark lips on a mouth a fraction open in sleep, long hairs touching her lip. A fine pulse beating on her temple, slow and steady, a little flag for her happiness.

Jamie smiled at himself as he stood out on the roof in the icy breeze, his head thrown back and his eyes closed. He would go down and sleep by her side: blissful, oblivious sleep. But not for a minute yet.

He opened his eyes to the moon, which hung high and blazed. Enormous silhouetted peaks were tipped with cold platinum, while the facing slopes gleamed so brightly they seemed lit from within the ice. From the gorges ran streams of rippling mercury, and the wind brought snatches of their rocky progress. It sounded altogether good to Jamie. He was grinning idiotically; a young heart brimming over.

Jamie was thus the only person in Jyeko to see the signal flare. For an intoxicated instant, he thought this a celebratory firework. But the flare was red, its burning malevolent. It arched briefly over the low, sullen barracks on the far bank. There was a glimpse of horsemen, of bayonets at the slope, closing on the garrison from three sides.

At the monastery, the first they knew about it was the gunfire. Across the river, a heavy machine-gun thundered. The gross sound barged into the music and killed it dead. The crowd, the players, the dancers all froze, listening, looking in fright at each other. In the side room, the monks laid their oracle half conscious on the floor. Some ran for the doors, others to the galleries above. Gathering out on the roof and the riverbank, the villagers stared across the water.

It was all very quick. A last despairing volley sputtered from the garrison but the horsemen wheeled regardless. Attacking infantry clamoured at the barred windows: moments later, the watchers heard heavy, crumpling bangs from within. Next, the gate was dynamited: a terrific blast made the Tibetans on the near bank cringe. Only one more minute of shouts and shots, and the drama was ended. In the strange quiet that followed, the villagers whispered to each other: *'The Communists'*. Then they crept away to their homes.

*

Part two

one

The Communists crossed the bridge the following morning. Colonel Shen was well informed: he knew that no Tibetan troops waited at little Jyeko, that no explosive charges had been set under the bridge. There was no need for heroics at dawn. The Colonel had a decent breakfast of rice and mutton, then led his troops over the river in the morning sunshine. He had perhaps one hundred and fifty infantrymen, led by thirty cavalry.

Some villagers kept to their houses with the doors barred, but many came out to watch and stood near the bridge. As the Chinese approached, these villagers began clapping energetically. The Colonel and his men were pleasantly surprised. No doubt they recalled their political cadres' assurances that the Tibetans were a people crushed by the most appalling oppression who would certainly welcome their liberators. So, in response to the clapping, the soldiers gave the villagers relieved, weary smiles. One or two managed a slight bow as they marched in. In this instance, ignorance was a great blessing: for Tibetans, clapping is a device to drive out devils.

Colonel Shen rode with the wary correctness of the unopposed victor, his uniform dusty but smartly worn. The villagers noted, however, that the soldiers looked a poor lot. This was the army that had swept away the Nationalists, with thousands of miles of arduous marching and scores of pitiless battles to its name, yet the men were miserably equipped and half starved, their boots disintegrating, their uniforms thin and shabby, scarcely adequate for Tibet. Certain village women were tempted to offer the poor things a decent sheepskin. The officers seemed fired with new-coined zeal but the common soldiers' eyes had a resigned look that the Khampas recognised at once. The Nationalist garrison, every one of whom had been killed in the night, had had that same look for years.

It was tempting to conclude that the latest bunch of Chinese was no different from the last. From the outset, however, the Communists behaved quite differently.

The Colonel led his cavalry straight to the village square; his infantry stopped at ease on the riverbank. With his captain as interpreter, Colonel Shen asked the villagers to assemble for an announcement. They had nothing to fear, he stressed. He and his men had come to set them free.

Cautiously, the people gathered, their first alarm abating somewhat. They noticed that the infantrymen had sat down in the sun, their bayonets sheathed. They saw that the cavalry were relaxed, their rifles at their backs. The Colonel was resting his hands on the pommel of his saddle and making an effort to look amiable – he'd rather lost the habit. In a few minutes most of Jyeko was there, whispering uncertainly. Then the Colonel spoke. He was here as a liberator, he said. The Khampa people had groaned under the rule of distant Lhasa whose laws were obscene, whose officials were corrupt, whose taxes were criminal. Their monks were idle superstition-peddlers who never dirtied their hands with work. The people had been condemned to backwardness, ignorance and disease because only thus could the effete aristocracy keep them down. Their Chinese brothers and sisters had determined to end all this.

When the Colonel paused, no one spoke. Only the horses stamped and tossed their heads.

The Colonel raised his voice: he required billets for his men, fodder for the animals but everything would be paid for at a fair rate. There would be no looting, no sacrilege in the temples, no insult offered to any woman. If any villager had a complaint against his men, he wanted to hear of it. He and the main body of his force would be marching on after this single day of rest, but he would be leaving a small garrison to secure the bridge lest the deluded fops of Lhasa dreamed of meddling.

The force dispersed. The infantry officers went among the houses requesting billets with a courtesy that left the villagers speechless. The Colonel made his way to the monastery and paid his compliments to the Abbot. And a troop of horses rode directly to Jamie's house. Clearly, they knew all about him.

Jamie, with Khenpo Nima at his side, was transmitting as they arrived. The generator puttered, the Morse key rattled, a frantic account of the incursion was flung into the upper air. Outside, Karjen heard the horses coming. For a brief, heady minute he thought of opposing the Chinese single-handed as his father would have done. His musket was loaded and propped by the fuel shed door. He began heaving the gates shut, but mercifully he was too stiff and slow.

A dark figure filled the radio room door, shutting out the sunlight. A grimy military hand was placed over Jamie's on the Morse key. He looked up, and a Chinese trooper grinned and said, 'Hello, English!'

Out in the bright courtyard, Jamie half expected to be shot at once. A Chinese captain with a short sword at his side dismounted from his horse, and turned to stare at him. Someone stopped the generator. Puton and Dechen were nowhere to be seen. The monk and the Ying-gi-li stood together in wordless apprehension.

*

'This is a sad, medieval country, Mr Wilson. I cannot imagine why Britain bothers with it. I have studied with the British, do you see? Hydraulic engineering for the Shanghai Water Corporation, work of which I was proud and all in British English which is quite the best. One could not be proud of this land full of serfs but no wheels. What do you think?'

Colonel Shen's eyes never left Jamie's and never blinked. Jamie supposed that a decade of civil war might well turn a man into an automaton.

'Well? Please explain it to me. What is the British Empire doing here?'

Jamie took a deep breath, then repeated an assertion that this man showed no inclination to believe. 'Colonel, I am a civilian under private contract to the Tibetan government.'

'Oh, Mr Wilson! I have information. You are a soldier. You

served in Malaya. I know it, you know it – '

'I *was* a soldier, Royal Corps of Signals. I don't deny that. I was demobbed in forty-eight, and I happened to be in New Delhi when this chance came up. Yes, the British authorities contacted me as intermediaries. But I repeat, this is a private, civilian contract.'

'"When the chance came up"? To be posted to this place is a *chance*? Really!'

'That's how I saw – '

'And what Captain Duan saw at your house was an American military radio. Correct?'

Captain Duan, standing two paces away, nodded curtly: 'The markings are US Army, sir.'

'The equipment was already in Lhasa when I – '

'Mr Wilson, I know all this. There are three American sets, for yourself and Mr Fox who has now fled from Lhasa, and for Mr Ford, who we shall shortly be detaining in Chamdo. The whole business is the work of Colonial Powers in collusion with the stinking and ill-named 'nobles' of Lhasa. I *know*.'

Jamie bit his lip. A Chinese corporal entered and murmured something to Captain Duan, indicating Jamie. The Captain smiled thinly. Jamie thought unhappily of Puton, with only Karjen between her and a troop of soldiers.

Colonel Shen, meanwhile, had not taken his eyes off Jamie. 'The People's Republic of China has every reason to mistrust your imperialist employers very deeply indeed, Mr Wilson. Even as we speak, the Americans are persecuting their own Communists at home while through their stooges at the United Nations they viciously assault the proletariat of Korea. Their British and Indian lackeys assist their conspiracies. Did you know, Mr Wilson, that there are more than a dozen American agents in Assam posing as missionaries? We have identified every one of them. Isn't that laughable?'

Colonel Shen's laugh, thought Jamie, had all the warmth of a Jyeko January.

'At any rate,' he said, 'I'm not an American.'

'Small mercies,' smiled the Colonel.

'I thought they were your allies,' said Jamie. 'They kept you going against the Japanese, didn't they?'

The Colonel merely sneered: 'The devious and changeable American is quite beyond belief.'

He seemed more concerned to humiliate than to interrogate. Suddenly Jamie became indignant. Why should he, a twenty-two-year-old radio operator from Inverkeithing with a taste for horses and watercolours, be taken to task on American anti-Communism by a Chinese colonel? Jamie didn't know any American Communists, he knew little and cared less about Korea or Assam. He just wanted to know what was going on at his house. Captain Duan had pronounced it a billet to his liking. Captain Duan could take a running jump into the pit latrine.

'Frankly,' said the Colonel, 'I do not think there is much more that you can tell me. I would seem to be the better informed. I strongly advise you to co-operate with me, Mr Wilson. I require your radio log immediately, with full details of those stations with which you are in contact. I cannot yet say what is to happen to you. I myself will be leaving in the morning to join our armies advancing on Chamdo. My liaison officer Captain Duan will be remaining here with his unit. You will find that he knows something of this dismal country and its language. When I have reported the situation to our commanders, instructions will be sent. You should prepare yourself, Mr Wilson.'

'For what?'

'Who knows? At a guess, we shall simply expel you. However, a protracted spell of re-education in the military prison at Chengdu is a possibility. I bid you good day.'

Jamie scurried home, frantic at the thought of the soldiers and Puton. But she was sitting demurely in the kitchen chopping vegetables. Dechen stood in the sun outside, watching three Chinese cavalrymen unsaddling horses and carrying bedding rolls into an empty storeroom. Their behaviour had been irreproachable.

It was the last Jamie saw of Colonel Shen. At six the next morning, the horses pulverised the ice on the track that led through the gorge towards Chamdo, with the Colonel leading. He had left just twenty men to keep Jyeko in check.

*

'Why the hell didn't you blow up the bridge?' Jamie asked Khenpo Nima. They were sitting on a rock at the village margin, staring at the river crossing.

'No dynamite here, Jemmy,' said Nima.

'So cut it down.'

'But it is made of iron.'

'Oh, for pity's sake ... '

Communist soldiers came and went busily. The villagers had timidly requested that the Chinese make themselves comfortable in the former Nationalist barracks. Captain Duan had replied in his stiff but frigidly clear Tibetan that he'd not been given charge of a bridge in order to camp on the far bank waiting for it to be sabotaged.

'And what am I meant to do?' grumbled Jamie. 'Wait for them to cart me off for brainwashing in Chengdu?'

He stared disconsolately at the soldiers, filled with dismay and chagrin. Here he was, the radio operator, supposed to pick up warning signals of impending danger. But it was he who had been wrong-footed. Now these Chinese had retuned *his* radio and were listening each day for the moment their own army's transmitter came on air!

By his side, Khenpo Nima picked at the worn fabric of his robe, lost for words. He'd had plenty of experience in evading malicious spirits, in circumventing theological impasse. Communists were different.

'We can send you to Lhasa in the night,' he began.

'No, you can't,' returned Jamie. 'They've put guards in my house. *They* think ahead. Beside which I've got Captain Duan billeted in my house. I couldn't pack a sandwich without being spotted, let alone a caravan for weeks in the snow.'

The two men walked slowly into the lane leading to the

market square.

Here, the Chinese had continued to behave remarkably well. When they came to the market for food, they paid promptly and in silver. In the grain shops, they thanked the merchants effusively; they even bowed to the astonished matrons behind the butter stalls. But the Chinese NCOs let their men do the shopping while they themselves stood watching like hawks. Clearly, orders had been given and would be enforced.

It was unsettling; nor were the villagers reassured by the posters. On the second morning, the soldiers went about Jyeko in pairs carrying paper rolls and thumbtacks. They stopped before the weather-worn gates of the houses, unrolled and pinned up large greyish photographs of a man with a pudgy, avuncular face, a radiant look and a red star badge on his collar, heroically portrayed from a low angle. There were lines of script below, but the villagers could not read it. The face on the poster was not unkind but, when the soldiers turned to the knots of watchers and mouthed a name, the Khampas returned only puzzled stares: 'Ze-dong' in Tibetan means 'Short Life': was 'Mao Ze-dong' a joke or what?

Passing through the lanes together, Khenpo Nima saw Jamie peer at the soldiers with deep suspicion. Half whispering, the monk said, 'Jamie, I do not think we have to worry so much. We have lived with Chinese before now. You see how nice they are?'

But Jamie gave him a look of such withering scepticism that Nima fell silent.

At Jamie's house, the same air of edgy, unreal courtesy prevailed. Two cavalry troopers and a sergeant had moved their kit into empty storerooms. Their horses crowded the stable shed. Captain Duan had informed Jamie, politely but with no hint of flexibility, that he would be sleeping in the living room. He made himself a comfortable corner with rugs and boxes arrayed about his sleeping roll. The man was quiet and punctiliously proper.

His troopers took turns to cook and did not interfere with Puton and Dechen. If anything, she found them easier than Karjen. They fetched fuel, cleaned up around themselves and were a lot less surly than the ex-brigand.

But, like Karjen, the troopers were always there. They produced a padlock and secured the radio room. At 1800 hours each day they made Jamie switch on and tune to the frequency they specified. But there was no signal from their commanders to the north, nothing but a blizzard of radio snow. The door would be firmly relocked. They did not prevent Jamie from leaving the house, but did not allow him to take his pony. At night, with Captain Duan in the living room, Puton kept to her own bed. And when she had shut her door, she pushed a heavy box against it; she had noticed Duan regarding her with an eye that she did not like.

Thus the first two days passed with no news. On the second evening, Jamie felt suffocated so he went to the monastery for a game of ping-pong. Rumour had suggested that the godless Communists would indulge in anti-clerical pogroms; Colonel Shen had merely asked for a note of the monks' names.

After the Colonel's departure with his main force, monastery routines continued: scripture reading, debating and divine services, consumption of buttered tea and barleymeal. Khenpo Nima compounded his herbal cures; others went back to painting wall hangings or the construction of ever-more-ingenious praying machines. They tried to believe that everything would continue unchanged. And, of an evening, they played ping-pong.

On Jamie's arrival in the assembly hall, the usual vigorous bunch of novices was gathered watched by rather more of the senior lamas than usual. For all the crowd, there was little talk. Each man brooded while waiting his turn to play. The bright *tock tock* of the ball was a blessed filler of an unhappy silence.

Suddenly, there was a stir in the passageway outside and the doors flew open. The players and watchers froze. In the doorway stood six Communist soldiers. They were not carrying rifles.

The soldiers looked round the hall, met by the expressionless scrutiny of two dozen monks and the surprised gaze of Jamie. For several seconds no one moved or spoke. All at once the leader of the group of soldiers – Captain Duan's lieutenant – laughed aloud and spoke in bad Tibetan.

'OK, we are come to play!' He looked round again, grinning expectantly. The Tibetans made no move. The lieutenant's smile tightened fractionally. 'We play well, all People's soldiers. We like it so much.'

The young monk who had been about to serve placed the ball on the table, his bat on top of it. Then he stepped aside, making way wordlessly for the Chinese. His doubles partner put down his bat and at the other end their opponents began to follow suit. Only now the lieutenant cried out, 'No, no, stay, please, for double! Mr Wi-lih-soh, you must play.'

The Tibetans had come to understand that tone of voice. Friendship and dominion, invitation and command: the tone of a father carrying a stout cane. So they played: a Scot and a clutch of maroon-robed monks playing ping-pong with Communist soldiers. The Chinese showed enjoyment and skill; only Jamie and Wangdu could begin to match them. But whenever a Tibetan scored a point, the soldiers would smile and chorus automatically: 'Very good shot!'

*

At dawn the next day, a young herdsman was driving a dozen sheep along the riverbank into Jyeko. The October morning was grey and cold, a light snowfall trickling from a dull sky. His thick sheepskins were lightly dusted with fine crystals that did not melt. He looked regretfully at the open pasture on both sides of the river beyond the bridge: the grazing was nearly gone. Six months of winter in prospect. His sheep looked similarly depressed.

He intended to sell the flock at market, possibly to these new Chinese soldiers who paid for food instead of expropriating it. The young shepherd looked across the river at the old barracks, shut tight against the cold. The ends of the bridge, supposedly under guard, were deserted. The men on the Sikhang side had been allowed indoors for breakfast while those on the Tibetan bank were huddled under the porch of a trader's house fifty yards off, trying to warm themselves with cigarettes. They glanced at the flock of sheep without interest.

As he neared the bridge, something caught the boy's eye. The great stone-and-timber piers that supported the iron chains jutted a yard or so into the water that swirled about in icy whirlpools. Mountain flotsam and village rubbish were caught there in a grubby tangle. But today there was something else, larger and darker than driftwood.

In a moment the boy was scrambling down to the water's edge. A man, face down, was bobbing gently on the flood. The boy pulled at him, feet slipping and scrabbling for purchase on the icy gravel as he heaved at the waterlogged coat. With a frantic effort he turned the body over.

He peered at the face, at once relieved and surprised. It wasn't anyone from his family's encampment. It was no one he knew. It was a Chinese soldier. In the same moment as this realisation, he heard shouts behind him. He looked up and saw one of the bridge guards pointing a rifle at him while two more were slithering down the bank. As they were about to lay hands on him, one cried out, pointing.

Two more corpses were no more than feet away, black bulks sailing past them in the opaline, ice-laden water and away under the bridge.

*

When Jamie emerged from his bedroom that morning, Captain Duan was already standing with a bowl of tea (unbuttered) in his hands. The room was dark and cold.

'You will not have to suffer this dreary place much longer, Mr Wilson,' said the Captain. 'I expect orders regarding you any day now. Unfortunately, our radio at Chamdo seems not to be established yet. Otherwise I would ask you to operate your set to receive your own marching orders.'

He gave a dry little smile. The door opened and Puton entered with a large dish of barleymeal that she placed on the packing-case table. The captain's look followed her intently. He said: 'She has fine features, Mr Wilson. Her deformity almost becomes her, don't you agree? As with Tibet itself, a touch of pathos enhances the appeal.'

Puton made no sign of hearing; it was Jamie who flushed with anger. But the Captain did not notice. He was watching Puton. She straightened, looking trustingly at Jamie. He felt his throat tighten, wondering what on earth he could do about anything.

At that moment there came a cacophony in the yard, heavy boots running across the yard, men calling: 'Captain!' Duan stepped smartly to open the door. Outside, his sergeant and a breathless infantryman stood speaking in low voices, urgent and anxious.

Still Puton looked at Jamie. He saw her mouth open slightly, as though she would speak to him. He felt his whole frame quivering with frightened need: he was on the verge of drawing her back into his room simply to bury his face in her neck and take in the scent of her thick hair.

Captain Duan bellowed an order: the troopers ran to saddle the horses. The Captain turned back into the room, his face murderously cold, all courtesy discarded. He pushed past Puton so that she stumbled towards the wall. He seized his revolver belt and was gone through the door. A moment later, Karjen burst into the room with news. The Chinese were strutting through the village hammering on gates and ordering the population to the market square.

A thin, bleak little snow drifted down on Jyeko market. The stalls were empty, the shops closed except for one that the soldiers had forced. The square was as crowded as ever, but the people stood speechless. The monks were all present; only the ancient Abbot had been left alone. Along one side of the square, ten infantrymen stood with their long rifles at high port, bayonets fixed. Blocking the riverbank exit were four cavalry horses, the troopers clasping their carbines across their chests. In front of them, Captain Duan sat motionless in the saddle. But no one was looking at these.

Two soldiers were at work by the empty, snow-dusted

stalls. They had ripped off several timbers and had constructed a crude vertical framework lashed together with cord taken from the shop. Two others held the young shepherd with his arms jammed up behind his back. When the timbers were secure, they stripped his coat off, then hauled him to the frame. They spread his arms wide and bound them to the rough wood, pulling the cords tight round his wrists and then across the palms of his hands. The boy stared about in wide-eyed terror.

From his saddle, Captain Duan watched without expression. When the shepherd was fixed, he made a small sign to his men to pause, then turned to the crowd. 'Three are dead! Three of your brothers, your liberators, your dearest Chinese friends are dead!' His voice was hoarse and screeching, his accent making the Tibetan phrases weird and harsh. 'Thus has Tibet rewarded them. Thus do I repay Tibet!'

The crowd was silent. At the back, Jamie and Karjen entered the square and stood on a slight rise under a wall from where they could see clearly.

The soldiers had found a piece of bamboo. This they split with a bayonet into long slivers. They took the helpless boy by the hand and the lieutenant pushed long slivers of bamboo under each fingernail. They pushed them hard, deep as they would go. A sigh went through the crowd of villagers as the boy screamed. Slowly, his fingers curled and uncurled, absurdly long. On the far side of the square, white-faced Jamie thought of Struwwelpeter. The back of his mouth flooded with saliva. He was going to be sick.

Then he heard the soldiers laugh. The lieutenant had gone into the shop, whose owner stood on the muddy step wringing his hands pathetically. The officer emerged with a clutch of paper prayer flags scrumpled in his hand. Pausing, he took out of his pocket a single coin. He handed this to the shopkeeper with a curt bow: all paid for. Stepping to his victim, he tore small holes in the paper flags and slid them onto the bamboo jutting from the shepherd's fingers. One flag on each finger. The snow alighted on the boy's head, his fingers curled and uncurled, fluttering their desperate prayers.

The Chinese soldiers howled with mirth. The cavalrymen gripped their saddle pommels to prevent themselves tumbling off with laughter. Those with their rifles presented could barely stand straight enough to menace the crowd. The Tibetans stood in utter immobility. At the back, Jamie sat on the ground with his head in his hands, retching silently. So he heard, but did not see, the contemptuous crack of the Captain's pistol.

*

two

Khenpo Nima wanted nothing to do with revenge. He saw the speechless rage that had taken hold of Jyeko, he understood it, and he grieved over it. He saw in the eyes a lust that prayer wheels would not satisfy, he saw the little groups that muttered in alleyways, the shufflings of barely suppressed rage and the muffled cries of ferocity. Khenpo Nima was no fool: something was smouldering, was being planned. The likes of Karjen, the Khampa merchants, the herdsmen and hunters were afire. He realised grimly that several of his senior colleagues in the monastery were inclined to consider the Chinese beyond the pale of Buddhist tolerance. No one had confessed to knowing anything about the dead soldiers in the river. But the monk saw the looks between men, the stares and silences that shouted across the village.

The young shepherd's body had been left draped until early evening. Soon after dark someone cut the cords and took the boy away. The Chinese did nothing to stop this but if Khenpo Nima hoped that passions might abate, he was soon disappointed.

Had the monk been in the market the following morning, he might have witnessed a curious discussion. In the shadow of an old house, a knot of Tibetans were whispering urgently, monks and village men, Karjen and also Jamie, listening to them. Jamie stood stiff with reluctance. The Tibetans were urging him in the direction of the monastery.

With the Colonel's departure, Captain Duan had moved his headquarters to the monks' assembly hall, though he still slept at Jamie's. He had taken over the ping-pong table as a desk and after breakfast was discussing food and forage with his NCOs. The monks were in the prayer hall clocking up prayers; Duan could hear the irritating mumbles. Then the guard on the door hefted his rifle to some newcomer, barring access. Captain Duan looked up and saw Jamie peering in, a monk at his elbow. After a second of scrutiny, the Captain nodded to the guard who let Jamie pass.

They exchanged stiff greetings, then the officer sat back

and waited. The young European was clearly ill-at-ease, groping for words. At last he began: 'You've had no news of what is to happen to me?'

'You are surely aware that no messenger has reached me yet from Chamdo.'

'I see.'

'As for the radio, Chamdo is still not transmitting. I have, therefore, no instructions.'

'Oh. Right, then.' Jamie glanced at the soldiers who waited round the room, their conference with the commander interrupted.

Captain Duan said impatiently: 'Was there anything else? You see that I am busy.'

'Oh. Well, there was one thing. The monks and myself, we'd like to invite you to the monastery.'

'We are already here, Mr Wilson.'

'Yes, but I mean for a game. Sports.'

'What sports?'

'Well, ping-pong. Table tennis. Your lieutenant said that you're all very good.'

Captain Duan looked up at the lieutenant in astonishment. The other man laughed. 'Sir, we have seen these people playing. Even their monks! They are not so good. I think we shall slaughter you, mister!'

Jamie managed a wan smile in return. The Captain peered at him, bemused and suspicious.

That evening, the first ever table tennis tournament in Tibet took place in the Jyeko monastery. A sergeant joked to Jamie that it was an 'international' tournament but Captain Duan curtly reminded them all that, as Tibet was a region of China, this was a fraternal, domestic matter.

Duan was far from a fool: exemplary executions do not commonly lead to ping-pong tournaments. But his men were growing bored and Peking's orders were that they ingratiate themselves wherever possible. He gave his assent – and instructions for extreme caution.

Shortly after dark, the assembly hall was crowded and ablaze with lamps. Butter-oil smoke belched up to join the ancient crust on the timbers. Captain Duan had graciously removed his papers from the table. Around the sides of the hall, monks and village men chattered. At the end furthest from the door, the Chinese soldiers gathered. They were alert, watchful, and they had very particular orders: while their comrades were playing, the others were to keep their weapons to hand.

Jamie stood beneath one of the high, barred windows holding the last of the box of white balls. Beside him, Khenpo Nima looked round the company. There were no women or children present; he wanted to know why, but found himself reluctant to ask. The Abbot had retired to the scripture library: 'Leave it to Wangdu,' his colleagues had said. 'Wangdu plays best.' As Nima looked at the glistening, intent faces round him, he found the smiles fixed too hard, the eyes too bright.

Wangdu stood forward. He addressed the company and included the Chinese, ostentatiously so. Tibet and China had always lived side by side, he said. There were great changes in the air, he did not know what the immediate future might bring. But if friendship were the guide, mutual prosperity would be found. Therefore he welcomed the Chinese to Jyeko monastery and hoped that ping-pong could bring understanding in its train.

Khenpo Nima thought: Wangdu is a shrewd man: he's heard the accents of the moment.

The first game began. Jamie and Khenpo Nima played a Chinese sergeant and a private; for all Jamie's efforts, they were soundly whipped. A second match went the same way. The villagers laughed and cheered Tibetan points but there were long awkward minutes when only Chinese soldiers applauded. The Tibetans began to glower. Friendship was not making great headway and the soldiers stood with a firm grip on their rifles. But certain monks went murmuring discreetly among the villagers: thereafter, the Tibetans applauded the Chinese with markedly greater generosity. Khenpo Nima noticed that the Chinese began to relax. One or two had slipped their rifles off their shoulders and had leaned them against the stone wall. When they finished a game, they returned in triumph to their comrades to laugh and chatter – but did not pick up their weapons.

A roar of delight: Wangdu had beaten the sergeant. For a moment, the soldier stood in idiotic immobility, unable to credit his disgrace. Wangdu, his face barely big enough to contain his grin, swaggered in front of his supporters, his robes swaying. The jabbering of monks, merchants and soldiers grew ever louder and the Tibetans began to move between the Chinese. Small sums of money were discreetly displayed. The soldiers were nodding and laughing at the certain bets. Now the Chinese group was fragmented, divided by villagers.

The NCOs began to debate among themselves as to whom should face Wangdu and Jamie in the doubles. Few of the soldiers now held weapons. The lieutenant was marshalling his team, and Khenpo Nima realised that the lieutenant was in charge because Captain Duan had left the room.

He saw Wangdu muttering unhappily to Karjen: the bandit seemed to be urging the monk to play, to continue. Jamie stood by the table holding two bats. He looked bewildered, lost in the babble that surrounded him. He glanced repeatedly over his shoulder as though for reassurance and instruction. Khenpo Nima saw beads of sweat on Jamie's brow, a hint of fear, very far from home.

'We are waiting!' called the lieutenant.

There was a sudden hush. Wangdu went to the table and Jamie held out a bat. His eyes were loud with alarms and questions. Wangdu took the bat and smiled: 'No worries, Mr Jemmy. We slaughter them now.'

He looked round the room, which had fallen still, every face intent on the game. Then he turned to the table and the two Chinese opposite. Wangdu toyed with the ball in his hand a moment, rolling it speculatively between his thumb and fingers as though contemplating a spin. He tossed it lightly into the air and struck it hard – not at the table but straight at the face of the Chinese player opposite.

When the Tibetans moved, the Chinese were staring at Wangdu, at the soldier who pressed a hand to his eye with an angry shout, and at the ball that ticked away across the floor. They were still staring when the first knives sank into their bellies, twisting and ripping even as Khampas flung powerful arms about their throats. The soldiers cried out, turning towards the stack of rifles against the wall only to find a phalanx of herdsmen in their way, bringing short cudgels down on their heads. The Chinese shouted with surprise and rage, then shrieked with fear and pain as they fell. Two soldiers burst out through the door and were at once pursued by a mob. For the first and only time in its history, the little monastery was defiled by screams.

In the centre of the tumult, Jamie stood frozen by the table. He still held a ping-pong bat. Khenpo Nima saw him gaze at the slaughter all around him – and slowly crouch to pick up the loose ball. Then Jamie backed away until he reached a stone ledge beneath one of the high windows with its heavy, vertical iron bars. As he sat down to watch the Chinese die, a frantic soldier leaped up by him, grabbing at the bars above his head. Knives were at the man's back, a dozen hands reached and tore at him. Still he kicked and screeched and pulled at the bars above Jamie, as though to haul himself out through the gap as the knives came on again.

At last the soldier gave up his grip on the bars, slumping and sliding down. A blade had breached his neck, and his blood gushed onto Jamie's face. Then he slithered to the floor, and there was silence.

Outside, shouts came and went in the lanes as the news ran through the village. Jamie heard it where he sat motionless beneath the window, ashen-faced and blood-drenched. Khenpo Nima, boggle-eyed, rushed away to find the Abbot. Throughout the hall, the men of Jyeko looked about them. At their feet lay a dozen soldiers and their NCOs, gashed and broken. Their killers did not exult, but stared in astonishment at what they had done.

*

three

Karjen, the veins on his flat balding skull distended, spat on the ground in front of a Jyeko youth and roared: 'Bird-brained baby!'

The young man drew back, looking round for friends, wondering if he should throw a punch.

Karjen gave him no respite to think it over. 'Why didn't you go after him? Don't you know how to ride a horse?'

'What difference does it make?' protested the villager. 'We killed his men, we laughed the bastard out of town!'

They stood before the gates of the monastery, a dry wind blowing grit in their faces. Jamie, his face newly rinsed, felt sick with dread.

'You tell him, Mr Jemmy,' said the indignant young villager. 'The Chinese Captain will be shit scared of us now, he won't come back in a hurry.'

'Not on his own,' said Jamie. 'The problem is, he'll come back with an army.'

'Well, we stopped him stealing anything from *your* house, at least.'

'How do you mean?' asked Jamie.

'He was in your house, Mr Jemmy. That's where he was hiding, stealing things. We scared the wits out of him!'

Jamie said not another word but started off at a run through the lanes.

Puton was in her room cradling Dechen, crooning comfort to her as the little girl tugged in fright at her mother's plaits. There had been sudden, horrible shrieks outside, murderous cries, two shots fired from a fleeing pony. Dechen was terrified; Puton's own fears had had to be stifled, drowned in a gentle song. Then they heard a scuffling noise from the yard and a curse: Jamie, pelting in through the gate, had slithered on the icy stones and fallen.

He appeared in the doorway a moment later. 'May I come in?' He squatted beside Puton's bed where she held her daughter.

'Have you heard what has happened?' he asked.

'They came here,' she replied, nodding. 'The Captain has gone, I don't know where.'

'Towards Chamdo, fast as he can. All hell's loose now.'

Puton pulled Dechen to her breast, closed her eyes and rocked backwards and forwards very slightly. Jamie put a hand on her shoulder. 'Did he harm you?'

She lifted her face a fraction. 'He did not touch us.'

Jamie waited. Surely that was not everything? He prompted: 'So what happened?'

'He came, and he was standing in the doorway there, just looking at me. Dechen was here. He did not say anything. Then there was noise, he ran out to the gate, he took a pony and was gone. That is all. He did not harm us.' She continued to cradle Dechen, crooning almost inaudibly into the child's hair.

Jamie said: 'But he'll be back, do you see? As soon as he and that Colonel find some soldiers. Once they take Chamdo, they'll come storming back here like mad things. We all have to leave, we have to be out before they come.'

He stood and moved to the open door. 'Karjen and some of the men are talking ambushes, waiting with their daft old muskets in the rocks upriver. They have no conception ... This is China they're up against! Why the hell wasn't there some defence? Prayer flags, for Christ's sake! Flags and fires, incense smoke and wind horses, what is that going to do against a million soldiers? That won't keep you safe!'

His voice trembled, beginning to crack. Puton looked up at Jamie. He had his back to her, but she glimpsed the muscles of his jaw clenching. He was trying not to gibber with ... what was it? She wondered. Exasperation? Dismay? Should she feel ashamed or thankful now? Jamie spun round, his boots scrunching the grit of the doorway as he returned to kneel by her. To her amazement, his eyes were radiant even as his face ran with tears. He put his hand out to her cheek. He said: 'We'll get you out, you hear? Just don't you worry!'

*

An hour later, all the village was back at the monastery's assembly hall. The corpses of the Chinese soldiers had been tossed gaily into the river to bob downstream to perdition. Patches of the floor were wet from a hurried sluicing. The Khampas stood in whispering clumps, brewing their anger, their anxiety and adrenaline. Jamie, in whom the instinct to keep life tidy was normally weak, busied himself a moment in freeing the ping-pong net from the bloodstained tangle into which it had been knocked. In his head there ran: Look after the pennies and the pounds'll look after themselves ...

The doors swung wide and the Abbot entered, flanked by his monks.

There was instant quiet. Pema Tulku, XIIth Incarnation of that name, Abbot of Jyeko, moved stiffly across the stone flags, sat on a rug-covered dais at the head of the hall and surveyed his people. They wanted to know what to do, and formed up in front of him expectantly. 'So,' he asked them instead, 'what will you do now?'

Out of the surprised silence, Khenpo Nima stepped into the open space. 'Blessed Abbot, we have let anger rule our hearts today ... '

'*Justice!*' someone called out. '*It was simple justice!*'

The people stirred, growling their agreement.

Nima raised his voice. 'I do not judge anyone,' he said, 'but such an action may not be reversed. You have killed, and the consequences shall not leave you, neither in this life nor the next.'

'Reverence,' cried Karjen behind him, 'don't tell me to start having regrets, please. When shits from China start pulling Khampa fingernails, I scratch back!'

The crowd heaved and pressed forward, murmuring their approval. The Abbot, however, said nothing, only observing them all through his bleary but shrewd old eyes. Khenpo Nima, isolated in the centre, looked around him. He had never known such viciousness in his friends.

Wangdu took a step forward. 'Khenpo Nima, we know that we are never free from regret. We must regret our previous lives, in which we bound ourselves to this wheel of suffering with wrong actions. But other wheels turn alongside our own, striking us, hurting us. These village people had no choice.'

'Ah, well put,' said Karjen, pleased that his instincts could be so elegantly dressed.

At his side, a burly Khampa wool merchant stamped his foot impatiently and shouted: 'I may or I may not come to regret killing Chinese – but I'm damn sure I'd have regretted *not* killing them!'

Delight boiled over from the men, their bloodlust turning to relieved laughter.

The women were calmer. 'Reverend Wangdu,' said one known better for her market bawdy than her philosophy, 'for myself, I have no expectation of blessedness just now. I daresay I shall be lucky to come back as a goose next time round. But what of my children? There are paths in life where the choices are all evil, where we must climb over the rocks to bring our children to safety.'

Jamie craned his neck to see an ugly, dirty, bloated creature, famous even in Jyeko for the stench of her body.

Khenpo Nima turned to his abbot. 'Blessed Abbot, there may be some here who consider that today we have outplayed the Chinese, that we have beaten them from our doors and done with them. They are wrong: devils do not die, they await their moment. Some here perhaps relish the demons' return; another chance to lop off their heads. But I say that as you swing the sword of hatred you will strike the little child that stands behind you.'

'This is unkind, Khenpo Nima,' called Wangdu. 'Here are people who fought only to defend their homes and their loved ones.'

'Justice! Exactly that!' shouted Karjen. At once, the anger boiled over once again; the women shrieked, a man roared, 'We've settled the score!' and his friends stamped their boots with approval. Khenpo Nima winced.

'Excuse me ... Excuse me,' called a voice from the side.

The room fell quiet. A group of women parted to let Jamie stand forward. He brushed back the hair from his forehead, bashful at addressing not only the whole village but the Abbot too.

'I just want to say this. I have to leave, you see? I can't stay, because the Chinese will be coming for me and for the radio. I have to go to India pretty quickly. Now, it's no business of mine what you people do, and I don't envy your position. But, may I say, I've seen a bit of war, I've an idea what armies do. I can tell you, the Chinese are going to be back very soon. And they'll be very, very angry. You see, it's not a matter of settling the score. It'll be more. It'll be annihilation. They won't fight fair, they won't stop short. That colonel and Captain Duan, they won't stop till they've wiped out Jyeko entirely.'

'If we can kill twenty, we can kill two hundred!' bellowed Karjen.

And his allies began a ragged recitation: '*Raiding parties! Ambush them in the ravines, trap them in the high passes! They can't trap Tibetans in the hills! When the bullets are finished, roll rocks on their heads!*'

This last was shouted by a young monk with a flushed face. Khenpo Nima winced again.

Karjen took a step across the open floor and clapped a grizzled hand on Jamie's shoulder. 'Mr Jemmy is a British soldier. He will show us how.'

'But it won't be two hundred,' said Jamie. 'It will be two thousand, and another twenty thousand right behind and aeroplanes as well. You've no idea what you're up against. You're brave and splendid people, but you must understand: you've killed Chinese soldiers. Now they're going to kill you.'

'What are you telling us to do?' called Wangdu sternly.

'You've no choice,' said Jamie. 'You have to leave Jyeko.'

No clamour greeted this, neither rage nor applause – only the dull silence of truth. Khenpo Nima looked to the Abbot. 'Only you can advise us,' he said.

'I can advise, but not instruct,' said the Abbot. 'Only your hearts can do that. For myself, the matter is clear. I am the Twelfth Incarnation of Pema Tulku, saint of this monastery. The spiritual health of this holy place is my charge, handed down through long ages. What has taken place here has been so terrible that only in retreat and prayer shall we begin to understand it. We are bound upon the wheel, all together.'

No one spoke. The old man contemplated his audience with small, watery eyes that, as they lighted on each one, did not leave until they had seen all that there was. So the villagers stood still as he examined them. 'I cannot abandon my monastery,' he continued gently. 'Many of you will take roads south or west. I shall remain here in prayer.'

The villagers hung their heads in humility. The floor at their feet still gleamed dully wet, where it had been washed. A woman took a scarf from her head, knelt and began to rub the flagstones dry. In a moment, a dozen others had silently joined her.

*

four

There were two leather trunks in Jamie's room. They had come from Lhasa covered in oilcloth and lashed over the massive ribs of a yak. They'd come stuffed with his warm clothes and personal things. Now they stood open, and Puton laid those clothes in them once again.

Puton's pride had never deserted her. She was of Lhasa family, she had grown up within a mile of the Potala. She knew that she was cultivated in ways no Jyeko woman matched. She had never flaunted it, but she was nobody's serf. So, as she packed Jamie's belongings, she wondered at herself. He'd not asked her to do it. She was acting like a wife, or a mother, even, packing her boy's case for his travels. The thought made her smile. She'd packed nothing of her own.

Her leg was hurting; she sat on the edge of the *kang*. He had said to her, 'We'll get you out, you hear?' What did that mean? That he was going to take her away? Or send her somewhere? What did he think he could do?

She considered her years of marriage and widowhood. Had it been *her* life at all? Hardly a single decision had she made. She had reacted, only reacted, to a stream of circumstance and commands from parents, her husband, her bullying aunts in Lhasa (all now dead), from a monk and now from a lover too. With her injury, she felt this still more intensely: she walked by grace of Khenpo Nima's skill, she ate by virtue of Jamie's patronage, and her future would now be decided for her once more.

She put out her hand to touch the furs on the bed. Had she been *so* passive? She had embroidered Jamie a scarf and entered this room with it in her hand. Much had followed. She had thrown him looks that had taken him by the throat. She had entranced him: she thought of the intense silence from just beyond the bathroom door. She had been the cause of that silence. If she had not often been the arbiter of things, she had sometimes been the origin.

But she was not deluded: sexual allure does not amount to self-determination. Indeed, free will does not figure much in the Tibetan Buddhist view of life on earth. Besides, she'd not kept love at bay, she'd soon succumbed. Even as she perched on his bed, her eyes watered happily, her cheeks ached with smiling.

She asked only the liberty to look on the inevitable with whatever face she chose. In packing her lover's clothes for his departure, she did no more than anticipate. That small power she did have: she saw what was coming, and always stood to meet it. That was her dignity.

Puton heard footsteps, took her stick and pushed herself to her feet. She unfixed Jamie's watercolours from the wall, wriggling free the hardwood slivers poked into the soft plaster. She took the dozen or more sheets, laid them inside the covers of the sketch pad and placed them in the bottom of the second trunk.

'What are you doing?' he said gently, just behind her.

'For your journey,' she answered.

Jamie put out a hand, still amateurish with her, wanting to toy and caress, hardly daring. He touched the side of her head, the thick black hair. 'You can leave all this to me,' he began. 'You should be packing for yourself, for you and Dechen. We're leaving at first light. The village is heading for Lhasa, then it's ten days to the border. We need food for at least two months' travel. That's if you want to come ... '

She turned searchlight eyes on him. She had no time for empty comfort, bland assurance, ill-considered options. He did his best to face her without cowardice. He felt quite giddy as though, with wolves at his back, he was diving off a cliff into a pool whose depth he could not gauge. He said: 'I'd like you to come with me to India.'

She regarded him with her head cocked and a puzzled frown.

He had made his leap and was not dashed to pieces yet. He swam a few strokes further. 'Would you come? I mean to say, would you stay with me there? You and Dechen? I'm pretty sure I could get telegraphy work there.'

But she was away through the door, across the front room and out into the darkness. *I've hit rocks!* he said to himself. *I'm broken and sunk!* Dismayed, mortified, he went after her.

She was standing just beyond the door in the freezing night. She heard Jamie's tread behind her but did not move.

'Is there ... have I said something I shouldn't?' he asked timidly, hurt. She remained with her back to him, quite still. 'Look, it's a hell of a thing. I can't stay here, you can't either. But we can ... I want you to come with me.'

He almost jeered at himself: begging for a family! But, standing there, it thrilled him astonishingly: a turn in his life with which he'd already fallen in love.

She turned slowly and leaned forward to rest her brow on his shoulder. As the moonlight emerged from the broken cloud, Jamie looked past her head across the frozen yard; the gate stood open. A form appeared there, a shadow stomping in from the street. Jamie knew it was Karjen. The stocky figure stood in the centre of the yard, peering scandalised at the two in the soft lamplight on the porch. Never was a silhouette so disapproving. Without a word, Jamie led Puton into the house and shut the door, leaving Karjen in the darkness.

*

Khampas and monks were running between their homes, their shops, their monastery, their stores ... It was the same in every house and yard: arrangements and packing, arguments, panic and stern words, entreaties, loans, quick repairs, the frantic preparations of people for flight. Food and fuel, treasures and thick clothes, cooking pots and currency, prayer wheels and weapons: everything was lashed and bundled, was too heavy, was discarded, argued over, rescued, thrown aside, reloaded ... In the moonlit lanes, Khenpo Nima overheard the desperation of families abandoning their settled lives for a bitter winter traipse.

He came to Jamie's gate and was surprised to find it open. He entered and saw a lamp flicker in a back room across the yard.

He heard gruff mutterings: Karjen, in a foul mood, was stuffing his scanty property into saddlebags.

Khenpo Nima looked again towards the main house. There were lights, but no tumult of preparation. For a moment he wondered where Jamie had gone. Then he heard a woman's playful shriek, a man laughing.

A fine snow was floating on the still, deep-frozen air. The crystals were less than powder: just an ice-vapour that settled gently on the yard. Moonlight came down in sheaves. Khenpo Nima sat on a small wooden bench on the porch, pulling his heavy sheepskin coat around his shoulders. He settled down to wait. From within the room behind him, piercing the solid shutters, the sighs and whispers came.

After a short while, a loud scrape announced that the shutters were being opened. Khenpo Nima stood up, took a step or two back to the edge of the porch and faced the window. A second later, the timbers swung back and Nima found himself face to face with Jamie, naked under a sheepskin wrap. The latter's face switched from intoxication to astonishment.

'Nima! Jesus!'

In the glowing room behind, Puton lay in an awkward curl on the bed, her head on a fat bolster of plain cotton. The *kang* beneath her was alight, the room warm. The furs were tumbled across her middle, tresses of black hair pouring over black nipples set on dark breasts. Khenpo Nima was dumbfounded: he had been blind to her. This woman whom he'd regarded as a poor despised cripple meriting his pity and nurture, she was a beauty. The wearying, fearful years had departed from her, her demeanour now that of joyful youth. Puton gazed towards Jamie at the window – then saw Khenpo Nima regarding her from the darkness outside. In fright, she pulled the covers up to her neck.

'There are some arrangements, Jamie,' said Khenpo Nima, remembering himself. 'We have little time.'

'Oh, there are so! Heavens! Look, don't stand there in the snow ...'

With a glance towards Puton he shut the window, seized a

pair of trousers and rushed to let Khenpo Nima into the front room. Jamie's face was flushed with an excitement that threatened to ignite the rugs around him.

'Pemba Tsering will bring you two mules later tonight,' said Nima. 'No one is in their beds, you see. And we shall have a yak ready in the morning for the radio.'

'I'll need at least one more animal, I'm afraid,' said Jamie. From the bedroom door came the sounds of Puton dressing and finding her stick. 'They're coming with me to India. They're my family now, Nima. I'm not leaving them.'

Khenpo Nima looked at him carefully, as Puton appeared in the doorway, her modesty restored. She stood facing Khenpo Nima. He saw in her look a strange wistfulness, neither thanks nor reproach, but: *This path you set me on: where does it end?*

'Are you able to travel?' asked Khenpo Nima quietly.

'Of course,' said Puton.

'Oh good …' began Khenpo Nima.

But Jamie had already rushed out past him, yelling 'Karjen! Karjen!' The surly brigand emerged from his room to be greeted by Jamie waving his arms and calling twenty instructions all at once.

Khenpo Nima came into the yard and looked back one last time at the house. Through the front door he could see Puton sitting. She was quite still, not stirring. She held up her head proudly, but her look was on the middle distance, half smiling, as though taking a last fond view of a dream.

*

At dawn, a sickly grey light entered the valley. At the edge of the village, a crowd gathered: villagers, mules, yaks and ponies. All were sagging under their loads; the men moved purposefully among the pack animals, lashing and tightening, heaving and straightening. The women gathered up their children, seating some on yaks to cling to the thick hair, or tucking babies inside their own coats.

Nearby, the gates of Jamie's house stood open. Jamie was

saddling ponies. Karjen was there, more taciturn than ever, settling the radio case and the pedal generator onto a huge yak with a ring of twisted juniper through its nose. Two other village men had volunteered to help: they were caravan-*bashis*, regular traders with spare tents. As Jamie worked, he saw from the corner of his eye that a knot of people now stood at the margins of the crowd, observing him. Perhaps two dozen villagers, in spite of all urgings and pleadings, had elected to stay with their homes and their abbot. Mostly they were old or infirm. One or two grasped their long muskets with antelope-horn rests as though resolved to hold the bridge against all China.

From the lane issued a throng of monks: at their head came the Abbot riding a pony led by Khenpo Nima. Regardless of the cold, the Abbot was in fine brocades. He had brought his establishment to join the exodus, and was here to bless their departure.

The pony halted; the Abbot began to speak. 'Travel with peace and hope in your hearts,' he urged. 'Do not be guided by illusory passions. Pay homage to the Dalai Lama and trust in his guidance. Do not be seduced by the manners of Lhasa.'

All those departing passed before the Abbot, who touched everyone on the head with a hand wrapped in a yellow silk scarf. Meanwhile his monks chanted, twizzled their staccato monkey-drums and spun their wheels. When he had done with the people, the Abbot moved through the caravan blessing the animals.

Jamie looked back to see Puton settling Dechen among the leather bags slung on a mule, swathed in sheepskin. Her own beige hat, of soft lamb's fleece, was low over the small face.

'How's the family? Ready?'

He went to Puton and drew her mouth to his own. This was the way to embark. They closed their eyes, still for a moment, hearing each other breathe.

'Hey, what's that for?' he said, alarmed. She was crying silently. 'We're away to India!' But she said nothing. She thrust her arms in through the front of his sheepskin coat and enclosed him, her hands seeking out the shape of him urgently as though to memorise his form.

'Oh, now! Come on ...'

He pushed her back a fraction and fingered the untidy mess of tear-wet hair on her cheeks.

'Hey, I think I might be needing this, don't you?' said Jamie. From his coat pocket he pulled the red scarf, its ends covered with her embroidery: *T4JW*.

'Give me,' said Puton. She removed it from his hand and tied it neatly about his neck. She tugged it firm – almost too firm.

He grimaced, laughing. 'Don't garrotte me ... That's fine.' Her fingers, fumbling and stumbling over themselves, wriggled it looser. He saw her eyes watering again. 'Now, then, it's time to go,' said Jamie, and he lifted her on to her pony, side-saddle.

From the field outside came a last flurry of bells and monkey-drums. The blessing was done: the Abbot and his diminished entourage had turned back into the village. The travellers were moving to their animals, mounting. The little procession came out from Jamie's yard: two well-laden mules which he led, walking in front with his pony, and Puton's pony with Dechen's mule tied to it behind. Jamie looked for Karjen and the radio yak, and went towards them.

He noticed a cluster of faces around Karjen that stared and looked away again. Then he saw others join the whispering with urgent hissings and quick glances at Jamie's party. He saw a woman urging Wangdu to something. The smile left Jamie's face. Wangdu took a step forward from the edge of the crowd, in front of Jamie.

'Jemmy, please listen ...' he stuttered. Then came silence: Wangdu could not finish.

For a second, Jamie paused, facing him. The monk would not look at him. 'What is it, Wangdu?'

But a different, louder voice called out, the voice of a man used to bullying: 'Send that woman back, Mr Jemmy. She doesn't travel with us.'

A brutish middle-aged Khampa, a man of means with a paunch to suit. The eyes were narrow and determined.

'What did you say?' asked Jamie softly.

'I said, send her back. We have quite enough to contend with, devils and storms and Chinese and all. We don't need ill-fortune riding in our midst.'

'What the hell do you mean by that?' snapped Jamie, reddening instantly. 'Her only misfortune was living among the likes of you.'

'Exactly,' said the merchant. 'That woman lived in my house a while. My mistake, which I sorted. This time I've got my whole family to look after and I'm not taking chances.'

'No one's asking you,' said Jamie. 'She's travelling with me, as my responsibility.'

'But you're travelling with *us*,' said the merchant.

He gestured at a dozen, two dozen men and women grouped behind him.

Jamie felt panic creep into his voice. 'You think I'm going to leave her behind?' he demanded.

'You, Mr Jemmy, can do what you like. I've no quarrel with you. But you're not bringing her in this caravan.'

Everyone was curiously still, even the animals. Jamie looked from face to face: each one implacable.

'Nima, for Christ's sake, what is this crap?'

'Jemmy, they spoke to me last night. I have tried, please believe that I have tried. You must know that I have cared for this girl! But every person here agrees, it is what the whole village says. They will not have her.'

'Well, they're going to have to think ... '

'Jemmy, you must understand! It is not Puton, it is the evil that attends on her. These people are fleeing for their lives.'

'And what of Puton's life?'

'The Abbot is here, there is plenty of food ... '

'Crap! Bloody crap, Nima! She's coming with me. If we have to ride half a day in front or half a day behind, I don't care. Puton, for pity's sake! Where are you going? Puton!'

But she had seen her fate, and pre-empted it. The moment that Wangdu stepped forward, she had stopped her pony. As the fat merchant was opening his mouth, she had turned and pulled

Dechen's mule after. And even before Jamie had begun his tirade, she was moving steadily back towards the house.

'Puton! What are you doing?'

Even as he howled, Jamie saw the mule and the pony pass back under the archway of his former home and disappear.

A stillness fell on Jyeko, stillness and the breathing of animals. Jamie gripped the reins of his pony and stared towards the distant gate, unmoving. His nostrils flared and the wind dragged the tears out of his eyes; otherwise he was motionless, stunned. For some seconds the village stood still in witness. Not a horse, not a dog made a sound but looked around the human faces. The fat merchant kept mute from decency. Khenpo Nima, by Jamie's side, put out a hand to touch him, but could not.

Then someone moved, swinging into a saddle – and at once the entire caravan stirred into movement, yaks and ponies, dogs and people, mules and monks streaming out on the track through the stone-walled gardens. Jamie barely registered that two men came to his side, one holding his mount's bridle, the other grasping him by the shin and lifting him deftly into the saddle. The pony moved off after the pack. In a trance, Jamie rode away from Jyeko.

*

Part three

They rode hard, not daring to glance behind them. A score of Khampa families with a dozen monks and a Scottish radio operator drove their animals forward in a clamour of shouts and whistles. The noise was unnecessary, since the animals moved readily enough, but it was preferable to the clamour of regret. In the centre of the crowd rode Jamie. On Khenpo Nima's instructions, two novices kept near to him. He did not appear to notice them, or anyone or anything else.

A short distance from the village, the trail began its diagonal climb up the mountain flank towards the first pass. The throng turned to single file on the narrow track. At the crest of the pass, two miles from the village and several hundred feet higher, the broad saddle was covered with a dusting of snow through which dead yellow grasses stuck. Here, the lead riders paused.

At last, they looked back. Almost everyone they knew was strung along the trail and climbing towards them. As each family reached the summit they, too, turned to gaze at the distant village, every detail visible in this thin, clean air. Nothing seemed out of the ordinary, except for the unusual quantity of prayer flags that still hung on every house, across every gate to keep the Chinese out. But scarcely a living soul was visible in the lanes. No children played, there were no dogs, no traders or market wives, no animals, no smoke from fires.

As Jamie and the villagers gathered in silence and looked down, a delicate sound reached them in faint wisps and snatches. It was a tiny ringing pain, trembling with unhappiness. A light wind was rising along the river valley, passing through the village towards the pass. As it went among the deserted houses, it had found a hundred little prayer bells on cords and springs in courtyards, windows and doorways. Touched and shaken, the shivering of these bells reached the people in the pass.

Khenpo Nima bit his lip and looked around the crowd. He saw a strong man raise a hand slowly to his face. A girl wept noiselessly and twisted a cloth tighter and tighter in whitened fists. Then a woman began to move, leading a mule with two children. She had turned round, back down the mountainside towards her home. A moment later, her husband started after her, hauling a yak on which all their possessions teetered. No one spoke, but Nima felt that everyone held their breath. In a minute, the family was a hundred yards below them, racing for Jyeko on lurching animals.

Khenpo Nima swung down off his pony and picked up a large flat stone in his broad hands. There was a high cairn at the crest of the pass. Nima strode towards it purposefully, pulling his mount after him. He slapped the stone onto the cairn with all the decisiveness and noise he could manage, shouting: 'The gods are victorious, the devils are defeated!'

They'd all cried it a thousand times, a tradition for the crossing of a pass. No one moved. Khenpo Nima surveyed them in dismay. Then Karjen stooped also and picked up a fat little boulder. He hoisted his rock to the cairn's top and bellowed the same: 'The gods are victorious, the devils are defeated!'

At last, the villagers began to stir. Everyone, every family found a rock for the cairn; even small children seated on yaks were given little stones and shown where to toss them. The cry was repeated, and repeated. So the village began to pick their way down the far side of the pass.

*

They travelled fifteen miles in the first day. The ground was hard and level; the caravan spread out, allowing the animals to nose for fodder. At dusk, they set up camp. Some of the shelters were huge, stout felt raised on ropes over outer poles, with all the appearance of black spiders in the snow. These were tents for wintering out, gale-proof and clan capacity. But many of the townspeople had only light summer pavilions, or the little ridge tents of brown hemp cloth the herdsmen carried to pasture, open to the wind at one end.

With fires lit and tea prepared, the villagers had time at last to talk, to reassure each other that they'd acted wisely. Khenpo Nima saw Jamie by a family cooking fire. Karjen was busily repairing a rip in the tent they'd borrowed so these people had given Jamie food. He sat in silence. The daylight failed, the herdsmen drove their animals together and volunteers stood watch. There were leopards in the hills they'd passed through. Brown bears, quick to kill mules, ponies, sheep, had been seen in the distance that afternoon. In the borrowed tent, Jamie, Karjen and a herdsman lay packed between bags of food and the boxed radio equipment. Around them, the children's cries died down, until the only sounds were the stamps and shufflings of ponies, gruff snorts from the yaks and soft speech at the watch fires.

So a routine began. It would take many weeks to draw near to Lhasa, even if the winter weather was kind.

They rose and ate at dawn, then began the elaborate business of repacking. The herdsmen were ready to move well before the villagers, and drove their ponderous yaks on to the trail while some families were still eating. Once re-formed, the caravan stayed together: the old perils of the road – bandits, wolves – were still there. Now many of the travellers were quiet, deep in their thoughts. Again they camped; again they moved on.

Mid-morning on the third day, there came a shout from the lead riders. A few hundred yards ahead, a small party of two or three families had appeared, leading pack animals on foot. At the sight of the Jyeko caravan, these people began to run. They turned off the main track to head across the empty plain.

'Perhaps they think we're Chinese,' said Khenpo Nima doubtfully.

Wangdu shouted: 'Akung, Norbu! Go after them!'

Several young men spurred away in pursuit; Khenpo Nima saw the Jyeko horsemen cut in front of the strangers, wheel about and lean down from their saddles to talk. While he watched, he noticed Jamie bring his pony nearer, ready to listen. Then the riders returned.

'What's happening? Do they take us for bandits or what?' called Karjen.

The young men's faces were flushed. 'There's news,' they began.

'Doubtless,' retorted Wangdu. 'Where are they from?'

'Near Chamdo. There's been a battle! Thousands of Chinese, they're everywhere! They've taken Chamdo!'

'Taken it?' growled Karjen. 'Somebody gave it to them?'

The information tumbled out in a tangle. 'They weren't prepared, everyone has left, they blew up the magazines!'

'For pity's sake,' interrupted Khenpo Nima, 'one thing at a time.'

The boys glanced at each other, then began again: 'Five days ago, Governor Ngabo heard that the Chinese had crossed the river at Batang, so he fled. The Khampas wanted to fight, they wanted the ammunition in the magazine. But the Governor wouldn't give it, and he fled. Then the Chinese attacked Chamdo at night, and now it's all over, finished.'

'What's finished?'

'They caught Governor Ngabo. The Chinese have got him. We've surrendered.'

'Speak for yourself,' said Karjen. 'That's what happens when you have a ponce from Lhasa in charge.'

They looked at one another and at the families in the distance, who again moved away south.

'Won't those people join us?' said Khenpo Nima. 'They'd be safer.'

'They don't think so,' the scout replied timidly. 'The Lhasa road is cut. And ... they don't want to be with anyone from Jyeko.'

'What's that meant to mean?' snapped Karjen.

'There was talk at Chamdo. They say a party of Chinese soldiers is missing – they went to Jyeko and haven't been seen. There was a captain who came into Chamdo riding alone, completely exhausted. There's a story that the Chinese were caught in the gorges, killed by rocks.'

The monks looked at Karjen, who shifted on his pony among a knot of dark-faced friends.

'They're saying Jyeko murdered them,' the boy added.

'There's soldiers searching. No one wants anything to do with Jyeko. We're bad luck.'

Out of the moment of silence that followed, there came a peculiarly shocking sound. It was Jamie giving a short, bitter laugh.

No one knew what to say, what to suggest. Wangdu rested his hands on the pommel of his wooden saddle, shaking his head. Khenpo Nima peered again at the party heading south, now drawing steadily away from them.

'Where *are* they heading?'

'Not to Lhasa. They're going to India.'

'India?'

'They say hundreds of people are gathering at Moro-La – '

'An army, to throw out the Chinese!'

'It's not an army. They're all going to India.'

'Leaving Tibet?'

'I don't believe that for a moment.'

'That's exile!'

'But that's what they're doing.'

Jamie had stopped laughing; he was looking from one face to another. They were floundering.

'Well, to hell with that!' said Karjen. 'Leave Tibet? No, thank you.'

'Look,' someone shouted. 'Look there! Back there!'

They all looked.

Above the pass they had crossed, far behind, there was a curious grey smudge on the snowfields that rose and discoloured the white clouds above. It was faint at first; they might have missed it. But as the moments passed, it became thicker, blacker, dirtier.

Someone murmured, 'Jyeko's burning.'

*

two

A pain gnaws: we pinch another limb for distraction. As the caravan moved on, the thought of what might have become of Puton in Jyeko was more than Jamie could bear. If he allowed his mind to slink back to her, he'd feel his throat tighten, his eyes sting, his brain throb, the start of panic ... and in desperation he would drag his unruly thoughts elsewhere. Thus he had given full rein to his less generous feelings about Tibet. This was not so hard: he held all Jyeko responsible for Puton's plight.

He rode in silence over the frozen ground, letting his pony find a path among the burrows of the pica. In the Jyeko throng, Jamie spoke to no one. These people did not look so charming now. The wind had stirred up white dust, filling the wrinkles on every face, leaving every eye bloodshot. Jamie felt no charity for any of them, neither monk nor merchant nor the children who had stoned Puton. His mind filled with grim images that he had, maybe, stored away for this moment of need. Things in Jyeko, in Lhasa; things that were not pleasant.

He recalled the beggar-criminals, miserable amputees. It was a routine punishment to manacle a man's legs and turn him loose without his hands, or his feet, or his eyes. Unable to work, he'd creep from shelter to shelter, begging food. Jamie had seen them in Jyeko: who had done that to them – Wangdu? The only 'police' were there in the monastery. One could not take a life in oh-so-Buddhist Tibet, of course, but he'd heard that monastic officials might flog a thief to within an inch of his life then dump him on a blizzard-swept mountainside at nightfall. It could not strictly be said that *they* had killed him. Just as it could never be said that a good Tibetan had taken the life of a yak or sheep. There just happened to be a profession of bad Tibetans, despised outcasts, to do the butchery for them. So much for tradition!

He'd heard whisper of other things: of pepper forced under eyelids to obtain confessions; of the ritual sacrifice of babies (could that *really* be true? Just now Jamie was disposed to believe it); of the huge Lhasa monasteries where, it was rumoured, a steady supply of young novices was buggered ragged by the monks. An Indian government doctor in New Delhi had worked in Lhasa and warned him, 'There's hardly a Tibetan doesn't have the clap. Believe it, sir! When their husbands are away they'll fornicate with his brothers – the nearest merchant, the meanest shepherd will do. I've treated ghastly things ...'

Jamie had been told things that he'd not credited – until he saw them in Lhasa. People copulating openly on rooftops in the summer sun. Monks from rival monasteries fighting in the streets with wooden clubs. The squalor of the city lanes where everyone upped skirts and shat as they liked. The filth of the houses, where women gave birth in piss-soaked stables then licked their babies clean. The sheer ignorance! A land without carts, without roads, without newspapers, without curiosity. Without maps, even: they scarcely knew the shape of their own country. Half of Tibet thought the earth was flat, and the other half didn't care one way or the other. As for Khenpo Nima's 'medicine' ...

Such was the catalogue that went through Jamie's sullen mind as he rode onward. He recalled, with an ironic shiver, how he had 'loved' the place, ignoring the horrors of its 'civilisation'. How he'd laughed along with bandits in Jyeko as they reminisced about killing people. How he'd spent so much time learning the language that he'd hardly considered what was being said. How he'd smiled indulgently at the Lhasa aristocracy with their foppish manners and stupendous brocaded robes, their giggling adulteries, their endless parties and staggering wealth wrung from countless serfs on never-seen estates. How he'd listened to justifications of feudal class and caste, of credulity, sorcery and superstition; how he'd 'understood'. Jolting along in his crude wooden saddle, Jamie grimaced at his own naïveté, at his gullibility. He declared to himself that the scales had fallen from his eyes: the place was medieval, and a stiff dose of China might be no bad thing.

He glimpsed, sour-eyed, the villagers riding near to him. Once, he had sat on a hillside outside Jyeko and mused in grateful affection. Now he could see them in one light only: they had condemned Puton. They had no charity, no shred of common decency. He wanted nothing to do with them. He would ride to Lhasa in silence.

But with the sighting of the smoke came a new desperation. If he relaxed, an unbearable thought of Puton's fate might rush into his mind. His entire body tensed with necessary anger; possibly by holding himself rigid he could block the reverberations of despair. Jamie wanted only one thing: to be out of Tibet as fast as possible. If it was true that the direct Lhasa road was cut, if they were forced to swing in a loop to the south near to the Sikkim border, that was fine by him. If it meant exile, he'd be delighted to assist. They could sweat and rot in refugee camps, feel their self-esteem evaporate and their blood curdle with malaria; that was entirely acceptable. He just wanted them to decide, then get on with it.

The caravan had come to a halt again. The crowd swilled, clumped and hardened about the core of leaders, who had dismounted and stood in a tight circle in the snow. Meanwhile the animals drifted aimlessly over the plain, because Jyeko could not decide where to go. Were they truly being hunted? Humble, backwater Jyeko? The westward road stood apparently empty and inviting, but perhaps a force of Chinese sat astride it somewhere, waiting for them, who knew where? To the east behind them, their homes were burned. To the north, the disasters at Chamdo. To the south ... what?

'So we push them out of the way,' snarled Karjen, his cronies growling their agreement. 'I think we've shown that we can deal with Chink soldiers.'

'This is a village, not an army,' sighed Wangdu.

'We have fifty good men,' Karjen tried again.

'Karjen, your old blood is all afire and your head's full of smoke,' Khenpo Nima reproved him. 'We have women, children and animals to protect. We are slow and noisy. We have no idea how many Chinese there might be. We *must* avoid them.'

'Isn't it obvious?' called another voice. 'We have to go after those people, whether they want our company or not.'

The other little party was still visible, drawing away rapidly to the south.

The weight of opinion swung back and forth. Was the long southern route possible? Probably. Had they enough food? Probably not. Did they know the route? Maybe. Was the pass at Moro-La open at this time of year? They'd know when they got there. It was uncertain, it was frightening. If there was one thing the Khampas knew very well, it was the difficulties of winter travel. Perhaps Karjen was right after all: they should move forward as fast as possible, and break past whatever Chinese force was on the Lhasa road.

'That is crazy,' said Jamie, rather loudly.

Everyone turned to peer at him. It was the first time he'd spoken up since leaving Jyeko. They were well aware of his feelings for them.

'Do you imagine the Communists are a bunch of incompetent peasants? You're up against something else now. They've just won a war beyond your imagination. They're tough, they're the biggest army in the world, and they're after you. If they've cut the Lhasa road, there's going to be hundreds of men, watching for the first sign of your yaks and your families coming through the hills, with horses, machine-guns, radios ... '

He stopped, suddenly thoughtful, and glanced at the pack animals behind him. Karjen stamped his feet and glared. The monks regarded each other warily, questioning. Wangdu began: 'Mr Jemmy, at least on the Lhasa road we know where they are. We can have scouts forward and feel our way towards them. If we go south, they could be anywhere. We might run straight into them and not know until they start shooting. They're not going to tell us in which valley they're waiting.'

'Well, they might,' murmured Jamie, frowning more thoughtfully still.

His tone was such that everyone fell quiet. Jamie was still staring at the pack animals.

'Jemmy ...?' began Wangdu.

But Jamie cut him short, shouting inexplicably: 'They will!

They bloody will!'

The villagers, bewildered, looked to the monks to explain. But Jamie shouted again: 'Nima, Wangdu, come and see!'

He strode towards his animals, the monks following uncertainly and the villagers' eyes on them. Jamie tugged aside the cords that half smothered the radio box. Without taking the crate off, he eased open the cover and peered inside.

'Look!' he said triumphantly, pointing at the radio that nestled in rolls of old blanket. 'The Chinese pre-set it for us.'

Khenpo Nima and Wangdu peered: it was the same radio as before. What did Jamie mean?

'They've left it on their military frequency.' He was laughing. 'Don't touch! I can read it off ...'

He grabbed at his own saddlebag, dug in it for a notepad, scribbled down the setting and held it out to Khenpo Nima. His eyes were shining with a hard glint of excitement and irritation: how could the monk not see the point?

'I don't understand,' said Khenpo Nima.

'They tried this frequency every day.' Jamie spelt it out, the contemptuous edge to his voice blunted by delight at his discovery. 'Six o'clock, regular as clockwork. They were waiting for transmissions, orders, don't you see? Their headquarters at Chamdo has transmitters and this is the frequency.'

'So?' asked Nima.

'Nima, we'll know exactly where they are, they'll tell us! We've got the pedal generator. We can check the radio each evening at six o'clock, we can listen to the orders, we can hear where they're sending their patrols and we can avoid them. It's like a spy, it will lead us to safety.'

A quick muttering began that might have been interest or incredulity. Jamie heard someone say, 'We've got our monks: they can use their divining bones.' And another, replying: 'It didn't work in Jyeko, did it? Maybe oracles can't detect Chinese, not being decent Buddhists, you know.'

They looked to Khenpo Nima: he might know the truth – he'd spoken to the radio each day, he'd seen it work. They waited for his verdict.

'But we won't understand what they are saying,' Nima began weakly.

'Who speaks Chinese?' shouted Jamie. No one stirred. 'You traders, some of you have been right down to Chengdu.'

The crowd stirred now, looking one to another.

'Come on, for pity's sake!' bawled Jamie.

Someone shouted, 'Jamyang Sangay!' and at once three or four others chorused, 'Yes, Jamyang Sangay, he knows Chinese!'

'All right,' called Jamie. 'Jamyang Sangay! Where are you? We need you to listen.'

'I'm here,' replied a rasping, arrogant voice. Jamie looked – and winced. Jamyang Sangay stood with his hands on his hips, head cocked sceptically to one side. He was a large, strongly built, corpulent man. He was the landlord who had turned away Puton.

'You're asking for my assistance, Mr Jemmy?' he said, with a distinct sneer.

'No,' said Jamie. 'I'm asking you to help all Jyeko. The Chinese will speak on the radio each evening. You just have to tell us what they say.'

'And why do we want to do that?'

'Because their commanders will be telling the patrols where to go. If Captain Duan really is after us, he'll report to Chamdo every day, so we'll hear exactly where he's going, and we can avoid him. This is an oracle that detects Chinese.'

Someone laughed; Wangdu glowered at them.

'This means,' said Jamyang Sangay, 'that we go the southern route, right? Which would suit you nicely: have us escort you to Moro-La so you can pop over the border?'

'You go along that Lhasa road and you get yourself cut to pieces,' spat Jamie. 'That would suit me just fine too!'

'Jemmy, please!'

Khenpo Nima stood forward between them. He turned towards the leering bulk of Jamyang Sangay. 'I believe Jemmy is correct. Those people,' he nodded to the receding specks of the other little caravan, 'they're heading for Moro-La, they say many others are also. They've seen the Chinese army in Chamdo, they know how bad it is. If there's a gathering at Moro-La, whether it's an army or even just people heading for India, that's the place to be.'

'Reverence,' said Jamyang Sangay, his voice more respectful, 'only you have seen this radio thing work. Tell us, please, are we to trust it?'

Khenpo Nima glanced at Jamie. He'd known him ... how long? A year? But what marvels in that year. 'We can trust Mr Jemmy absolutely,' he said. 'The radio can guide us if you will assist, Jamyang Sangay.'

The big merchant peered a moment at Jamie, then nodded. 'All right, if that's what everyone wants.'

A ripple of excitement spread through the villagers.

'Look at this, please,' cried Jamie loudly. Jamyang Sangay's pony stood near his own. From its bridle hung half a dozen white silk prayer flags. 'These are yours?' he called to the merchant.

Jamyang Sangay narrowed his eyes, frowning. 'Certainly. They ask for Lord Maitreya's blessing,' he replied.

'Then, excuse me, but the radio needs one.'

Before the merchant had realised it, Jamie had untied a flag from the bridle and was heading for the radio mule.

'Now, just a moment!' huffed Jamyang Sangay.

'Please.' Jamie held up a hand. 'Just watch.'

He pulled open the lid of the case again, extracted three sections of lightweight aerial and fitted them together with quick, practised hands. He tied the white triangular flag to one end, then jammed the aerial down the side of the pack. It stuck straight up, the flag caught at once by the wind.

'Follow this!' cried Jamie. 'Follow the radio flag!' He cursed the villagers, their teetering indecision. They *would* go: he would push them, drag them! He marched to his own pony, swung up into the saddle with the mule's leading rope in his hand and pulled both animals barging out of the throng. He pointed the pony southward and shouted: 'Moro-la! To Moro-la!'

'Moro-la!' bawled Khenpo Nima firmly, striding towards his own animals. The obedient novices went straight after him, and the decision was made. The caravan turned south.

*

The ground began to rise. The wind knocked and buffeted the riders, exhausting them, while the sky ahead took on a lurid purple, thick as swags of velvet. Across these sombre drapes flickered distant lightning.

The wind gusted and picked up the snow in handfuls to throw it in the Khampas' faces. The crystals were small and hard, like sharp sand. They rode with their hats lowered and the horses hung their heads, tossing and blinking with discomfort. The picas stayed fast in their burrows, the griffon vultures and lammergeyers kept to their crags.

In the caravan, all conversation ceased. Jamie tugged the red scarf tighter at his neck and pulled down his hat until the fur pricked his eyes. He could hardly see the way ahead but the pony trudged onward. There was little escape from his thoughts. He sank into his coat like a winkle whose shell would not save it from the pin. Brooding, he felt sick with grief; he thought it unkind that he should be afflicted simultaneously with petrifying cold from without and nausea from within. His senses were cruelly occupied by memory: of the touch and scent of a breast topped by a near-black nipple, of dark slanting eyes, of fluids and scents. He was scarcely aware of present physical sensation except the swill of saliva in the back of his mouth, that told him he was near to retching with misery. He paid no attention to his riding. The reins hung loose in his hand and his body subsided, shivering. He folded in on himself, as though he might have curled into a ball on the saddle and slept.

He was roused by men calling and by the caravan halting for the night. He saw that they had made some progress, that they were not so far from the mountains. He realised how cold he was, chilled to the bone, so he dismounted and threw himself into the business of tents, fires and the radio. He'd dragged Jyeko into the southern route with this promise; he'd have to play it out.

He heaved the radio case inside the black tent with the box that held the pedal dynamo and assembled it; then he went outside and erected the whip aerial. He saw Khenpo Nima watching him, and called: 'Nima! I need someone to crank the generator. Quickly!'

In the spacious tent, an energetic but nervous young man set his back against a saddle pack and his feet on the pedals of the dynamo. On a rug by the radio sat Khenpo Nima, Wangdu, Jamie and his least favourite Khampa, Jamyang Sangay, all cross-legged. Others crowded in. Shortly before six, Jamie waved at the young man to start pedalling.

The flywheel spun, a low whistling coming from the covers. There came a low sigh of satisfaction as the dials began to glow: this alone must have efficacy against the Chinese. As Jamie touched switches and knobs, an electric hiss filled the tent. And then, suddenly, voices.

'Eh? What's that?' Jamyang Sangay sat back in surprise.

'Listen!' commanded Jamie.

The voices were startlingly clear.

'What are they saying, Sangay?' someone whispered.

'I can't make it out,' said the merchant plaintively.

'Listen to them!' snapped Khenpo Nima. 'It's Chinese, isn't it?'

'Yes, yes!'

Flustered, Jamyang Sangay frowned and stared ferociously at the radio. The listeners strained to catch the words.

'That's Chinese all right,' a woman said. 'Where are they?'

'Hush, for pity's sake!' cried Jamie.

'Sangay, listen!' commanded Wangdu.

The stream of messages continued, rapid and staccato. Jamie glanced at Jamyang Sangay questioningly; the merchant was concentrating furiously and leaning forward as though to listen with the very pores of his cheek.

'Something about Batang? Something about transporting ammunition up from Batang. Who's this talking, then? Calls himself Yellow Nine ... '

'They'll use code names.'

'What?' Sangay grimaced. 'Now I've got Yellow Two.'

'Listen, Sangay!' Khenpo Nima shuffled closer, his nerves fraying.

There was silence for a moment, then another voice began, clearer.

'Now what's he saying?'

'Ssssh!'

'"Blue Nine, where are you? Blue Nine, where are you?" Why do they say everything twice?'

'Blue Nine,' whispered Jamie. 'That's what Duan used in Jyeko.'

'Murderous shit!'

The villagers cocked their ears; if it was Duan, his voice was unrecognisable.

'Where is he, Sangay?'

'I don't know, do I? I'm listen … Gyamotang! He says he's in Gyamotang, that's on the Lhasa road. That's exactly where we were going!'

'Ah!' A warm breath of approbation from Khenpo Nima, who patted Jamie's shoulder.

'Listen! What's his orders?'

'He's waiting. The other fellow is asking, any signs? Any riders? … He says, "Negative contact." He wants to wait two more days. Then east. He wants to move east.'

'Towards us!'

'We're off his road now.'

'Sssh!'

'The other man says that's good … Now it's about ammunition from Batang again. That's it.'

The dynamo man lifted his feet off the pedals, which turned for a few seconds more with a dying hum.

'Well!' said Jamie to the company. 'You see? We'll hear every move he makes.'

'Jemmy, well done,' said Khenpo Nima quietly, and the villagers chorused: 'Well done!'

'Send a message to Lhasa, Jemmy!' cried Karjen. 'Tell them we're coming!'

'Greetings to His Holiness!' called another.

'Tell the Chinese to screw themselves!' shouted a youth.

'Karjen,' began Jamie, 'if I transmit, who will hear?'

'His Holiness.' Karjen smiled, delighted.

'Maybe. Who else?'

'All the spirits!'

'And?'

Karjen subsided, looking uncertain.

'The Chinese?' asked Khenpo Nima.

'Just so,' said Jamie. 'Nobody touches this transmitter – or they'll track us all the way to Moro-La.'

That night Jamie lay in the dark under his swaddling of quilts and furs, listening to Karjen snore. A dull satisfaction stayed with him. This was how it would be: he would set himself to it, escape and survival, the road to India. He would not abandon anyone, he would get these people to Moro-La: it would occupy his mind and garrison it against misery. After Moro-La they could do what they bloody well liked.

Outside the tent, the wind had not given up. Over the taut fabric it tossed hard grains of snow with a dry sugary rattle. It whispered the threat of the winter road. The temperature was plunging; Hector whined piteously. Without leaving his bed, Jamie reached out and opened the flap a fraction. The mastiff slipped inside at once, shook off the snow and lay by the radio. The huge dog, trained to knock a man from a running horse and a match for most wolves, was reduced to a shivering heap peering round pathetically in the darkness. In his nest of furs, Jamie drew up his legs for warmth. For a terrible moment he thought of fires, and then of fireplaces and houses and houses on fire and then ... Mercifully, exhaustion claimed him.

He slept fitfully. But the whole chilly camp woke early, creeping out into a clinging grey mist. By Khenpo Nima's baggage a mule lay frozen on the ground, its eyes clouded over.

*

They moved among low foothills. In the black tent at evening, the radio confided that the pursuing force remained at Gyamotang. On the third day, the Chinese commander told Chamdo that he had new information. Nomads reported a large party going southward towards the mountains. He, Duan, was taking that route in the morning, towards the Mar-jya Kou valley.

'Where we are now,' observed Khenpo Nima.

'Well, let's get out of it,' said Jamie, turning off the radio.

'It depends which way he's coming in,' said Nima. 'If he's coming from Gyamotang, he could be in front of us. But he might follow the route we came.'

'In which case,' said Jamie, 'if we turn round we'll run straight into him.'

Khenpo Nima trailed his finger across the matting, tracing a ghost map.

'We can travel just as well in the Dre-Kou valley, the next one south. Is there anywhere we can cross over?'

'At Shang,' called someone.

'Where's that? Before or after the river?'

'Before. He wouldn't see us.'

At first light, the caravan went deeper into the Mar-jya Kou valley. Three men with rifles and quick ponies were sent a mile ahead as scouts. Time was against them. The Chinese cavalry would be moving at twice the speed of the caravan with its yaks and baggage.

Mid-morning, the outriders came trotting back to point out a cluster of deserted stone animal pens on the valley floor ahead. That was Shang. Above them to the left, a narrow sheep track led to the saddle in the hills that they should cross into the parallel Dre-Kou valley. In front of them, the Mar-Jya Kou turned a corner, passing behind a long, barren spur.

They began to climb in single file. Two thirds of the way up, almost at the smooth brow of the spur, the scouts halted suddenly. One began to run back down the hill, calling, 'We can see them! We can see the Chinese!'

The caravan leaders crept to the crest and looked down. In the middle distance, little more than a mile away, were crags of silvery-grey gneiss in which the quartz sparkled. At the foot of these crags, almost hidden, was a large encampment of soldiers: trim tents, horses tethered in lines and pyramid stacks of rifles.

'They've got machine-guns, look,' said Jamie. The villagers at his side were silent with awe.

'We'd have ridden straight into that,' someone whispered.

'Well, for heaven's sake, don't let them see us now.' Jamie grabbed at Hector who was strolling on the skyline.

'Everyone dismount!' cried Khenpo Nima. A moment later the muted call went down the caravan, 'Off the path!'

Stumbling on the icy slope thirty feet below the crest, exposed for just fifty yards, the animals were dragged into a trot, villagers heaving at the leading ropes and slapping at their rumps, hurrying them over the crest to safety with their loads swaying. Crouching in the snow at the top, Jamie and Karjen, Wangdu and Khenpo Nima peered back at the soldiers who were hunting them. The Chinese hadn't stirred. Karjen grinned broadly and began to laugh. 'Ha! They've lost us. They're sitting on their arses just where they *said* they'd be sitting on their arses. Excellent! Ha!'

'Wonderful!' said Wangdu.

'You see?' beamed Khenpo Nima. 'That's Jemmy's radio, our oracle. Isn't that fine?'

Jamie smiled with narrow eyes. 'It *is* rather useful,' he agreed. 'Come on, Jyeko, let's leave them far behind.'

*

three

So a cat-and-mouse game was played out in the mountains. The Jyeko caravan moved deeper into the protective maze, climbing towards the watershed and the high passes, hoping to emerge from the farther slopes well to the south and clear of the Chinese. The rolling grasslands were long forgotten now. The valleys were deep wounds slashed into the Tibetan massif, lined with black rock and scatterings of dwarf rhododendron. There were half-hidden cols and sunless gorges, pockets of iced-over marsh through which the yaks' hoofs smashed into greasy mud, and waterfalls like frozen mares' tails. The narrow paths wound this way and that, round spurs and over ridges, and could readily plunge or leap five hundred feet at a turn. At times they would glimpse a powerful torrent glittering a thousand feet below them. They'd see it foaming, but would not be able to hear it.

The pursuing Chinese were more mobile than a train of slow-moving yaks, but were not used to the terrain. Neither side had maps, since none had ever been drawn. The Chinese had crude, small-scale plans; the Tibetans had a smattering of local knowledge. Sometimes the soldiers could pick up the trail left by the yaks, mules and ponies, but mostly the high winds threw snow about and covered it. The Chinese sent out scouts, but their ponies slipped and stumbled on the precipitous and icy tracks just as the Tibetans did.

The troops were men from warm, lowland plains, ill used to floundering in snow-clogged gullies. They clambered cursing up to ridges, hoping to spot the fleeing caravan and cut it off, but they never set eyes on it. At times they came perilously close. Once the villagers were obliged to hurry for concealment in a gorge. They had to search for fuel and fodder, and this made them vulnerable. The radio was erratic here. Each evening they strained to catch the Chinese commander's reports, tried to relate what they heard to the landscape they saw about them, and agreed a route for the next day. Each morning they moved off at first light, praying that they had made the right choice. West and south they aimed, but more than once they were almost trapped and had to double back and look for another trail.

At first Jamie thought them worryingly undisciplined. They argued incessantly: two men spent a week furiously disputing the ownership of a yak that might or might not have been purchased for the journey. Those ready first in the morning would start off without waiting and might well have got lost in the steep twistings of the valleys. But after a while he noticed that no one went more than half a mile or so from Khenpo Nima, Wangdu and the other monks, who themselves travelled in a compact group. And, within an hour, they had all formed up behind the radio mule, which travelled at the head of the party, its antenna and flag whipping and cutting the air. It had become a mascot; they followed it as obediently as tourists follow a furled red umbrella through cobbled streets.

Jamie saw other things. A laden mule was stumbling up the snowy track led by an old woman who was herself staggering. A family came from behind, took the rope from her hand and removed all the baggage from the mule while the old lady stood mute. Having distributed the load among their own animals, the family lifted her onto the mule and continued with her in tow. A man shot a musk deer and presented roast meat to every child in the caravan that night. A pony, suffering badly from the cold and poor grazing, could no longer carry its owner. It was not abandoned, but was allowed to follow at its own pace while its master took the wooden saddle and carried it on his own back until the pony regained some strength. So the village went on together.

They climbed towards the Siekan-La, a pass at eighteen thousand feet surrounded by towers and pinnacles of iron-stained limestone. The track became narrower still, no more than steep erratic steps stacked there a century before. Snow pockets hid crevices into which feet and hoofs jammed. The animals protested and refused; the people cursed and struck at them, heaving on the ropes. At dusk, nearing exhaustion, they gained the pass.

'Once again, the gods are victorious and the devils are

defeated,' puffed Khenpo Nima, hoiking a rock out of the muddy snow and dumping it on the cairn. Two or three gruff villagers followed suit.

High in the far distant haze, the interminable complexity of the Himalayan ranges was heaped, peak after ridge after gorge, with snowfields shining in a palette of pale blues according to their angle in the sun. Below in the middle ground spread a region of broad valleys. There would be some scanty winter grazing there, and the trail would not be an endless icy clamber. But there were many cold miles to descend, and a choice of routes: two deep ravines curved downward, both with deep snow drifts and, way below, sprinklings of juniper and larch that gathered into thin forest. They chose the southernmost.

On the descent they slithered and scrambled uncomfortably. The track dropped suddenly from ledge to ledge, between boulders and over little runs of frosted scree. The animals peered, balked and resisted, eyes big with fright, and their owners held their tails to steady them. People sank to their thighs in snow, or twisted their ankles between wet boulders, or slid on the muddy paste stirred by the pack animals. Hector sprawled awkwardly and gave Jamie reproachful looks.

The incline eased and the long column spread out once again on the thread-like trail that descended the valley. By late afternoon they had regained the tree-line: first the dwarf rhododendrons, then a few brave larches, a scattering of fir. The caravan picked up a little speed, their shoulders lifted and they felt warmer in both their spirits and their feet. The river drew near on the right hand, now shrugging off its ice casing and running cheerfully. Through the trees they glimpsed the open plain again; beyond that, they would begin the ascent towards the pass at Moro-La. The sight buoyed them ... and then they stopped short.

At least, the head of the march stopped short. The long column behind did not react instantly and threatened to telescope into the leaders. An anxious call of enquiry came from the rear, and met an urgent order for silence. Everyone strained to see.

Where the long spurs of the mountain met the plain a

short distance ahead, a larger river debouched from another steep gorge to the right, and the two joined force. There, on flat ground above a bend in the stream, were the Chinese soldiers.

'What,' asked Wangdu, 'are they doing there?'

'Waiting for us, I'm afraid,' replied Jamie. 'I thought we heard them say somewhere else.'

'Nupkong,' said Khenpo Nima. 'They were meant to be at Nupkong.'

'Perhaps this is Nupkong.'

'Wherever it is,' said Jamie, 'there they are and we almost walked straight into them. So what do we do? Go back?'

Everyone turned to look behind them. The trail climbed, steeper, narrower and colder with every yard, until it disappeared into the mist.

'I can't see that being very popular,' observed Wangdu.

'*I* can't see that we have a lot of choice.'

'We can attack!'

'Hush, Karjen.'

'Well – '

'Talk sense, man. Look at them!'

They all regarded the camp below. It was well organised with machine-gun nests behind stacked rocks, well-drilled lines of tents and fires, the horses tethered in the rear. There might be eighty or a hundred soldiers, and two or three civilians were visible: reluctant guides perhaps. By one larger tent in the centre, a tall radio mast had been erected.

'Is that Duan?' wondered someone by Jamie's elbow.

'Who knows? He won't be able to hear Chamdo too well with the mountains on top of him. He probably wouldn't even try to transmit from here. Waste of time.'

'You can see he doesn't know where we're coming from,' said Karjen.

'How do you mean?'

'He's facing the wrong valley.' They all turned to Karjen, who shrugged in a superior way and continued, 'Just look how his guns are placed. He thinks we're coming down the other river.'

Jamie kicked himself in chagrin. *He* was meant to be the trained soldier, but it took a retired bandit to point out the obvious: the northern valley was broader, easier, the preferred way to the pass. And all the Chinese guns were trained on it.

'We're behind them!'

'Don't get too excited. They'll turn round fast enough when they see us.'

'*If* they see us.'

'A hundred or more people and four score animals? They might notice something.'

They surveyed the landscape. Certainly, the Chinese were not actually on their path, which kept close to the foot of the mountain. At no point was it less than three hundred yards from the Chinese. But it was completely exposed – like marching across a shooting gallery.

'So, let's wait here and attack in the dark,' proposed Karjen, enjoying his new-found celebrity as a military pundit.

'Karjen, we are not commandos,' retorted Khenpo Nima in irritation. 'We have to turn back.'

'They might hear us even then,' said Wangdu, 'and come after us on the trail. Imagine: they'd shoot us in the back one after another, all the way up the line. We have to get round somehow.'

'Put socks on the yaks,' a woman called softly. It was Tsering Norzu, a market harridan. She stood now with her hands on her hips and a challenge in her eyes.

'Socks?' queried Nima.

'Socks, Reverence, socks, like Mr Jemmy wears. We tie cloth round the animals' feet and ankles.'

'What for?' enquired Nima, still confused.

'So they'll be quiet. Then we go at night, right past the camp. There's no moon.'

'Ridiculous.' Karjen spat. 'I can't see why we don't attack. We can get close up along the gully after dark, then cut that shit Duan to pieces. They *are* facing the wrong way – '

'Karjen!' hissed Khenpo Nima. 'I will not listen to that talk any more. We are here to save our families, not to butcher those young men.'

'But they're Chinese!' protested Karjen.

'If you persist in this evil, Karjen, that's what you'll be in your next life: Chinese.'

'So what *do* we do, Reverence?'

Khenpo Nima looked unhappily at the camp below, at its machine-guns, stacked rifles and poised brutality. Everyone waited, hanging on his next words.

'We'll bind the animals' feet, and go past at night.'

Tsering Norzu grinned cheerfully at Jamie – and he smiled back.

They waited on the path. They could not move for fear of making a noise or catching a soldier's eye. Nor could they cook: smoke would betray them instantly. So they sat in the snow behind the thin screen of trees, shivering, murmuring. They tied the animals to branches and prayed there'd be no whinnying or protest. The men muttered that they'd cut a mule's throat if it started to bray. They passed handfuls of dry barleymeal to each other and ate it with a little snow to soften it. They hushed their children, pulling the smallest under their heavy coats. And they waited.

Jamie pulled the radio mule close by, taking down the top sections of the flag mast before they caught in the branches. Hector, his long legs going into the drifts like spikes, curled up in the snow. Jamie had in his pocket a little dried fruit that he'd brought from Jyeko market; he tossed Hector a fig which the dog nosed then ignored.

Sitting in silence, Jamie let himself think of Puton, keeping this to a sternly practical level. How might she have coped with their journey so far? Not without considerable difficulty. She could ride easily enough, but there had been little chance of riding for much of this last week. He envisaged her struggling up over rocks, or her stick becoming snagged in roots, or Dechen whimpering and her mother unable to carry her. It would have been hard. But she would have done it somehow, they'd have managed. He could see her in his mind's eye on some precipitous trail, and pride filled out his imagination. It was less awful to think of her thus than to speculate on what had actually happened.

He considered the people around him. Two weeks before, he'd been hardly able to look at them without wanting to spit then burst into tears. Time and the route had dulled his fury and despair. Not that he was any happier, but one cannot traverse Tibet in a spasm of misery. His anger near exhausted, like everything else.

Over these weakened defences, a touch of admiration had begun to creep upon Jamie: at how little complaining there had been; at the dogged endurance, the resourcefulness and resolve, the unquestioning redistribution of fallen loads, the promptness with which the women now dug into the packs for cloth to cut up and bind the feet of the bemused pack animals, with quick whispers and suggestions exchanged. At the stubbornness of good humour. He thought, I have often needed help – and it has generally come before I've had to ask for it.

But then the cold took hold of him. It brought back his sadness, the enervating despondency of memory and loss. It wearied him so deeply that he seemed to sleep as he sat, with dulled but open eyes fixed on the ground in front of him. He remained thus a long while as the darkness deepened. When at last Wangdu whispered to him, 'Jemmy, it is time now!' he shivered profoundly, then snapped back thankfully to full attention.

In the starlight he saw figures rise from the ground, silent and expectant. A whisper went back: 'No hurrying, no running. Pick your way slowly, carefully, don't fall!' They began to move at a snail's pace, the column stretching like elastic. The villagers stepped carefully over roots and rocks; the animals plodded softly, their feet swathed, making little fuss. They emerged from the last tree cover. To the right, a dozen campfires spilled small pools of yellow into the darkness. Black silhouettes clustered by these, or moved between them. A most unpleasant image haunted Jamie: a mule stumbling and slithering noisily in the rocks, a Chinese flare drenching the night sky with phosphorescence, catching them on the open path. A machine-gun would start at one end of the column and turn towards the other ...

The caravan crept onward, the noise of a hundred or more people and their pack animals little more than a rustle, a soft thumping that the river sounds absorbed. No child's cry, no pan clanging, no rocks kicked aside to crash into the gullies. Only, once, a small snort from a pony – but they did not stop moving and the Chinese flare did not burst out.

Still Jyeko crept along the path.

*

They travelled on for three hours more and then stopped. They were frightened of losing each other in the night. If a family went astray now, not only might they perish, they might also fall into Chinese hands and give the whole caravan away. So they halted and rested as best they could, huddled by the baggage without putting up the tents. They allowed no fires until dawn, the hour when the light of the flames was lost and a faint mist concealed the smoke. Filling themselves quickly with barleymeal and thick buttered tea, they stripped the bandaging from the animals' feet and their own boots, remounted and set off again, sagging with weariness.

At the head of the caravan rode Jamie, tugging the radio mule and its quivering flag mast. As they pulled away from the resting place, a Khampa youth rode up and clapped Jamie on the shoulder: 'Hey, Mr Jemmy, we fooled the Chinese! Brilliant, hey?'

But Jamie gave him such a scowl that the young man backed off, puzzled and hurt. Jamie rode on, nodding drowsily in the saddle, the radio mule's flag bobbing in the cold morning air.

*

four

The Chinese had wasted no time in returning to Jyeko.

There was, after all, little to prevent them. Captain Duan had arrived at Chamdo in time to see the Commander of the Second Field Army (PLA) receiving the surrender of the Lhasan Governor, Ngabo Ngawang Jigme. The first stage of the occupation was over already.

General Wang was feeling expansive: eastern Tibet had capitulated in less than a week with hardly a battle worth the name. When the PLA had closed in on Chamdo, chaos had ensued. Ngabo, an aristocrat of smooth manners and weaselly policy, had fled the town, taking his officials and every available horse in a desperate scamper westward. Abandoned, betrayed, beside themselves with rage, the Khampa levies had run amok, looting and destroying everything remotely connected with the rule of Lhasa.

For many years, a cruel story persisted about the fall of Chamdo: that there had been no battle, only fireworks. The Chinese, it was said, had set off a splendid display of rockets and crackers in the hills above the town that had panicked the Tibetans. In fact, Governor Ngabo had not required sparklers to send him flying. He'd turned tail before the enemy arrived. The humiliation could not have been more complete. Around Ngabo's residency, the tents and bivouacs of the Second Field Army now clustered.

Chamdo was a shambles, with many buildings burned in the rioting, the military magazine blown to smithereens, the radio station wrecked. But here, as in Jyeko and every other town they had captured, Chinese policy was to woo the Tibetans: nothing to be seized without payment, nothing looted or razed, no one shot out of hand. Captured Tibetan soldiers had been handed their rifles back (empty) and were then filmed presenting them to the Chinese with fixed smiles of 'Friendship', after which, they'd been given a little money and told to go home. It was, to the ferocious

Khampas, utterly bewildering.

Captain Duan, exhausted, cold, famished, had ridden from Jyeko in sixteen hours overnight, but he requested an immediate interview with General Wang. In the course of this, he presented an account of events at Jyeko and gave his surmises as to the fate of the dead soldiers in the river. Forty minutes later, he emerged with the command of a punitive expedition and the rank of major. At dawn the next morning he was on the road back to Jyeko.

He arrived the following afternoon to find the village virtually deserted. He rode through the familiar lanes, half expecting a sniper's bullet. With every yard, every familiar lane, Duan's anger intensified. Such humiliation! Fooled and butchered! He was not at heart a particularly hard or ruthless man; at least, he had not been born such, and in another time might have enjoyed a peaceable career in hydraulic engineering like Colonel Shen. But the desperate decades of civil war had taught him that his personal survival was largely in his own hands. If he must be zealous, he would not flinch. Thus, zeal had become a way of life.

His men now smashed open the doors of every house but found almost no one. A handful of Tibetans were rounded up and taken to the monastery. There, just three monks remained, attending the very elderly Abbot who sat motionless and watched the troops with tiny, watery eyes as they waited for the Major.

Duan's progress through the village had led him, naturally, to the house where the radio had been installed and he himself had lodged. On reaching the gate, he found it shut but not barred. He dismounted, put a shoulder to the old timbers and opened it without difficulty. Again, he half expected a welcoming fusillade, but was met with silence.

The British technician had obviously fled with the villagers. The door of the radio room was closed but, in the shed next to the stable, Duan could see the bulky generator on its stone foundations. Not something you'd carry away in a rush. In the stables themselves, however, Duan was surprised to find a mule and a pony. The animals stirred uneasily. He came out into the courtyard, momentarily uncertain.

Then he saw the child. Dechen was standing in the doorway. She looked at him with the same clear gaze as her mother. Duan heard a voice call, 'Dechen?' A moment later, the woman was there and staring in frozen alarm at the Chinese officer.

Duan regarded them without speaking. Then he took a few steps towards them, his Tibetan speech awkward still but his manner punctilious. 'Good afternoon,' he began. 'I daresay you remember who I am.'

The woman said nothing, but pushed the little girl indoors behind her.

'I am surprised to find you still here,' Duan continued, 'after all your compatriots have fled.'

'I am unable to travel,' said the woman. Duan saw once more her misshapen leg and stick. He also noted again the two sturdy-looking animals in the stable.

'I would have thought some arrangement could have been made. In a Chinese village you would have been better cared for. You'd not have been left alone.'

'There are others here,' said Puton.

'Yes,' said Duan. 'We have found them. Incidentally, I have had the honour to be promoted since we last met. I am a major now. I shall lodge here again tonight.'

He watched carefully for any reaction. She made none.

'Do you have any objection?' he said.

But she turned inside the house, leaving him there.

Major Duan watched her go in some surprise – not least, that he had *asked* her if she had objections. This was a punitive expedition, for heaven's sake! He took a few short strides to the doorway. She was clearing the room, gathering up some belongings and pushing them into large saddlebags. 'We are not here on a courtesy call!' Duan barked at her back. Puton straightened and looked at him again. He continued, 'It may not have escaped your notice that a number of Chinese soldiers have died in your disgusting hovel of a village. Men who brought freedom to Tibet.'

'I am from Lhasa,' replied Puton. 'This is not my village.'

'So, you won't be upset at its fate.' Duan spun on his heel. As he did so, three of his troops barged in through the gate – then saw him and stopped, unsure what to do next.

'These people are to be left undisturbed,' said the Major. 'I shall be lodging here tonight.' He called over his shoulder to Puton, 'Make up a bed for me in this room.' Then he marched out of the gate.

As Duan departed, Puton subsided onto the empty packing case that stood in the centre of the now shambolic room. Jamie had taken his most precious and useful belongings, but had been forced to leave much behind: the forsaken books, equipment and surplus clothing were heaped in desolation. Puton had pushed them roughly together, clearing space for herself and Dechen.

She regarded the untidy jumble with a weary shiver. She had expected that the Chinese would return, though their speed had caught her by surprise. She had expected Duan's return too, and had tried to gauge what that might mean for her. She'd recalled the silent stare he had been giving her the moment before they heard shots and shouting and he had run for his horse. She had tried to convince herself that he would be too busy at his commander's behest to notice her again. But she had not predicted that he himself would be in command.

So: once more, her fate was out of her hands. A shiver of dismay passed over her. All she could ever do was rise to meet the future as it closed on her. Taking this resolution literally, she stood, took a deep breath and decided to prepare food and tea; that at least might mollify the Major. She looked about to locate Dechen. She missed her – then saw that the little girl had gone into the main bedroom and was sitting on the *kang*, which Puton had lit to warm the house. Her daughter, on Jamie's bed. Puton's heart shrank, her eyes stung, her throat tightened. She bit her lip and went to the kitchen.

She tried to stifle her terrors with activity. A week ago she had almost forgotten fear: she had been lifted above it, borne up by delight. But in Duan there was a quality that brought the terror screeching back into her head. It was his piercing watchfulness, as though he sought the weaknesses in everything and everyone he laid eyes on. She had felt that gaze laid on her.

*

At the monastery, Major Duan spared himself the effort of haranguing the few remaining villagers. Nor was he going to butcher them. No slaughter of reprisal: General Wang had been coldly precise on this point. The assumption must be that the guilty had fled; those left behind, mostly elderly and infirm, were probably innocent. Thus, the gathered rump of Jyeko was curtly informed that the following morning their village would be destroyed. They themselves could go where they pleased: to seek shelter in other villages, to starve, beg, freeze or whatever, it now being late October. They would be permitted to take only what they could carry themselves; the PLA had need of any pack animals. The Abbot and his attendants, however, would be keeping Duan company. He had an idea that they might be useful in due course.

It was now nightfall and Duan's exhaustion was catching up with him. (By PLA standards he was an 'older' officer, past his fortieth birthday.) He gave instructions for the morning, ordering his men to billet themselves in the plentiful empty houses. Then he returned to Jamie's compound escorted by two junior officers and a bunch of troopers. On reaching the gate, however, he dismissed them all to occupy the house next door. Duan entered alone.

He noticed at once that no bed had been prepared for him. His tired mind prickled as if at a challenge. He stepped back onto the porch and saw a light in the kitchen.

'I requested you to make me up a bed,' he said from the doorway, his voice more coldly questioning than ferocious. Puton was tucking dung fuel into the stove under a pan of steaming water. She straightened, sitting silently on a crude three-legged stool that Jamie had made for her. She didn't look up, but said: 'There is the *kang*.'

'Excuse me; I observe that the *kang* is occupied by yourself and your little girl. It is no business of the People's Liberation Army to deprive a mother and child of their bed.'

But the Major's insistence that she sleep in comfort was less welcome than it might have seemed. With him installed in the main room, she was trapped. She'd have given much to return to her old quarters with a simple brazier for warmth.

'If the meal is ready, I shall have it now,' said Duan.

He ate exactly as Jamie had done, off the upturned packing case. She began to clear a space by the wall for his bedroll, feeling the eyes on her back as she worked. With her stick in one hand, shifting the junk was a laborious business. Major Duan said nothing: he neither berated her slowness, nor offered to help. He merely observed her.

'We shall be leaving in the morning,' he said, as he washed down the simple food with unbuttered tea. 'You also.'

She turned sharply and stared at him. What was this? Where was he dragging her, and why? Major Duan enjoyed the effect. 'I would prefer to stay in Jyeko,' she said.

'But you tell me it is not your home.'

'I have made it my home.'

'You informed me that you came from Lhasa. I shall be accompanying General Wang to Lhasa shortly. It is my duty to see you safely returned to your family.'

'I have no family,' she said desperately.

'All the more reason why I should look after you. Such is the obligation on the People's Liberation Army: to ensure the welfare of all Tibetans.'

'Thank you, but I can – '

'*Everyone* will be leaving tomorrow. I do not think that you can look after yourself in a deserted village, do you? Besides which, I cannot imagine why you should be so fond of a place in which you have apparently been heartlessly abandoned. Can you enlighten me on this point? You are, may I say, a well-made young woman.'

She was flummoxed; she began to mumble something

about 'My daughter ... '

'Your little girl, of course, will be with us,' said Duan. A delicately sharpened edge came into his voice. 'I shall be delighted to have your company on the road.'

Her mind spun, her wits tied themselves in knots, her guts writhed and tightened. She could not think her way ahead of this. She put out one hand to the wall to steady herself and heard herself breathe quickly.

Duan said: 'Now, I have had several rather tiring days. I must sleep. If you have completed those preparations, I shall turn in.'

So Puton passed this unhappy night in Jamie's bed with Dechen. She slept poorly at first. There was no way of locking the door. She could perhaps have dragged the small writing table in front of it; this would not have withstood determined shoving, but she'd have woken at once with the noise. She had sensed, however, that the more challenge she offered to Major Duan, the more interested he became. She resigned herself to dozing fitfully and at last found a deep, weary sleep.

She was awakened by a sharp rapping. Instantly, she sat up and stared – but no one entered. As Dechen stirred drowsily, other sounds reached them: the crisp call of orders and reporting, horses in the yard, boots and equipment on the porch. She opened the window shutters; the compound was full of soldiers. She shook Dechen awake and went to the door. There was no one in the front room. As Puton reached the doorway she heard Major Duan's voice just outside. There he stood, his junior officers on the porch step below him receiving their instructions. In his hand, Duan held a bowl of steaming tea.

At the sound of Puton's stick, Duan glanced over his shoulder. 'My men have taken the liberty of preparing breakfast in your kitchen. I woke you because we shall be leaving in approximately one hour. You should pack essential belongings at once. We shall bring the two animals in the stable for you and your child.'

Puton backed indoors without a word. She was appalled at

herself. Once again, the Major had pre-empted her. She returned to the bedroom and began to stuff warm clothing into panniers as fast as possible. Dechen watched, as unblinking and silent as ever.

Shortly afterwards, she heard more shouting of orders. Most of the soldiers now left the yard at the trot, harried into action by their NCOs. Puton led Dechen cautiously to the kitchen. A pan of tea still simmered. They ate quickly.

When they returned, Major Duan was in the house once more, packing his own two leather satchels.

'Ready for our departure?' he asked, his voice kindly enough.

'Where are we going?'

'Eventually we shall come to Lhasa. On the way, however, I am obliged to seek out your village friends and hold them responsible for terrible deeds. This will not be a happy proceeding. But after that, I shall be taking you to Lhasa.'

'Why ... do you take me?'

'Oh, not only you. The Venerable Abbot shall ride with us. He will be acting as an intermediary, do you see? Towards you yourself, though, I feel a particular duty. You will accept my protection, will you not?'

She tried once more to think her way past him, to be ahead of his scheming so that she could turn and face her fate. She began, 'I am an ordinary Tibetan woman, no more.'

Major Duan shrugged. 'It is a central creed of Communism that we value the ordinary and the humble above all others. You won't refuse my assistance, surely.'

Almost every ounce of Puton desired to scream out, *Yes! Yes, I refuse it!* But deep within her, one self-preservatory particle whispered, *Go along ... just for now ...*

She said, 'I want no special treatment. Only for my girl.'

'I'm afraid that "special treatment" for anyone would be a tall order in the coming days,' replied Duan. 'There will be some hard travelling. You will have a military tent for yourself and your daughter that will be placed next to my own each evening. I would not have you exposed to the inadvertent roughness of the common soldier. We leave very shortly.'

Thus, again, the terms of Puton's life were dictated. She had no expectation of triumphing over this state of affairs. Hearing it from a Chinese, however, had an uncommonly aggravating effect. Like lemon juice on an oyster, it made her twitch helplessly.

'I wish to travel in the entourage of His Holiness the Abbot,' she said.

Duan dropped the two satchels by his side and straightened, looking at her piercingly. He took two strides to the door of the room and shut it. His movements never ceased to be crisp and drilled. Almost before she knew it, he was standing close to her.

'You will listen carefully to what I say. There is no one else who can or will do anything for you. Is that clear? Tibet has fallen apart. There is no defence, there is no future that is not China. Now, you will be in my personal care. I ask you to consider well, and understand.'

He put out a hand and took a light hold on her cheek and jaw. 'I shall not harm you in any way,' he said. 'Nor shall I touch you again without your consent.'

She was rigid, every muscle locked tight, as she stared back at this sudden man. He let go her face and gave a quick, almost sheepish smile. 'All in due course,' he concluded.

A moment – and he was gone from the room. Little more than one hour later, Puton and Dechen rode out of Jyeko just as they might have done days earlier, in the midst of men and animals. Only this time the Abbot was with her and, behind them, Jyeko was ablaze.

*

five

The radio intercepts were almost reassuring, and the leaders of Jyeko gathered each evening to listen intently. Jamyang Sangay declared that the blundering invaders were exhausting themselves in chasing up and down searching for the caravan. The villagers were under no illusion that they could outstrip Duan, but his men and animals would not be finding the weather any more comfortable, or the grazing more plentiful than they were. They were ahead of him, and that was everything. With watchful outriders behind the caravan, they felt confident that it would be Khampas ambushing Chinese and not *vice versa*. They'd slaughter them all over again!

Khenpo Nima did not like such talk, but he kept his distance and rode on with his own thoughts. It had not occurred to anyone that Duan might divide his forces.

It was now the second week of November. As the crow flies, the caravan was perhaps little more than fifty miles from the border with Assam, but that meant little on the ground. Even at Moro-La, where the ways divided, the villagers would be only halfway to safety. A turn due south would lead Jamie through the passes to India. Those heading for Lhasa, however, would still have more than two hundred and fifty miles to go.

They trudged along broad valleys, riding when they could but increasingly going on foot. The mules were in poor condition, debilitated and slow. The ponies were so famished that they had begun to bite each other's tails and blankets. They could be given tea-leaves and some barley but the people's own rations were hardly generous. Even the yaks, whose horny, barbed tongues could pull up almost anything that grew, were now lethargic and reluctant to move.

Each evening the temperature plunged further and the winds gathered force. A steady gale set in and continued for several days. The cold blast drained energy from the caravan, leaving people and animals without reserves. By day, the weaker pack animals began to stagger. A pony's eyes would glaze sadly as it saw the village party draw away, and its head would sink down. A man would turn back to the forlorn thing and cut its throat, rather than leave it to the wolves that would terrify it before tearing it apart. The redundant packsaddles were ripped open, and the hay stuffing shared out as fodder.

Ravens and griffon vultures were on watch now. One morning, after a night of seventeen degrees of frost, two ponies and a mule were dead. They were found on their sides in the thin dust-snow, rigid, necks and legs outstretched. From one, the eyes had gone already; ravens were hopping towards the next corpse, to enjoy the delicacy warm and soft. The people shouted curses at them. The mastiffs had a fine meal.

'The weakest die, which means that the strongest are still living.' Karjen shrugged.

The radio mule, meanwhile, with perhaps some sense of its greater dignity, showed no signs of giving in. At nightfall Jamie swathed it in blankets and in the morning it stomped along admirably, its mast and pennon swaying at the caravan's head and the people dutifully following.

They reached an expanse of thin pasturage, the dry grass long enough for the ponies and mules that trotted unstoppably in all directions and gorged themselves. The Jyeko women cried, 'For pity's sake, let them eat!' so a rest was called.

Wild creatures seemed to be flourishing in this bleak place. They saw a herd of mountain asses, white legs trotting in the distance. There were antelopes that sprang away, their smooth fur a lustrous satin that turned to velvet as the wind brushed it. The outriders went after them with Chinese rifles and brought in enough for everyone's supper. There were wild yaks far off, and the tracks of wolves.

Jyeko made camp, setting up the black tents and lighting fires. For once they made no effort to wait until dusk. If it was fated that the fires be seen today, then so be it. The people needed warmth, buttered tea without stint, their clothes to be thawed and dried.

There were streams around the camp, frozen into flat glassy snakes. The villagers began chopping up the ice to boil. With the radio tent up and Karjen hobbling the animals on the best grazing, Jamie sat on a saddle peering into the flames. He felt little tongues of heat penetrating his face; his cheeks and lips were badly cracked with cold.

'Jemmy,' said Khenpo Nima beside him, 'with luck we shall reach Dengkol tomorrow, where there is a village. After that, just two or three days to Moro-La.'

'I'd rather not talk about luck,' said Jamie coldly.

Nima peered sideways at him and frowned. 'You think about Miss Puton?'

'Oddly enough.'

'Oh, that was very bad luck.'

'Which, I suppose, proves the whole notion. If she had the bad luck to be left behind, she would obviously have been a dangerously unlucky person to bring along.'

'Well ... ' murmured Khenpo Nima, taken aback. There was half a minute of silence. 'Jemmy, you see that woman who is breaking ice there?'

A dumpy woman was bent with her back to them, smashing at the ice with a small rock. When she turned, Jamie recognised her by her hare lip: she had once stood with Jamyang Sangay, shunning Puton.

'I know her,' he said, and looked back at the fire.

'Some three years ago,' continued Nima, 'this Tesla had a husband. Her man Norsam, he was a wool trader, an ill-made person quite as coarse as she. But they were contented in their way. Now, Norsam came home one afternoon saying he had something in his eye. He thought it was a grain of sand. Tesla looked but could see nothing. The next morning Norsam's left eye was red and swollen and his vision was bad. He sat in the house rubbing his eyes and rubbing again, and perhaps with rubbing he moved the grain of sand to the other eye because by the evening that eye was sore also. Still, Tesla could not see the grain of sand and she began to worry because his eyes were worse.

'So she spoke to a lama who said that during a festival in Jyeko when the devils were being driven away one of the evil spirits had looked for somewhere to hide. And this spirit had seen that Tesla's store of luck was low, and had sought a way into the household. Now, normally this would not be dangerous but in this family – so the lama told Tesla – there was a little chink in their fortune through which the evil spirit had crept. Those very words: a tiny gap in their fortune. So Tesla now believed the evil spirit had entered their home through the gap in her lip.

'They called in a physician from Chamdo who charged dearly. Norsam lay in a fever. By this time, his eyes had hard growths in the corners that were growing towards the centre, closing his eyes and throbbing with pain. This so-called doctor looked at Norsam's eyes and took out a small knife. He cut the growths away, as roughly as a nomad butchering a sheep. Tesla tells me that her husband never made a sound. The doctor told Tesla to pray hard – as if she hadn't been! He gave her some potion, and left with his pay.

'When he had gone, Norsam asked Tesla what the doctor had said, and did it agree with the lama's diagnosis? The poor man begged her to tell him why he was suffering so. Tesla began to weep, to confess that it was all her fault that the evil spirit had got among them. Norsam lay listening in silence. Then he turned his back to her and he never spoke another word. He died a few days later.'

Khenpo Nima stopped speaking; the two men sat side by side looking into the fire. Jamie dropped another piece of dried yak dung onto the embers, which burned with a sweet scent.

'What are you telling me?' he said at last. 'That her luck was even worse than Puton's? I can't say I'm impressed.'

Khenpo Nima shook his head. 'I wonder only, what should this woman believe? Why *did* her husband suffer so? Was it all caused by a grain of sand, something so small that she could never find it? I have taught her myself that these things are prescribed in our destiny: if her husband's wheel had turned thus far, his death was certain and no guilt of hers. But still she would ask, why should

147

he suffer such bitter pain?'

'Deep matters, I'm sure,' grumbled Jamie.

'Oh, yes, but no deep explanation could make her happy. Tesla is a vigorous but simple woman. She sees life in terms of butter and barley, fire and money and wool. She listened politely to my doctrines, but I am afraid they had little force for her. So, she was left with a choice: either she inhabits a perfectly hostile and unpredictable world, having no notion of what malignancy surrounds her, what might strike her next, or she clings to the explanation of the little gateway in her lip that she can plug up again with prayers. Are we surprised that she has chosen the latter?'

Jamie glanced towards the woman who was now packing ragged shards of ice into a pan and perching it on three stones over a yak-dung fire. But he said nothing.

Again, they sat in silence until Nima said, 'Jemmy, I do not wish you to leave Tibet filled with hatred as you are.' Jamie looked at him sharply – he continued: 'Consider, Jemmy, whose luck is more in question here? You, with no job and no lady? Or one hundred and thirty people from a burned village who must walk to Lhasa?'

'They're doing well enough.'

'Really? We are giving our barley to the animals to keep them strong but still they freeze to death. Most families are on short rations now, did you know? They are eating once a day only. Few have any butter left. Some have a little cheese, most do not. We are even short of tea.'

'I had no idea,' Jamie mumbled, not entirely truthfully.

'No?' replied the monk gently. 'Well, of course, *you* they will always feed.'

Thirty yards off, Tesla of the hare lip put a few handfuls of barley into a nose bag for her mule. The animal hung its heavy head, looking weakly towards Jamie. Khenpo Nima got to his feet to walk away among the villagers.

'Nima,' said Jamie quickly, looking up, 'what happened to Puton's husband?'

'Oh, yes, there was an accident,' said Khenpo Nima wryly, 'in the gorges.'

'He was a taxman, wasn't he? People hated *him*, didn't they?'

Khenpo Nima spoke quietly: 'Our sufferings spring from our desires, Jemmy. Do not be ruled by desires.' He began to walk away, tall and strong.

He was some yards off when Jamie said clearly: 'You brought her to me, Nima.'

Khenpo Nima walked on.

*

In the morning, a weak sun came out and tried to warm them. The light steel tubing of the antenna took on a faint gleam as it flicked and bobbed rhythmically above the radio mule. They were climbing again.

Towards midday the caravan paused. In front of them, stretching several miles along the valley, was a narrow frozen lake of ice tinged with greys and greens. A steady wind streamed over the valley floor from the peaks ahead. It picked up tiny spicules of ice that stung their faces; as these blew across the lake, a faint humming rose from the frozen surface.

'Nomads, Jemmy!' shouted Wangdu. Jamie looked along a treeless shore of ice-bound boulders. Two miles ahead, he glimpsed a cluster of three or four black tents.

'Typical.' Khenpo Nima smiled. 'There are friendly houses at Dengkol just at the lake's far end but these nomad people stay apart.'

Buoyed by the thought of company and news, the scouts trotted ahead. Jamie let his eye survey the mountains that pressed on the south shore, the steep shoulders of black gneiss banded with quartz. They seemed lifeless, frigid and deserted. No birds, no plants, no mountain livestock that he could see. There might be leopards, even bears in the vicinity; if so, they were huddled out of sight. The barren aspect made Jamie shudder, made him more susceptible to the bitter cold. He noticed idly that the outriders had stopped short of the tents and were now returning at a fast trot. Jamie saw Khenpo Nima frown and stare ahead. The riders were calling, their shouts thin and barely comprehensible in the wind.

A knot of villagers came together in sudden conference. The faces were dark, looking along the shore with narrowed eyes.

'What is it, Nima?' Jamie asked.

'Something is wrong there. Come.'

A dozen riders were moving forward; Jamie went after them, seeing them bring muskets and rifles off their shoulders. He caught up just as the riders slowed to a walk, rising in their saddles, peering ahead and then all around the hillsides. Nothing moved among the rocks except wisps of snow. The group trotted forward again. Seventy yards from the tents, on the near side of a frozen stream, they stopped, stared, dismounted. Then the men stepped gingerly across the strip of ice.

There were three large tents. One had been cut to ribbons. It hung in strips from its guy lines, teetering at wild angles. Cords and fabric flapped pathetically in the wind; snow had penetrated the rents, settling on despoiled property. The inhabitants were spread about on the ground. Death had reduced each figure to a shapeless dark bulk. As the Jyeko men moved wordlessly among the corpses, two startled dogs backed away from a heap at which they had been tearing. Only here was there any colour, any crimson. Two quick shots from a carbine knocked the dogs off their feet.

Jamie stood at the edge of the campsite shivering. He saw what might have been a woman sprawled face down with her legs at a ridiculous open angle. Just beyond her reach, a much smaller bundle lay still. Although the child was possibly five or six feet away, the mother was almost touching it, because her arm had been severed and lay midway between them. Nearby, four adults lay together in an untidy pile, apparently executed together. Other corpses were scattered at random, killed as they ran. A Tibetan musket lay apart, its long prop twisted off; someone had tried to fight back. Perhaps that had been the mistake.

The Jyeko villagers came together slowly, backing away from the scene.

'You remember these people?' Wangdu asked Jamie. 'We met them on the road. They said *we* had the bad luck.'

Jamie pointed: small dark shapes marked the far end of the lake. It was possible to make out movement.

'Chinese,' said Karjen. 'I think we shall go and cut their throats.'

*

Even by Tibetan standards, Dengkol was a small village. The homes were built of stone, thick-walled, squat and grey, pierced by a random scatter of tiny windows shut tight with red-brown boards. The parapets of the flat earthen roofs were topped with thick fringes of scrub juniper, like eyebrows. The skulls of horned animals guarded the corners together with ragged little white and yellow prayer flags, flickering on short poles.

A *mani* wall ran for some hundred yards parallel to the foot of the hill. Four feet high, it was built entirely of rocks inscribed with sacred texts and blessings. Not so long ago, they had apparently felt inclined to celebrate at Dengkol. In summer, it was doubtless a lovely spot.

Just now, a squadron of Chinese cavalry was in possession, their horses tethered behind the houses, smoke belching from the hearths. The soldiers bustled about the doorways like bees at a hive, getting inside for warmth whenever they could. In front of the houses were the usual neatly stacked rifles and a light machine-gun in an emplacement of boulders, pointing along the lake shore.

'Where are the Dengkol people?' whispered Wangdu, lying flat on an outcrop of granite two hundred and fifty feet above.

Aben, the Jyeko herdsman at his side, pointed to a round stone enclosure some five feet high. 'See that animal pen?'

A thread of smoke was visible, climbing the height of the circular wall and at once torn away by the wind. From time to time,

Tibetan hats could be glimpsed moving about inside.

'They've been pushed out to make room in the houses.'

The reconnaissance party rejoined the Jyeko caravan, halted in the shadow of tumbledown crags two miles distant.

'We can't get round them this time,' said Aben the herdsman. 'Even if we went all the way round the other side of the lake, we'd still end up at Dengkol.'

'We could wait until they move away.'

'Wait where? I've got yaks and mules that'll bellow all night if they get no grazing.'

'In my opinion – ' began Karjen.

'Karjen wants to rush them head-on,' laughed hare-lipped Tesla.

'Well!' spluttered Karjen, piqued. He had been thinking of something along those lines.

'No good,' observed Jamie. 'They'll post sentries, and the rest will stay in the houses. They're like fortresses, those buildings. Once the shooting starts, how would you get them outside?'

'That's the problem, getting them all outside.'

'That is not the problem,' said Khenpo Nima emphatically. He drew himself up to his full and impressive height in the centre of the ring and looked the villagers straight in the eye, one after another.

'I'll tell you the problem. It is that we are getting ever more embroiled in slaughter.'

The fighting men did not groan audibly because they were too respectful of Khenpo Nima. They looked at the ground instead. Other villagers peered at him, troubled. Someone murmured: 'Are we just going to forget the people in the tents?'

'What do you want? *More* revenge?' Khenpo Nima cried out.

'But it's Duan! *His* throat's ripe for cutting!'

'This isn't Duan,' said Jamie. 'This is just a scouting patrol.'

'Does not one of you remember our Abbot's words as we left home?' demanded Nima. '*Nobody* remembers? Shame, Jyeko!'

'Travel with peace in your hearts,' a young voice said. The

teenage boy blushed madly as they all turned to him.

'Exactly.' Khenpo Nima nodded. 'And do not be guided by illusory desire. Remember now? I tell you, there is no greater illusion than vengeance. Remember this, Jyeko: we are in our present plight because we tried to take revenge.'

From among the crowd, Jamie watched Khenpo Nima carefully. Such was the monk's presence, that the villagers fell quiet before his arguments. But it was not the silence of acquiescence. In the suspended instant that followed, Jamie knew that a contrary decision was taken.

'Khenpo Nima, dear friend ... ' began Wangdu, shaking his head.

Aben the herdsman took it up. 'What choice do we have, Reverence? We can't go back, we can't sit here. We have to fight them, I believe.'

'I'm no warrior,' said Jamyang Sangay, 'but we have to face the moment, I'd say.'

'But you are village people! You are farmers and traders, wives and lovers, fathers and children! What are you thinking of, throwing yourselves at trained soldiers with a machine-gun?'

'We are Khampas!' shouted Karjen.

'That's it!' came a quick chorus, 'Khampas don't fight shy!'

A flush of fervour went through the village. They stamped their cold feet and looked at each other with keen smiles. Jamie thought, how remarkable that these people could be inspired by a superannuated bandit.

'Excuse me,' he began, 'can we talk sense a moment? How do you propose to take on these soldiers?'

'We creep up,' said Aben, 'through the rocks, then behind the *mani* wall.'

'Aben! Every stone is a holy prayer!'

'Well ... '

'You still have to get them outside,' insisted Jamie. 'You have to get thirty Chinese soldiers off their guard, out in front of those houses. They're not going to come out because Karjen's shouting at them.'

Another silence. Rawhide boots shuffled.

'Maybe Mr Jemmy could do it for us, though,' observed Aben, 'if he wouldn't mind.'

Jamie blinked at him. The Khampa was a pleasant young man, a far-from-wealthy herdsman with too many children, always straight-dealing, open, helpful. His cheerful wife Drolma stood alongside him now, and Jamie remembered the family house that had been open to him, with the best hospitality that they could manage. He recalled seeing one of Aben's children sleeping in his lap: how it had filled him with envy. Jamie said: 'What could I do?'

'Well, get the Chinese outside the houses.'

'How, for heaven's sake?'

Drolma said, 'We'll think of something, Mr Jemmy.'

Jamie looked unhappily at her strong, wind-scoured face. That was the sum of things, wasn't it? Aben and Drolma were here and now, on a freezing lake shore half-way to Lhasa. If they were to save themselves and their children, they had to think of something.

'Aben would follow anything you were willing to try,' said Drolma again.

Jamie shivered with a pang of fear.

'Yes? Like what, exactly?'

*

The Chinese sentries were longing to retreat indoors out of the wind. The only approaches to their position could surely be seen well enough. The narrow space between water and mountain face was strewn with rocks and rubble through which barbarians could creep: it was that way the machine-gun pointed, along the line of the *mani* wall that followed the foot of the cliff.

Behind the two sentries, chatter came from an open door, where the supper was on the fire. Suddenly one of the men tensed, nudged his comrade and brought the rifle off his shoulder. The second followed his look, then blinked, screwed his eyes against the blowing dust and looked again.

Plodding towards them was a large yak whose long horns were draped with white scarves. On the back of the animal rode a most peculiar figure. It was a tousle-headed man without a hat, whose clothes were covered in scarves and pennons in red, blue, white and black. They were draped from his belt, his neck, his sleeves, his feet. From his ankles and wrists hung bells. As the yak stomped forward, the rider flapped his lower legs and the bells chimed in a haphazard, rhythmless way. The man started something that might perhaps have been singing.

One of the guards shouted into the house behind him. Faces appeared at the door. After a second of staring, a soldier sprinted to a second house, saluted from the doorway and ducked inside. From both buildings, more soldiers began to emerge, peering in astonishment at the approaching rider. The newcomer was flapping his arms up and down, waving his colourful pennons and screeching like a tone-deaf jackdaw.

Two or three soldiers grabbed rifles from the stacks; most simply watched curiously. They'd not had much novelty lately. Besides, if this was an attack, it was heavy cavalry of the silliest variety.

'What the hell is that?'

'A lunatic. Country's full of them.'

'He doesn't look Tibetan.'

'He's singing, sort of. Doesn't *sound* Tibetan.'

'Sounds like gibberish.'

'Sounds foreign.'

The song soared and wailed. It was not exactly gibberish:

Birds in their little nests agree
with Chinamen but not with me!
Birds in their little nests agree
with Chinamen but not with me!'

Howling and yowling: no tune at all. The arms gyrated like windmills.

'A foreigner, Captain! Is this the British, Wi-lih-soh?'

The Chinese Captain stepped out of the house, buckling

on his revolver belt. His entire troop of cavalrymen now stood about watching, starting to grin and guffaw. Wi-lih-soh drew nearer on the decorated yak, flapping his arms ever more frenetically and shrilling again: 'Birds in their little nests agree with Chinamen but not with me!'

The Captain frowned and shouted, 'Get him down!'

But they never did. The loud crack of a rifle seemed to explode at his right hand – and half the sentry's head was blown away. A second later, the air broke apart. The gunfire was astonishingly close; the troops dithered, dazed, perplexed, where or how was it ... until they began to fall. Then the Jyeko men came through gaps in the *mani* wall, bellowing and rushing, a crowd of them with knives and rifles outstretched. Soldiers still on their feet dived for the gun stacks and tugged in clumsy desperation at the bayonets in their belts, swearing furiously. Two Chinese raced for the machine-gun, cried out and died short of it. The horses reared and heaved at their tethers, panic-stricken as the Tibetans clamoured among the soldiers.

Karjen killed the Captain in the best traditions of his family. The enraged officer had ripped his revolver from its holster. His quick firing struck home: a Tibetan fell, a second. He raised his pistol at Jamie – then uttered a peculiar engorged cry. Below his eyes, the bloodied tip of an antelope horn suddenly appeared from out of his own throat. He peered at it, amazed. He staggered a step or two, trying to look behind him, trying to lift the revolver again. But a strong hand seized and wrenched the gun from his fast-fading grip and the Captain tumbled forward to the ground with the long sharp prop of Karjen's musket jabbed right through his neck.

It was over: it had taken less than a minute. The Jyeko men stood half crouched, turning about as though more Chinese might yet rush them from behind. But nothing happened. Only, in front of them, the startled yak trotted away along the shore, its rider prone and lifeless along its back with Hector the mastiff pelting after and baying furiously.

'Jemmy! Jemmy!' called two Khampas, running. They

sprinted as best they could in soft fur boots until they headed off the yak at the waterside. 'Jemmy?' they called anxiously again.

Then the rider lifted his head, white with shock, saying, 'Jesus wept.'

*

six

There were Tibetan casualties: some of the Chinese had reached
their weapons after all. They were hardened soldiers; they'd not
fought all that long civil war to be knocked down without kicking.
Several Tibetan men had wounds and to these Khenpo Nima now
went busily with his cures and dressings. There were two fatalities:
one was a forester who'd lived in the woods downriver from Jyeko.
The other was Aben, shot twice in the belly. His wife Drolma knelt
by his side weeping in silence while he died. Her four children
stood ten feet away, clinging to each other. At last, other women
led them away and came back for the stunned young widow.

The Jyeko people made camp, and the spoils of the fight –
clothing, rifles and ammunition, pots, precious food, animal tack
and, above all, the ponies – were soon being shared out by an ad
hoc commission of two monks and Jamyang Sangay. The latter
perched his fat buttocks on a boulder and presided with an air of
flatulent self-importance.

But there was no triumphalism, just chores to be done.
Youths led the half-starved Jyeko animals round the back of the
hamlet to gorge on the rough grazing beyond. Others rigged the
cumbersome tents or scoured the vicinity for fuel. Someone
handed Jamie a wooden bowl of tea. He received plentiful smiles
and pats on the back: a gruff, workmanlike approval, as though
he'd done a decent job in fixing a tumbledown bridge.

He wandered slowly through the camp, keeping his hands
pressed to the warm bowl. The wind threw grit against his coat. He
turned to gaze abstractedly over the frozen lake. From time to time
the ice moved and cracked, and the noise startled the camp dogs,
who bayed at it. Spurts of ice-dust flew up at random, as though
some invisible giant schoolboy scuffled about idly in new boots.
He looked north along the lake shore. There, ponies were dragging
the thirty Chinese dead in clutches by their heels, to be dumped for
the wolves.

Where can Duan have got to? wondered Jamie. These were

just scouts, with no radio, so they couldn't keep in contact unless they were pretty near. There might be a thousand Chinese over the brow of that hill!

He let his eye wander over the emptiness. In every direction there were hostile tracts without population, maybe no one at all for fifty miles. But if he looked back towards the camp, he saw the urgent bustle, the toil of survival. He saw the children taking nosebags of barley to the mules and ponies, the women marshalling their depleted resources of butter and salt, men reorganising the packs for tomorrow – and Drolma, silently feeding her smallest child. The tenderness, the love uncomplaining.

Enough: Jamie's tea bowl was empty and cold. He returned in the direction of the radio tent, feeling a trifle guilty as he saw Karjen struggling to rig it on his own. Close by, yet another of the impromptu debating circles that directed this expedition had formed.

'Jemmy,' called Wangdu, 'this Dengkol family have heard more talk of a great Tibetan army of resistance, which is forming to the west.'

'They believe their village friends have gone that way to join.'

'They think at Moro-La!'

'We will know when we get there.'

'Maybe.'

There was hesitancy in the voices: not the buoyant confidence of victors. They'd begun to reckon a cost.

'But they are also reporting that everywhere is at peace,' began a bald, tubby man. 'These village people say it.'

'Rumour, counter-rumour.' Jamie shrugged, stooping to tie off a guy line. 'Who told them that?'

'The Chinese soldiers.'

'Oh, come on! That's called propaganda – "We bring you peace, brothers"!'

The bald man hesitated, then persisted: 'If there's peace everywhere else but a war party at Moro-La, well ... do we want to go there? Get mixed up in all that?'

'You can't go back,' said Jamie.

'But things may have changed.'

'Not for this caravan I'm afraid .'

'That's awful. Everywhere at peace except us, except Jyeko.'

Karjen stomped into the discussion. His voice seemed to grow even deeper and rougher in winter, like two boulders scraping together. 'The Chinese idea of peace won't be mine, and if there's a gathering at Moro-La, it's for good reason.'

'Right! That'll be something to see!'

There was a pause – until the bald man muttered: 'I'd like to get home. I've seen enough people die today.'

'Now, listen to me!' Wangdu was losing patience. 'As Jemmy says, we can't go back. We'd all like to, but just you forget about that. Don't you remember the smoke of Jyeko? That wasn't a cooking fire, that was your houses.'

A tightness took hold in the back of Jamie's throat. They all fell silent a moment, looking at the ground.

'We do have a choice to make,' began Khenpo Nima. 'It's this. Duan is still looking for us, so which route do we take now?'

'Let's wait till we've tried the radio again,' said Jamie. 'We might get a clue where they are.'

'Yes, Jemmy!' Khenpo Nima suddenly put an arm around the young man's shoulder. 'You tell us, you have led us in a wonderful fashion today.'

'Me? That wasn't even my idea ... '

But there was a chorus: 'Bravo, Mr Jemmy! You sing them to death every time!'

'We'll listen at six,' called Jamie. 'Trust the radio.'

'Trust the radio oracle!' cried Jamyang Sangay, its interpreter.

'Trust Mr Jemmy's oracle!' cried Jyeko in response.

They broke up, and Khenpo Nima came to Jamie, leading him a little apart.

'Jemmy, you know, there is another way for you. These people say that there is a direct trail from here that would take you to Assam. It is not so easy, because there are high passes, but they would be willing to guide you. Also we can send two Jyeko men to help. You want to do that?'

Jamie was startled. He had a sudden visitation of warm forest humidity, a ringing of cicadas. The wind blew it away as quickly. He peered at Khenpo Nima. 'So, we'd part company here?'

'If you like, Jemmy.'

Jamie stirred the grey, frozen pebbles with his boot. He could hear the strong voice of the monk held in check, all prejudicial emotion kept at bay. He replied: 'I don't know that I *do* like. I mean, I'd reckoned on coming with you to Moro-La.'

There was a silence between them into which the sounds of the camp came on the wind. Jamie looked out across the lake, where the little spurts of ice-dust still twizzled in the gusts.

Khenpo Nima peered closely at him. 'You must decide, Jemmy. Moro-La is a longer way for you, and hard travelling from here. We shall have to climb high, and the cold is coming. Are you sure?'

'I'm sure. We've come pretty far together, haven't we? I mean, I want to see you there, safe and so on.'

Three weeks previously he'd have abandoned the lot of them without compunction. What had happened to him?

Before he found any answer, Khenpo Nima began again. 'Shall I tell you the other news? It is only rumour, of course, all of this. But maybe – only maybe – Miss Puton will be at Moro-La.'

Jamie's face turned ashen, then crimson in an instant. The blood had drained, then rushed back, like a wave that sucks away from a shingle beach before it thunders in again. He whispered: 'She's there? Nima, you were going to let me take a different route to India, without telling me this?'

'But, Jemmy, it is just rumour ...'

'Nima, I can't believe you would have let me do that!' He looked around the windswept camp, his heart pounding, his eyes seeing nothing. 'Then they're all right!' he whispered.

'We'll listen at six, Jemmy,' said Khenpo Nima.

*

Major Duan did not have anything like all the radios he would have wished, as Jamie had surmised. They were rare and precious, these portable transceivers (they were mostly of American manufacture, captured from the Nationalists). Duan had sent out four squadrons of fast cavalry to look for traces of the Jyeko caravan, but only the larger groups had a radio set. The two smaller parties were instructed to make physical contact at four-day intervals to report on any findings. The matter was becoming uncomfortably urgent.

This was because General Wang, in his bloodless, chilly way, remained resolute in the policy of 'friendship' towards Tibet. Peace was breaking out everywhere: that was the line. After the capitulation of Governor Ngabo near Chamdo, there were few pockets of resistance. Muja Depon, the only Tibetan commander of any military astuteness, had been captured with Ngabo. The few troops elsewhere had mostly been trapped by hugely superior numbers of Chinese, disarmed, given money and told to go home. The tactic served gloriously in its main object: to leave the Tibetans dithering and uncertain of their friends. Half the Khampas, always easily turned against Lhasa, had sided with the Chinese from the outset.

So there had been no need of reprisals, or the taking of droves of prisoners, no titanic battles or wholesale destruction. Indeed, with the surrender of Kham, the Chinese had not marched on Lhasa but had declared an end to hostilities. They began immediate 'fraternal' discussions with the fifteen-year old Dalai Lama, who continued to rule the bulk of the country. Throughout the east of Tibet, meanwhile, Chinese brigades asserted their authority but continued to pay exaggerated respect and generous prices. Political instruction had begun, with Khampas and nomads listening dazedly to beaming Communist cadres extolling the overthrow of feudalism – whatever that might be. Chinese tact had faltered at times: attaching radio masts to the golden spires of monasteries had not gone down well. There was great need of delicacy and caution.

All in all, General Wang did *not* want a zealot cutting his way through the south on a vengeful bloodletting. The Jyeko murderers must be brought to book, obviously, but it must be done promptly and with all possible restraint. Duan was already prosecuting his vigorous search much further west, much nearer Lhasa than General Wang had intended: this bellicose sweep was undercutting the claim to 'peaceful liberation'. So the General had sent Major Duan a simple instruction: you've got two more weeks.

Duan was not a man to betray his exasperation readily, but the Jyeko caravan was proving vexingly elusive. He had placed units across their path time and again – and always they had turned aside, or doubled back, or cut across, or by some other sleight-of-hand had slipped five or six score people past him. Had he been inclined to superstition, he would have described it as uncanny. Had he been a Tibetan, he might have suspected the ancient lama who now travelled with him of sending out psychic warnings. Duan was more inclined to wonder whether spies or his own troops' incompetence were to blame. At least, until there came the awkward revelations about the radio and the generator.

On his return to Jyeko, he had instructed his men to crate up all the radio equipment and dispatch it to General Wang for military use. The work had been done the following morning by a squad under a sergeant. As Jyeko burned, two heavy boxes had set out for Chamdo strapped to mules. Duan had thought no more about it until, on one of his irregular visits to headquarters at Chamdo, he had seen the crates in a store shed, apparently untouched.

'Does the General have no use for those?' he asked a lieutenant in some surprise.

'It's a petrol model, sir,' said the lieutenant. 'We have only diesel here.'

'But the radio?' insisted Duan.

'Sir?' The lieutenant looked puzzled.

A faint chill touched Duan's stomach.

'What is in that crate?' he asked.

'Generator, sir,' came the reply.

'And the second crate?'

'I believe it is equipment for the generator, sir, loose items that were packed separately.'

'Open it!' snapped Duan.

When the lid was off, one glance was enough to make Duan's nostrils flare with anger – mostly at himself: he had never checked. There was no radio here. So, the imperialist hireling Wilson had taken it with him. And that suggested a horribly simple explanation for the elusiveness of the caravan: that Wilson and the renegades had been listening to his transmitted orders. Was it possible? Certainly, if Wilson had any sort of portable power supply: the man was a trained military radio operator! The stern Major Duan felt humiliated and secretly violated, as though he'd caught someone reading his diary.

He returned to his own headquarters, encamped by the Lhasa road. From here he was following an approximate diagonal south-west, which must cut across the route of the Jyeko caravan unless they had fled wholesale to India. 'Diagonal' was a relative term, of course, since the mountain ranges hardly allowed for niceties of direction. The core of Duan's detachment moved slowly but at frequent intervals he dispatched search and intercept parties to scour every possible pass, side valley and river crossing. Often he had sensed that they were within a few miles, or less, but they had never set eyes on the Tibetans. He had felt so certain that the trap at Nupkong would yield results. But no, nothing. And now he thought he knew why.

In his camp there was an air of uncertainty, of indecision. The Major knew that the indecision was his own, and felt that he was being watched. In the command tent, Duan placed his thumbs on the edge of the table and leaned once again over the inadequate sketch maps from which he was working. His officers watched him in apprehensive silence: things were not going so well. But they did not understand Duan's particular ill-humour at present; he had not mentioned radios since his return. As they waited for their commander's thoughts and instructions, a less military figure entered carrying a large black kettle of tea. Puton limped across the tent without speaking and placed the kettle on a wooden box at the back with a grimy collection of tin mugs. Duan's eyes flicked up at her and back to the map, so quickly that none of his staff caught the look.

'They must cross the Pang-chen range to the south of us,' the Major mused aloud, 'which gives them the choice of only ... three passes? No, four. How high is Nangpe-La? Fifteen thousand seven hundred feet. What is this one, nearest India?' His searching finger traced and stabbed at the crudely hatched contours.

'Moro-La, sir,' said an officer, 'fifteen thousand three hundred and sixty feet, usually open until January. There's also Jewe-La and another here, but we don't have the name. I believe Jewe-La is the usual trade route, sir.'

As Duan listened, he was aware that Puton was hovering by the tea things without good cause. Listening also, of course for scraps and names. 'We cannot cover all of them,' he thought aloud, 'not with sufficient force. We have to make a best estimate of which route they will select. If only we could influence that choice.'

No one spoke. Puton poured tea, very slowly. Duan noted this; usually she left it to the junior officers, taking herself out of the tent as fast as possible. Duan pondered a moment, then said: 'Transmit a radio instruction, Sergeant Lin, as follows: "The two companies marching towards Moro-La are to go no further, but should return immediately to a position west of Nangpe-La."'

The staff officers dared to frown and glance at each other, puzzled. For a few seconds, there was silence. Then one foolhardy young man found courage to say: 'Excuse me, sir, we don't *have* two companies heading for Moro-La. Actually, sir, we don't have any —'

'Your critique of my orders will doubtless be most interesting at some other time, Lieutenant,' said Duan icily. 'However, for now you will see to it that the transmission is made exactly as my request. Transmit at four and at six this evening, and repeat in the morning.'

'Yes, sir.'

Duan looked up. The staff officers were watching him, intent but anxious. He thought that he detected one or two feet edging in involuntary retreat from him: really, he had little time for young men who could not stand their ground. He suppressed a desire to say something withering. Behind him, he heard a small rattle and a dribbling sound. Puton had overfilled or knocked over a cup, he guessed. She, too, was nervous, wasn't she?

'Take your tea, and leave me now,' said Duan. The officers moved towards the box of cups, grateful for the dispelling of tension. Puton moved to the doorway. Duan snapped: 'You, stay! There's a mess to clear up, so wait.'

The other soldiers departed quickly, breaking into low chatter as they walked away from the tent. Major Duan sipped at his mug and watched Puton as she tried to wipe away the splashed tea with her sleeve. 'Tell me,' said the Major, 'did your young Britisher have any means of powering his radio other than the petrol generator? Look at me, please.'

Puton regarded him with an expression of dumb ignorance.

'Don't understand what I'm talking about? Well, perhaps not.'

The woman gave no hint of understanding. It was infuriating: to think that the wretched British youth might have been listening to his every word. Duan recalled Wilson in their interview at Jyeko, impertinently trying to demand that he take his radio with him when he was thrown out of the country. If he was now lugging it through the Himalaya but was unable to turn it on, this whole supposition would be a colossal red herring. And he, Duan, would be making a perfect fool of himself with his nonsensical order to non-existent companies.

Duan moved round the table and sat gingerly on a folding stool. Puton remained standing by the low box, resting on her stick. The Major tugged off a boot and shook out some grit. 'Now, tell me how the old man is today.'

'A woman may not speak to the Abbot,' she replied, 'but I understand that he is weary.'

'I daresay he would be. He has been propagating nonsense for fifty years. I do not grieve for him. Do you believe in his teachings?'

She said nothing.

Duan's eyes returned to hers. 'Or do you, perhaps, find British philosophy more agreeable?'

Still she did not reply. He terrified and unnerved her, this major. He watched her so intently, so expectantly. He had ordered a little tent to be erected for her and Dechen only feet from his own, while the Abbot and his attendants were always camped on the far side of the troop. She was positioned by Duan, as though he expected she would shortly flow into him, like two droplets of mercury touching. He made no demand of her, never abused or forced his attentions on her, had never so much as touched her: he watched and waited for her like an incontrovertible fact that sooner or later she would have to accept. She picked up the kettle and turned as though to leave. Before she knew it, he was standing in front of her.

'Do not put your faith in cracked vessels, Miss Puton,' said the Major. 'When a bowl is well made, it rings true.'

She gazed up at him; she was becoming used to his cryptic talk. It induced a terrible lassitude in her. Her resistance was seeping away into the cold gravel.

'All Tibet will acknowledge this in time,' said the Major. 'We are happy to wait.'

*

Part four

'Moro-la, Moro-La!' sang Jamie, striding through the Dengkol camp. 'Karjen, come on, we're on our way.'

Karjen blinked. Dawn was scarcely come: what was all this? He'd have everything packed in due –

'I'll do the tent, Karjen, you go for the animals.'

Before Karjen could reply, Jamie was tweaking guy lines off the rocks and the tent was subsiding. Nearby, reluctant figures were creeping about in the thin mist.

'Nima, good morning!' Jamie saw the lama sipping at a bowl of tea. 'We should be moving. If we want to make Moro-La – '

'Yes, yes, we shall be ready.'

'Nima, the Chinese are returning to Nangpe-La! We've a chance, you see? Got to grab it!'

'Chance, yes.' Nima shivered, experimentally moving the muscles around his eyes to see if he'd had enough tea to crack the ice there. He looked round the caravan. He knew what was being whispered. There were those in the group who thought of little except going home, rebuilding Jyeko (wasn't there peace now?). It wasn't mutiny, just exhaustion.

The night before, a tense, thoughtful group had gathered in the radio tent. A vigorous young man cranked the dynamo, the lamps had glowed, the crackling and tapping had slewed in and out of focus. Jamyang Sangay had interpreted the Chinese order: they were turning back from Moro-La.

Jamie's face had lit up: 'There's our opening!'

He'd looked round the company, searching the dubious faces, trying to understand how they could possibly be wavering now. Khenpo Nima understood very well.

'We shall have to move quickly,' Wangdu had said. 'We've almost exhausted our food, even with this Chinese stuff. There will be nothing for us in the passes ahead. We must reach friends – and we shall not be able to wait for stragglers.'

With this chill observation to send them to their beds,

they'd agreed to continue. Only the Dengkol family refused to leave their homes, dismissing all entreaties and warnings.

In the colourless dawn light, Khenpo Nima said: 'Jemmy, remember, this will be hard travelling. You must carry some food ready.'

'How, ready?'

'You have some barleymeal? You make little cakes with tea. Then place this inside your clothes, you see? Right inside, out of the cold. You can eat them as you go along, in the worst places.'

Jamie peered at him, his ebullience momentarily chastened.

'The worst places? I see. Right, then, barley cakes in my clothes. Where's Karjen with the mule? Karjen!'

Jamie scurried away among the white-frosted boulders.

Half an hour later the mountain peaks were touched with new gold but Dengkol lake skulked in shadow. The cavalcade was packed, mounted and still shivering with uncertainty. Knots and sub-groups had formed. Like a truck stalled on a hill, the caravan might start rolling backwards at any moment. Their plumes of breath were the liveliest thing among them.

Jamie appeared from behind one of the houses, urging on his tired pony and leading the radio mule with Hector padding at his heels.

'All ready?'

No one spoke; not even the pack animals stirred. Many people would not meet his eye. Jamie looked around the company, his gaze darting anxiously from face to face.

'A few more days more,' he cried. 'Then you'll be safe!'

Still there was silence, still there were those who looked away. A fleeting panic touched Jamie, but in an instant he brushed it away. He reached into the radio mule's panniers, pulled out the whip aerial, jammed three sections together and thrust it into position down the side of the bag. The prayer flag still fluttered from its tip.

'Follow, Jyeko! To Moro-La!'

And the stalled pantechnicon spluttered into life; the

reluctant knots fell apart and the caravan began to stream through the hamlet and onto the westward trail. In silence, the Dengkol family watched them go, then turned indoors.

The valleys were now broad scoops in the mountains. Two hours' climb from Dengkol, they were back in the snow. Occasional outcrops broke the sweep of the snowfields with dark blotches; otherwise, all around them was a gritty white. Up this, the mass of people and animals came in a narrow column. From the crest of the first pass, they looked deep into the tangled mass of the range, fold on fold of white hills across which the incessant wind flowed unimpeded. Between these ran pencil-thin frozen streams. No break for pasture in the rise and fall, no hint of flat ground. The landscape was oddly featureless. Though Jamie could see fifty miles in some directions, he could make no sense of the watersheds, and was relieved and thankful that certain Jyeko men moved on without hesitation, following a scattering of rock cairns along the ridge.

The weather was deteriorating. The sky had not brightened all day, but from dull beginnings had grown steadily sullen. From cloud so heavy that it seemed on the point of collapse, spurts of snow, hard and very fine, drove into their faces. Jamie saw people stop, families tying tufts of wool in front of each other's eyes to break the stinging impact. He tugged his fur hat down as far as he could, inched the red scarf off his chin and nibbled one of the little pats of barleymeal that he'd placed inside his shirt.

They made camp in the poor shelter of a turn in the stream. Setting up tents was a fight, with whole families hanging onto the black cloth lest it be blown over the mountains. They stacked their belongings in tall crescents for protection: heaps of striped woollen packs and leather saddlebags, the shrinking sacks of barleymeal, rugs and bundles and even the occasional musical instrument, all heaped as high as possible and topped with wood and leather harness. The wounded, white faced with pain from riding, were lowered gently into the shelters. Gusts of dry snow, fine as flour, hissed on the fires. It puffed through the tiniest holes in the tents and powdered the contents. The yaks shuffled through the snow nosing out a thin meal of short-tufted sedges. The children were sent foraging for any scraps of dry grass the ponies might eat; they were becoming less choosy by the day.

That evening, a family announced that they had run out of barleymeal. They had a tiny quantity of butter, a little tea and salt: nothing else. They declared that their silver charm case was on offer to whoever would give them a bag of meal.

Their neighbours glanced round uneasily and Khenpo Nima at once objected. 'And what will you sell to your so-called friends when that food is gone? Your daughter? This is not going to become the survival of the richest.'

There was some half-hearted applause from the nearby fires. A collection was begun, a handful of meal from here and there dropped into a bowl. But, in the process, it became clear that a dozen other families were in almost the same condition and would soon be asking for themselves.

'Then it's time we killed a yak,' said Khenpo Nima sadly.

'This one,' said Drolma, pointing to her animals. Jamie frowned: the young widow would need her meagre wealth more than most. But Drolma insisted: 'My husband is dead and there is less to carry now.'

'Listen,' said a gruff voice, 'I'd like a word with you about this.' It was Jamyang Sangay. He waddled towards Drolma, wagging a finger of disapproval. He was moving slowly, Jamie noticed, was looking grey-skinned and weary. Jamie watched the muttered negotiation, saw surprise on Drolma's face and was about to curse his old enemy when he saw awkward smiles.

'Right,' announced Jamyang Sangay. 'I'm buying a yak off Drolma, and we eat it. Anyone object?'

'I saw your face, Jamie,' whispered Khenpo Nima, 'but you should know something: you see the yak the men are going to kill? Over there, look. It's one of Sangay's, not Drolma's. He's just pretended to buy one of hers and has given her the money anyway.'

'Why?' asked Jamie, bewildered.

'Why, Jemmy? What sort of a question is that?'

That night, the tents were so stiff and heavy with ice that they buckled, creaking as they sagged. The wind found chink after chink, seeming to stab new holes in the fabric. The dogs shifted uneasily; friends clung to each other in heaps.

In the morning, several mules and ponies were dead. Debilitated, starved, they could not survive these nights. They froze, fell, swelled up, all in silence. There they lay in the morning, hard as iron with their legs outstretched. One pony had died standing, its body fluids turned to ice. On rock outcrops nearby, the ravens waited.

The villagers regarded their reduced pack trains and comforted themselves without conviction: 'The strongest are still living.' The animals looked anything but strong. They dropped their heads dismally. Long icicles hung from their nostrils and their weeping eyes. Someone 'burned' a mule's nose, stupidly offering barley in a metal bucket that touched and tore the skin.

Small children and the elderly were the riders now; there was also a growing number of sick. The caravan picked itself off the frozen ground and tottered stiffly into the march.

'Today I shall issue some medicine to these people,' said Khenpo Nima. He searched his packs and brought out a cloth bag, then stood by the trail issuing everyone who passed with a small grey-brown pellet. Jamie saw that each recipient nodded gratefully and ate the pellet at once.

'Don't I get one?' he asked, as Khenpo Nima was about to replace the bag without coming to him. The monk peered at him thoughtfully, then shrugged and held out his little pouch. Jamie took the rough pellet and swallowed it with a grin.

'Yes, yes,' said Khenpo Nima vaguely. 'Why not? It will keep you warm.'

'What's it made of?' Jamie asked.

'Our Reverend Abbot's faeces,' said the monk.

On they went, the dogged radio mule and its flag leading the way from cairn to cairn, the animal itself wrapped in a yak-hair blanket. Jamie stumbled: the cold was taking hold of his brain, seeming to crush it. He knew that he was turning inward.

He began to feel inside his clothes for the little barley cakes he'd placed next to his flesh, hot and wrapped in a piece of cloth. Delving under layer on layer of fur and wool, down to his own belly, he found the cakes and extracted them. They were frozen hard.

The two men just in front of him came to a sudden halt. Jamie followed their look. Not far below the ridge on which they trudged, the broad river was white, still and noiseless. Some two hundred yards ahead, the gravel banks of either shore were joined by an irregular dotted line, black shapes in the ice, unmoving.

A herd of eight wild asses had tried to swim the river. Why they had attempted it? Perhaps, half starved, they'd believed there might be fodder on this near bank. Perhaps they had been driven by wolves. They had come into the water one after another, breaking through a crust of ice that was forming rapidly as the wind screeched down the valley. Jumping and breaking, floundering weakly with their legs being tugged away underneath them by the current, they'd slowed, their strength failing. And there, in line astern, they'd halted, just as the wind ripped the last movement out of the water and it froze solid. There they would remain, pecked and torn, until the spring thaw.

Family by family, Jyeko went past the spectacle, shrinking from it, goading on their own faltering beasts, following the radio mule.

'Tonight,' said Khenpo Nima glumly, 'we shall be practising *tummo*, the yoga of inner heat.'

*

They camped that night in the lee of a ridge, on sloping ground that in summer would have been pasture. The snow was thin and patchy, and the children began grubbing after desiccated yak dung for the fires. The tea was cold moments after it was made. Jamie had set up the radio mast but, as the wind intensified, there was no gathering, no consultation, only blue, swollen faces. They fed the animals, then crept into their tents and cowered.

Jamie lay in his heap of furs listening to the gale. He was effectively alone: Karjen was fast asleep, exhausted, and the herdsman had gone to a relative's tent. Over Jamie's head, the tent flexed and shuddered, reverberating like an old drum; the guy lines moaned dismally. Hard snow was tossed against the sides with a hollow rattling. The incessant noise got to you, dulled you, killed sensible thought with its interruptions, its attrition. What if the tent split or the ropes failed? What would he do? He pictured himself not moving, but remaining in his bed under the collapsed heap, not caring if he suffocated, Hector mute with misery beside him.

It was long weeks since they had left Jyeko. If they survived this blizzard, *if* they were ever able to move again, they might make Moro-La in three days. There he would find Puton! He would leave the villagers to their troubles and take her south to India, to safety. In his deepest core, that fire still burned and propelled him. His brain was too deadened by cold to sense it directly; still, it was there. But, as the wind battered his tent again and again, Jamie now felt his nerve begin to fail.

He had kept a butter-oil lamp alight for the weak reminder of warmth it gave. In the shadow behind, he glimpsed the radio pack and, beyond that, the dynamo set. It was more than a month since he'd tuned it to anything other than Lhasa or the Chinese military, since he'd had any other company through the machine. He wormed one hand out from his covers and twisted his arm to glimpse his watch, then found the strap of the cloth pack and eased it open. Tugging the stiff canvas downwards, he looked at the brittle, cold dials. Lifeless: no glow for him. The dead eyes of the radio reproached him. He'd given them no chance. Ungratefully, he'd blocked the world out. More than a month since he'd listened.

He slipped out of his covers, trying to ignore the cold. At his side, Hector raised his head in surprise (they weren't going *outside*, surely?). Before he could think better of it, Jamie was squatting alongside the radio, heaving his jacket close about him with one hand while the other tugged at the pedal generator. In a moment he had the dynamo set connected. Near Karjen's head was the coil of wire from the antenna that snaked in under the tent's edge. Jamie grabbed at it, the action drawing a cold draught into his clothes that made him shiver uncontrollably for several seconds. He pulled himself together with a stretch of his collar and shoulder blades, set his back against the tent pole, flicked two switches and began to pedal.

The slow, steady turn of the flywheel distracted him, so that awareness of the chill receded. The dials warmed and shone again. There was nothing but watery hiss from the Chinese frequency. Perhaps they too were all huddled in bed. He twisted the tuning dial, passing over shrill and uncouth music. On, through a chatter of coded Morse from India, gabbling voices – Japanese, Dutch, goodness knows what – until he reached the frequency for Foxtrot 5 Sugar Dog, position Rosyth, Great Britain. It was Mr Dinsmore's regular time: what was he doing? There was nothing. Oh, what was he doing, was the man on holiday, had he taken his mousy wife and spotty brats cycling or what? Jamie pumped the dynamo in a fury. How *dare* he be away from his set? There was no sound, nobody there. He touched the control ever so delicately, a feather tap to left, to right. Nothing.

Another fit of shivering overcame Jamie. He forgot to keep his legs moving and the dials' glow began to fade. He shook himself and started once again to pump and pump: he'd put a volt or two through Dinsmore, he'd wake him up! But nothing happened. And after some thirty seconds of only wind and the whir of the flywheel, Jamie let his feet go still. The ratchet on the flywheel clicked noisily and Karjen stirred. Suddenly Jamie felt his eyes swell with tears – and in a moment he was weeping, shaking silently, weeping for everything, weeping for his farness from everything.

Nearby, Hector opened his eyes again and watched, puzzled. A succession of rapid but profound sighs lifted Jamie's chest and shoulders and dropped them again, as though his lungs were trying to expel a lump of wet arsenic. He returned Hector's unhappy stare, glared with frustrated loathing at the radio – and then, all of a sudden, sat up straight. His eyes lit on a small switch by the tuning dial. He cursed, he nearly laughed, he lunged for it. He was on the wrong frequency band.

Once more, he pedalled. Immediately, there came a slow stammer of amateurish Morse. Jamie listened, and found he was listening to a shopping list, a music request programme, almost. An expatriate Scot with the BAOR, asking Mr Dinsmore to post gramophone records. He wanted Rimsky-Korsakov, *Scheherazade*, with the Hallé Orchestra. And Musorgsky, *A Night on the Bare Mountain*, if you please! *Break, break*, tapped Jamie rudely. *Please, let me in!*

A brief silence, then: *Go ahead.* There was the very slightest hesitation in Jamie, accompanied by a surge of nausea. Mr Dinsmore, Jamie signalled, this is Tare 4 Jig William, Tibet, over.

– *Tibet, we've been trying you every week! Your parents...*

– Mr Dinsmore, this must be very quick ...

Hardly two minutes later, Jamie was back under the covers, shivering enough to come apart at the seams. He thought he'd die of shivering. He tugged the red scarf tighter round his neck, fingering the embroidery, and lay curled up, working desperately to believe that his chest was naked against Puton's back, her buttocks in his lap, the front of his thighs snug against the rear of hers, his forearm close about her chest. Forcing this into his mind, he managed to find an idea of warmth – and slowly the shivers subsided.

*

'Your young British says that he is going home,' said Major Duan to Puton, the triumph in his voice bitten back, barely discernible. 'He's an exceptionally foolish young man. We shall be meeting him at Moro-La. He will go home if and when I send him.'

She was giving Dechen her evening meal, seated on a woven saddlebag at the door of her tent. They both held wooden bowls of barley cooked in the Chinese field kitchen. All across the wide camp, soldiers stood or squatted by their fires, shovelling the same studge into their mouths. Puton glimpsed the Abbot of Jyeko, seventy yards away, seated on a thin mat on the frozen ground and attended by his monks. The old gentleman was weakening daily:

this journey was too much for him. His attendants fussed about him with more tea and more furs. Puton had attempted to join them, hoping that her duty to the Abbot would gain her admittance and shelter but the monks had looked uneasily at Major Duan behind her and had driven her off with a cold scowl.

'Well?' said Duan, standing over her now, irritated. She looked up at him, trying to keep the sullenness out of her voice. The cold fact gripped her: this was her protector, and Dechen's.

'How do you know this?' said Puton.

Duan smiled, as though he'd been waiting for the opening. There was a packsaddle by them and he perched on it. Some yards off, three infantrymen glanced in their direction, at the almost domestic scene: mother, child, guardian.

'He has been speaking on the radio. I have been expecting him to do so, and now he has given himself away. He tells his friends that he will be in India in ten days. Therefore, he must be close to the border. I am certain that he is near Moro-La.'

Puton felt sick with depression. China was swarming over her, hanging over her face like a wet cloth that suffocated. She felt that her very eyesight was slipping away: that, when she looked about the hills among which they were camped, she no longer recognised Tibet. A last flicker of rebellion stirred in her. 'He is not going home. He will stay in India.'

'Oh!' said Duan, raising his eyebrows in mockery. 'So, he'll be raising a force to come and rescue Miss Puton. I must flee, I think.'

Crushed again, crushed so easily. Puton took the empty bowl from Dechen and refilled it with tea. Duan watched her, penetrating as always, his voice calmly insistent. 'He is a spy. He knows what it means for him to be caught. You must understand that he is running away.'

She saw, in her mind's eye, Jamie receding over a high pass, taking her courage away in his saddlebags. Still she did not look at the Major: it was the last of her resistance.

'For you, all that time is now over,' said Duan, quite gently.

At last, her eyes filled with tears. She tightened her jaw as best she could, hoping to stem the flow. But inexorably the tears billowed up from deep within her. Dechen, cuddling her bowl of tea, regarded her in mute horror. Her mother's face was awash with misery, the dam broken.

Major Duan raised his hand. With the back of it, almost imperceptibly, he brushed the wet hair off her face. It was the first time that he had touched her since Jyeko.

'We shall be leaving for Moro-La at first light; your tent and bags must be packed tonight.'

She peered at him through her tears.

'Bring your bedding to my tent after your meal,' he said.

*

When Jamie crawled from the radio tent at dawn, he was virtually alone. Only one or two dark figures had emerged elsewhere in the camp, creeping about like ghouls in lumps of stiff sheepskin. The cold slashed at Jamie's furs and defences, and for a second he thought of turning straight back inside. Then he saw the radio mule.

He had wrapped the animal in two heavy blankets of yak hair for the night, and fed it over-generous handfuls of barley. He had thought the mule was still hardy; unlike most, it had seemed to stamp and shake its neck with some vigour. But it now lay a few feet from the tent, ice on its lips, the red and green halter stiff on the snow. Only the eyes had not yet been taken, for the wind did not allow the ravens to move in.

'Oh, shit,' said Jamie aloud. 'Shit!'

He looked around anxiously. His pony was still alive, miraculously, but he could see other slumped shapes that would be perished pack animals. There was precious little sign of life from nearby tents. In the distance a figure was struggling to light a fire in the lee of a crescent of bags. Khenpo Nima's face appeared, half buried in a fur hat, scanning the dreadful morning.

'Nima! We have to get moving!' shouted Jamie. But Khenpo Nima retreated back into his tent. 'Nima! Karjen, come on!' Jamie opened his tent and shouted angrily, 'Karjen!' Then he stood straight and roared above the wind, 'Jyeko! Jyeko!'

Still the gale blew. There had been no fresh snowfall in the night, but the dawn sky was dark purple and the clouds streamed in a hectic torrent eastward. They'd be marching into the wind again.

Crawling from their shelters, the villagers grubbed about for fuel. The large black nomad tents had a fire within, but half the village were forced outside and huddled as close to the ground as they could. They searched for flints, trembling with cold, striking sparks with frozen clumsiness into the tinder, puffing at the wisps of smoke with little bellows of soft marmot skin. When the pot of ice was positioned on the fire, most people disappeared back into their tents.

'Oh, dear God,' thought Jamie, 'we have to move.'

'It is bad,' said the monk, standing upright at last and peering about the miserable camp. 'See this lady? Dawa, how is the salt?'

At the next tent, a woman had managed to coax up flames. She was crouched by the fire with a small leather bag at her side into which she dipped her hand. She brought out a pinch of greyish salt.

'You see, Jemmy? If the salt is dry, it will crackle on the fire. Then there is no snow coming. But if it is wet ... '

The woman held her hand over the fire; the salt trickled into the flames – and made not a sound.

'If there is much snow today we shall have trouble,' said Khenpo Nima.

'Nima, get them out, get them moving! You must do it! I heard the Chinese last night, you understand? I listened, I heard them, I heard them say Moro-La! Moro-La, that's where they're heading too, do you understand me? Are we going to wait to see who gets there first? Do you understand me, Nima?'

Jamie reached down and heaved out the guy lines supporting the radio antenna. It collapsed instantly under the gale. He seized the steel sections and lifted them, holding the antenna like a musket from which the wind horses galloped hysterically, the flag flicking loudly at electric speed. He drove Khenpo Nima among the tents. He took him by the hand and pulled him through the snowy camp from shelter to shelter: *Tell them, Nima! Tell them to move! These ... Now these ...* On they went, Jamie pushing Khenpo Nima on, past dead ponies, dogs with their hair quivering in the wind and their eyes streaming, astonished villagers looking up at them, frightened children: *Tell them to move, Nima! Jyeko, Jyeko! We're leaving now, we're leaving!*

He bellowed and bellowed as he strapped the radio onto his own pony. The people of Jyeko crept from their tents and, almost in spite of themselves, followed suit. He jammed the antenna into its accustomed position, and began the march.

*

Later that day, when the wind was thumping and the sharp snow grating their faces, Jamie saw a woman collapse. He was walking sideways at the time, as was half the village, because the gale made it difficult to breathe. The woman was just behind him leading a famished mule. She had been stumbling along for hours, not stopping, not complaining. She must have spent all her reserves of energy on keeping up speed near the head of the column, for fear that if she slipped to the back, she'd be lost. Suddenly, it was too much and she sank down.

Jamie stopped and tugged his pony off the trampled path to let others pass. He let go of the leading rope (the animal wasn't going anywhere) and went the few steps back to the woman. She was feebly trying to prop herself up on her elbows, but had not the strength to lift her head. Jamie crouched beside her and, with a clumsy heave, sat her up. Her eyes rolled and wandered, unfocused; her head lolled. Jamie looked round. The caravan trudged past them unseeing, as though in a collective daze, until a bulky figure leading a yak paused by them.

'Leave her, Mr Jemmy,' said Jamyang Sangay. 'It is the only thing. I think she is not the first.' He looked back down the caravan, as though there might well be a long line of the fallen. Then he plodded ahead.

Jamie remained beside the defeated woman. He pulled his pony towards her. With his stiffly gloved fingers, he unlashed the two panniers that held the radio and the generator. These thumped into the snow by the pony, which started nervously. Jamie dragged the woman to a standing position, grasped her round the waist and attempted to heave her over the pony – but he lost his balance, and they both fell in the snow. Through the wind he heard her moan softly. Then there were other arms under his, and he stood again quickly. Someone (he never saw who) helped him grasp the inert figure and haul her upright, then onto the pony's back. There she slumped.

Their unknown helper moved on ahead as Jamie panted for breath. He reached down to the radio pack and tugged the cords free. In a clumsy, makeshift manner he bound these around her waist and under the pony's girth, then tied the ends to her wrists. The woman lolled on the animal's neck without gripping but at least she did not fall. The radio lay on its side in the snow. *Tibet, we've been trying you every week! Your parents ...* Jamie stared at the set a brief moment. Already a snowdrift was forming round the case: in five minutes it would be covered. He left it there. But he tugged the antenna free and jammed it into his own belt so that it stuck high up over his head, the flag buzzing in the wind. Then he pulled at the pony's leading rope and returned to the path.

*

two

The pass at Moro-La is broad and smooth, a relatively easy passage at sixteen thousand, three hundred and sixty feet. It is quite well used, although dangerously exposed in winter and surrounded by vast expanses of heavy black scree flogged and scoured by the gales. Traders fear the sudden, engulfing blizzards for which the pass is infamous and generally prefer Jewe-La well to the north.

In the very centre of Moro-La, an enormous onion-shaped *chorten* shrine stands, the size of a house, its windward side pitted and blasted. Beyond, a thousand feet below the *chorten*, lies a more tranquil plateau of high alpine pasture that in summer is spattered with trumpet gentians and purple dwarf delphiniums. From the pass, the panoramas are grand even by Tibet's superlative standards. Herds of wild ass and antelope move freely on the broad slopes, with their dedicated predators – bear, wolf, snow leopard – never far distant.

On the pasture table, three trails meet: that which climbs up from Kham in the east; that which leads due south to the Brahmaputra river crossing and thence through forested valleys to Assam and India; and the way westward to Lhasa, a hard trail winding through the colossal central ranges.

In 1950 an antique fortress still stood by the Lhasa route. Kantu-Dzong was some miles from the division of the ways, down in the wide valley below. In Tibet's thin air it appeared quite near but took three hours of walking down the snaking path to reach. It was a small castle, owing its strength to position more than to impregnable design. It stood high on a shelf of glacial moraine, two hundred feet above the hamlet and hard up against the mountain flank. At the rear, the castle simply moulded itself to the steep hillside, trusting to the forbidding crags behind for protection. But from the front it looked like stone castles anywhere, a mass of walls and towers. It has been destroyed now, blasted to ruins by Chinese artillery in the awful, despairing revolt of 1959. The howitzers had a little problem with its masonry, which was on a quite massive scale. But the guns still took only a morning to demolish a fortress that had controlled a broad tract for four hundred and fifty years.

In 1950 the district was peaceful but, quite recently, Kantu-Dzong had been the headquarters of a minor warlord. For generations this family had been a source of much irritation to the government. Several of the grandest dynasties in Lhasa had long claimed to own land in the vicinity but had rarely tried to enforce their revenues. At last, the exasperated grandees of the Cabinet had imposed a new governorship.

The present incumbent, Dorje Gangshar, now waited by the cairn of Moro-La, seated on a sturdy white pony and watching the caravan of Jyeko villagers creep up the long valley towards him. He was a tall man of around fifty, every inch the disdainful aristocrat with narrow eyes set close together, full lips and a long heavy nose. His sleek black hair hung in two thick queues through which traced fine coloured threads. On his head perched a hat of fur, eight inches thick and very wide like a huge cake or hairy poultice. On top there was a little brass finial, polished and gleaming, perhaps for lifting the poultice off the noble pate. His ears were pierced, bearing long pendants of silver set with turquoises that looped loosely and joined under his chin. His hands were long and manicured, and positively clanked with rings. His fur gowns were surmounted by wraps of old Russian brocaded silk, their deep blues decorated with white and gold clouds. All this gleamed and glowed most beautifully for the sun was out on Moro-La. Unusually for the place and the time of year, it was a lovely day.

Dorje Gangshar was not smiling, however, for his present situation was an unhappy one. He had no liking for the vulgarly brutish Khampas and had some urgent travelling to do himself. Behind him, out of sight over the lip of the pass, some thirty or more companions were halted at the trail divide: his family, and a party of their servants and retainers. They had lit fires and made refreshments while waiting for him. But he himself was constrained to wait for this exhausted rabble to drag itself up the pass. He had a message to deliver.

As the caravan drew near, Dorje Gangshar could make out

the British technician Wilson, who was walking in the lead group and was curiously marked out by a pole with a little white flag attached. They had met in Lhasa once, though it would have greatly piqued Dorje Gangshar's vanity to know that Jamie did not remember him. The nobleman remarked that few of the approaching party were riding their animals up the pass, and thought this peculiar. It is a maxim in Tibet that a horse that cannot carry a man uphill is no horse, while a man that rides downhill is no man. Personally, Dorje Gangshar could see little value in transport that could not carry him in all directions. He did notice that the ponies, mules and yaks were over-laden. So, these people had not brought sufficient animals with them, were ill-prepared, careless, reckless: Khampas, in a word.

Painfully slowly, they drew close. He saw that some were injured, were riding or stumbling with help from their companions. He saw upturned faces intently scanning the skyline. Some of the leaders now saw him silhouetted there. Weary as they were, they waved enthusiastically. Dorje Gangshar had a sudden, uncomfortable feeling that they had been expecting to see him. To his certain knowledge, no such appointment had been made. At last, those at the head of the column reached the top of the climb, quickened their paces for the last few yards and stood before him, puffing and grinning, their hands hanging from the leading reins.

'Well, good day to you, sir, we're here! We're from Kham, from Jyeko, just arrived, come to join you, there's a hundred and thirty of us and this is Mr Jemmy.'

There were three lamas, a number of coarse-featured men who looked as though they'd been sleeping in a stable, and the young Britisher. The latter was beaming with what looked terribly like hopeful expectation. Oh dear, thought Dorje Gangshar.

'I am Dorje Gangshar,' he announced haughtily. His voice was distinctly nasal.

'Oh, yes?' said one lama.

'Governor of Kantu-Dzong,' the nobleman added, since they'd apparently not made that simple connection.

'Ah,' said the lama, a tall fellow quite well-made, who

seemed to command some seniority. He was now taking in the finery that sat upon Dorje Gangshar and his inane grin was changing to something less impertinent, less brazen. 'We are honoured to greet you, sir,' he finally got round to adding.

Behind this group, more of the procession was about to reach the summit. The British youth, Wilson, was almost stamping with excited anticipation. He glanced from one to another of his companions, as though willing them to ask questions. At his side, a grim mastiff glowered at the Governor.

'Sir,' enquired a second lama, a man with a strong, pugnacious face, 'might I ask who else is with you here? We've heard of a great gathering.'

'My family are waiting for me below,' countered the Governor, 'with their people.'

'But everyone else?' said the monk.

'Is there an army?' some oaf blurted out.

'There is indeed. I am charged with delivering a message to you,' said Dorje Gangshar, as loftily as he could.

'Right, we're expected!' the oaf interrupted.

'From Major Duan of the People's Liberation Army of China.'

The new arrivals fell suddenly silent; they stared at the Governor, some with their mouths hanging open. Their fellows continued to press up behind.

'That officer is waiting for you at my residence of Kantu-Dzong, which I regret to say is in his hands. His message to you is this: you have the choice of surrendering to him forthwith, or of taking the road to India that lies before you, or complete destruction. Should you, incidentally, take the India option, I shall require you to wait until my family are ahead and well clear of your animals.'

There were some seconds of silence. The steadily growing knot of people in front of Dorje Gangshar turned with exaggerated slowness to regard one another, taking in this news.

'And you, sir, are going to India?'

'Just so.'

'You'll be coming back?'

'What business is that of yours?'

'Governor, forgive my friend, we only thought – '

'You should be thinking about your answer to the Chinese commander, don't you think?'

'We have to send him an answer?' muttered a flat-headed old cuss with a filthy beard. 'Why don't we just cut his balls off?'

'For the very sound reason,' said the Governor, 'that he has some two hundred and fifty soldiers with him, some in the fort itself and the rest encamped on the plain. You'll see them soon enough. I repeat, he is waiting for your answer, and if you have any further questions will you put them now so that I can be on my way?'

'So,' one of the monks looked puzzled, 'will you be taking our answer back to him yourself?'

'I am not a postal runner. These will do it.'

With that, the Governor gestured with a long bejewelled finger to the rear of the massive *chorten*. The Jyeko leaders edged forward a yard or two – and gaped in amazement. Seated on the lowest ledge of the structure, quietly smoking cigarettes, were three Chinese troopers. Their ponies were tied to a denuded flagpole twenty yards off. The soldiers saw that they'd been spotted and grinned at the villagers with amusement.

Karjen made a most unfriendly noise in his throat and started to unfasten his sheepskin.

'Before you do anything crass,' said the Governor, 'I should point out that Major Duan has several hostages, your own people.'

Khenpo Nima turned quickly: 'Who?'

'The Reverend Abbot of your monastery, as I understand. A very dignified and holy gentleman, but somewhat debilitated from his travels. Indeed, he is quite unwell. There is a small retinue of his also.'

A ripple of excited mutters spread among the travellers, and quickly ran back through the caravan as the tail end came into view over the brow of the pass.

'There is also a woman of good family from Lhasa who, for reasons I did not trouble with, was apparently in the east and now travels with the Major.'

If the Governor had been observing Jamie closely at this moment, he'd have seen a graphic instance of blood draining from a face, then flooding back in a great blush and draining away once more. But the Governor disdained to look closely at any of these Khampas or their associates. He merely remarked, 'I trust you will think carefully before putting those persons to any awkwardness. Now, if you will excuse me ... '

Dorje Gangshar gathered the reins of his white pony and began to tug it round. The throng of Khampas gathering before him was getting to be oppressive, their nasty dogs too inquisitive. Some of them had run fifty yards forward to a point where they could look down to the Governor's travelling party waiting below, and were peering rudely at his relations. It was time that he made his way directly to his family and got them all on the road once more. He was about to kick his pony that way when, behind him, a woman's voice called out, tinged with a new insolence: 'Caught by surprise, were you, Governor?'

Dorje Gangshar hesitated, then jabbed his boots into the pony's flank.

'Governor, what happened?' called another female.

'We heard there'd be a Tibetan army here.'

'Were you in charge? Where's everyone gone?'

'We've come to kick out the Chinese, Governor.'

Dorje Gangshar did not look round but walked his pony away without expression or hurry. Suddenly, right in front of him, a burly woman with all the personal charm of a yak stood in his way.

'Governor, can you answer us, please? What's happened to the resistance? Why are you leaving?'

'Tsering Norzu, for pity's sake!'

'Remember yourself!'

(These hasty exhortations came from the men.)

'They've got hundreds of boxes down there!' yelled a younger woman on the farther crest, who stood gazing down at the encampment below. 'Taking plenty of loot, are you, Governor? Lots of silver? Plenty of finery for India, I hope?'

Dorje Gangshar, while trying hard to avoid the faces that swarmed about him now, could not ignore the anger, the fury riding on exhaustion. The three Chinese soldiers dropped their cigarettes, unshouldered their rifles and looked nervous also, backing away from the crowd towards their own mounts. The Khampa men were clustered around the *chorten*, squirming with feudal embarrassment. Their appalling women, however, were beginning to get both in the Governor's way and on his nerves. More and more of them were trotting alongside him then in front, walking backwards as they turned to face him. He began to feel alarmed, and discreetly urged the pony into as fast a walk as dignity would permit.

'Oh, Governor, come on, don't run away.' The squealing female voice was twisted with sarcasm.

'We *need* you, lordly sir!'

'Like we need a whack of smallpox.'

'Or Chinese clap!' A vicious screech. 'You're not Chinese, are you, sir?'

'Governor, are you really Chinese? Tell!'

At last, the noble legs began not so much to kick as to flap frantically. His mount trotted with several women jogging alongside. When the pony reached the descent, Dorje Gangshar urged it on down the path. Someone started throwing snowballs after him. The first missed; the second exploded with a pleasant *phut!* against his brocaded back.

'Get off!' bawled the women. 'Get off and walk! You want to kill the horse as well?'

'A man who rides downhill is no – '

The hoary maxim stayed unfinished – but proven. There came a gasp, then a gale of delighted mockery from the women now lining the crest of the pass: Dorje Gangshar had fallen off his pony. The stocky, sure-footed beast had been coping admirably with the unfamiliar business of carrying a man downhill, until its frantic rider took a snowball on the back of his neck, flapped his thighs and lurched forward all at once. The pony tripped, going down awkwardly onto its knees. Immediately it staggered to its feet, mercifully unhurt, but Dorje Gangshar tumbled among the drifts and rocks. He picked himself up, grabbed for the reins and a moment later was stumbling away downhill in a swirl of snow and blue robing, pursued by jeers and snowballs.

'Gracious,' said Khenpo Nima. 'I'd never have believed that.'

Around him, the men of Jyeko stood speechless.

*

The three Chinese troopers were so alarmed that they remained by their ponies seventy yards off, rifles loaded and ready in their jittery hands. They were smoking furiously, further betraying their nerves. Jamyang Sangay told them to wait while Jyeko's answer was considered, and gave them to understand that it was only the inherently superior civilisation of Tibet that saved their throats from a prompt slitting.

In the centre of the pass, the people of Jyeko gathered in a ring in the bright sunshine, debating passionately. Their animals had been left to mill about among the snowy boulders, looking in vain for something to nibble.

Well apart on the western edge, Jamie stood staring fixedly in the direction of Kantu-Dzong. The uncanny clarity of distant Tibetan views was perhaps enhanced by the intensity of his attention, and certainly by his imagination. It seemed to him that he could see every pebble on the pathway leading up the slope of rocky detritus to the gate of the fort. He believed he could count the soldiers going up and down the hill, and their field guns and tents surrounding the little hamlet below. He half believed that he could see Puton in the (completely hidden) courtyard.

From time to time, his gaze would pan across the grandeur of the landscape. The farthest mountains hung like pale drapes in various tones of misty blue. To the south, separated by a hundred peaks and ridges, a hundred valley troughs dark with forest drained into the Brahmaputra and thence to India. Nearer, between Moro-La and the Tibetan upper reaches of the river, were bare hills of colour: caramel, russet and damson topped with sugary snow. Among these led the trail down which the discomfited ex-Governor, his women, progeny and serfs were now making their way.

Always, though, Jamie's look returned to Kantu-Dzong, and the haughty nasal voice of Dorje Gangshar came and came again like red ants in his brain: *A woman of good family from Lhasa, who was in the east and now travels with the Major...*

'What are you thinking of, Jemmy?' said Khenpo Nima at his shoulder. Jamie waved in helpless silence towards the fort. The monk sighed. 'My little blue poppies grow in the heights above that castle.'

'I'm not thinking about flowers.'

'Oh, no. But, Jemmy, you can go home now,' said Nima, indicating the group receding along the trail. 'You can accompany the Governor, you know, you can go straight after him.'

'Thank you so much.'

They watched the fleeing aristocrat together for a moment.

'Rings on his fingers and bells on his toes. Dragging his servants with him. Do you suppose he asked *them* whether they wanted exile in India?' Inexorably, Jamie's eyes were drawn back to the distant fort.

Gently, Nima began again: 'Perhaps, Jemmy, there is now come a time when you cannot see her again ... '

There came a sudden roar from the debating villagers.

'What are they saying?' asked Jamie.

'Some are for India, some for surrender, still one or two say we should return to Jyeko. Some have a crazy thought of attacking the fort.'

Jamie looked at him in faint interest.

'How could they do that?'

'You know what they are like, Jemmy, those like Karjen and, I'm afraid, Wangdu. They say they cannot lie down quietly now, that they must rescue our abbot from this Duan.'

'Rescue?'

Again, the flurry of impassioned words. Jamie could see Wangdu struggling to manage the dispute, and the pack of charged faces around him, insisting, entreating.

'Don't you agree, Nima?' said Jamie. 'I do.'

'What is that, Jemmy?'

'You cannot go home. Duan's not going to be very civil if you surrender to him. You might as well try to kill him first, don't you think?'

With that, Jamie turned on his heel, heading for the circle. Khenpo Nima followed.

The arguments had gone round at least twice. Among those advocating a new life in India, Jamyang Sangay had been most forceful. For this he had been taken sternly to task.

'*You* have the means for it, Sangay. You've the money to make a new home and a business. Fine. What about Drolma, or Tenzin Drema, or Tesla, or Pemba Norbu? What are the poor people to do in India? Break rocks?'

More shouts, more vehemence: the three Chinese troopers were starting to edge towards their ponies.

Wangdu said: 'For me, there is no life that is not Tibet. For me, Tibet is where I ride as I please, where I play or pray or pay homage as I must. If I have to flee through the storms, or hide in the little valleys or creep past campfires in the dark – or abandon my abbot to the Chinese! – then this is not Tibet.'

'I shall go to the Abbot.' Khenpo Nima spoke out. 'I see no reason why this Duan should have harmed him. But *you* must save yourselves! Your lives are sacred, and if you stay here to fight you will throw them away most sacrilegiously. There is no shame in making your lives anew wherever fate takes you.'

'No shame,' called Jamie, 'but no future, no hope.'

'Jemmy!'

'Dear Nima, forgive me, but you know nothing of India. Your people will be exiles and refugees. I tell you, the world is crawling with exiles and refugees. No one will give a damn! *No one* is going to fight China for you. You'll sit in a muddy camp full of mosquitoes, eating sticky milk sweets, forgetting what Jyeko looked like and waiting and waiting, sweating your lives away, getting sick, having babies who will never – ever! – breathe the air of these mountains.'

The crowd all round him gave a low murmur of dismay. Just then, scarcely a soul would have gone to India. A woman spat in disgust: she probably did not know what a mosquito was, but she wanted none of them. Jamie said: 'Or you can try for Lhasa. There's Chinese waiting just down the road; it means a fight. But if you don't stand up to Duan, the Tibet you know is finished. It will die ...'

'We can make peace!' cried Khenpo Nima, stepping through the ring to face Jamie. 'We have lived in peace with the Chinese before.'

'They'll break Tibet apart, Nima, now or next year. They'll do it sometime. They'll finish Tibet for good.'

The tight-pressed people in the ring began to sway, to stagger. Khenpo Nima glared at Jamie, livid with anger. 'You tell these villagers to go and die, Jemmy? And you can go home? We don't like that, Jemmy. You just leave now, please, you just go after that filthy governor at once.'

'Are you giving me orders, Nima?' He faced the monk squarely.

But a woman intervened, demanding: '*Are* you leaving us now, Mr Jemmy?' Shrewd and hideous, she was looking right into his eyes. 'Going away to your own people, and leaving us?'

'*You* are my people,' said Jamie.

'Very nice,' snapped Khenpo Nima. 'Now you answer that person.'

Jamie felt suddenly content with this. He said: 'If you choose to fight, I'll be with you.'

'Yes! Yes!' spat Karjen, stamping his foot in deep gratification. By him, the novices slapped their hands together by their thighs, as if to say the debate was won. Gruff herdsmen and half-starved traders cheered. The women of Jyeko looked Jamie carefully up and down, checking for the crack in him. Seeing none, they nodded in slow approval. But Khenpo Nima felt his own world cracking and crumbling.

*

The Chinese troopers carried away with them a small leather pouch containing a letter written by Khenpo Nima on a page torn from Jamie's sketchbook. This respectfully informed Major Duan that, as night was now falling, the people of Jyeko would be with him in the morning.

As soon as the troopers went over the brow of the hill, the Khampas began redistributing captured rifles and ammunition and debating how best to mount a surprise attack. There were perhaps fifty men of fighting age among the villagers – and how many Chinese at Kantu-Dzong? Two hundred and fifty? Never mind: Jyeko was burning anew.

Surprise was clearly of the essence. Ironically it fell partly to Khenpo Nima to provide the means. Wangdu announced that Nima knew the route by which they could come upon the rear of the fort and over the low wall at the back.

'Through the valley of blue poppies,' Wangdu said, 'where our abbot once taught Khenpo Nima and myself to gather the rarest flowers. We can reach it along the ridge from here.'

'Won't it be guarded, Reverence?'

'It's nothing but a little trail among the scree,' said Wangdu. 'The Chinese won't even know the valley is there. They don't know about Tibetan poppies, do they?'

'And it leads right into the fort?'

'To the back wall. Khenpo Nima, you have been more recently than I: you know the place?'

'Know it?' whispered Khenpo Nima. 'It is a secret corner of my heart.'

Khenpo Nima looked like a man who had been bitten by something venomous, whose veins were even now starting to shrink and shrivel as the toxins crept towards his heart. When he spoke again, his voice was as thin as that of a man twice his age and half his presence. 'I will instruct you, Wangdu,' he said. 'You need have no fear of getting lost. But I shall stay with the families, who will have need of prayer and courage tonight.'

He moved away to his own pack animals, his novices going after him. Admiring and delighted, the people went back to their preparations.

Jamie had no delusions of his own heroism, or his credentials as a warrior. He'd never fought in a pitched battle, never killed anyone: he was a radio operator, a technician. When some eager young Khampa thrust a captured Chinese rifle and two pouches of bullets at him, he'd nodded gravely, laid these on the snowy ground by his well-stuffed knapsack and regarded them thoughtfully.

'How can you do this, Jemmy?' said Khenpo Nima. Jamie looked up and saw the monk looming over him. Beyond Nima, the villagers busied themselves in the fading light. The first of the pack animals was already making its way off the pass down to the lower meadow to wait. Jamie saw the men stoking hurried fires for a last hot supper before the assault group departed. Nearby, two waved at him to come and eat with them.

'How can I do it?' he hazarded. 'Well, I suppose because we'll all be together in this.'

'Jemmy, how can you urge these people into hopeless fighting? Just go away!'

'Thank you so much,' bridled Jamie. 'You spent no little time trying to persuade me to sign contracts and stay forever, as I recall.'

'Which you never did, because you thought of nothing but your own desires.'

'Nima!'

He had never seen such anger in Khenpo Nima; he realised only now how bitter were the eyes turned on him.

'You have persuaded these people into a bloody fight so that you can rescue your lady friend. That is all you care for now!'

'Nima, that is not so!'

Or was it? Flushed, dismayed, bewildered by the monk's ferocity, Jamie stared tight-lipped at Khenpo Nima. He felt defenceless against the tirades of the tall lama, who now paced back and forth in front of him. He stood by his pack, gripping the

Chinese rifle in confusion and self-doubt. The man's presence and fury made Jamie feel small. Khenpo Nima stopped pacing a moment and stood staring at the dilapidated fortress in the distance. The light was going fast, the cold was back. The sun's thin winter warmth had fled the moment its beams passed off the big cairn.

'Nima, you're so angry,' Jamie offered, 'and I can see why, everything blown to buggery, all your best principles, your world – but I've not done it.'

Khenpo Nima said nothing. Jamie caught a glimpse of the monk's strong face as he peered at the valley prospect below. The wind was getting up once more: it hauled Nima's coat and robes tight against him as he leaned into it, and pressed his eyes until they watered. Is he weeping? Jamie wondered. He was about to speak some words of reconciliation when Khenpo Nima turned and walked away from him.

One hour later, the villagers had all left the pass, and the fighting men of Jyeko took the narrow trail that led just below the ridge, heading north. With them went Jamie, a Chinese cavalry carbine over his shoulder. Looking back, he saw Khenpo Nima in the last glimmer of light, solitary, gazing after him. There was, even in that silhouette, an unhappiness that seemed on the brink of calling out to Jamie, calling him back to say some last thing. But the call did not come, and they never spoke again.

*

three

Major Duan reread the note that announced Jyeko's forthcoming surrender, then sat back on his folding stool, his shoulders against the stone wall. In front of him, a fire of yak dung burned with its sweet smoke. It was nearly midnight. Most of his soldiers were asleep; outside the open door of the room, his orderlies were forcing themselves to stay alert. No doubt they were wishing he would go to bed likewise. After all, did he not have a woman in tow?

Duan was tired, certainly, but his mind raced and rattled over the rocky trails of Tibet. For these paths had led him to act in ways at which he was not a little amazed. He was not himself, he'd begun to think. Perhaps it was the altitude. The peasantry of Sichuan, knowing nothing of barometric pressure, believed Tibet to be suffused with poisonous exhalations from the ground. These fumes, they believed, were the cause of the fearful headaches that lowlanders always experienced on the plateau. Duan had begun to wonder if they weren't right. He sat staring into the flames, puzzling over his own behaviour.

What was he doing, giving the murderous primitives of Jyeko a chance to escape with their lives? They had butchered his troops, yet he was prepared to let them take themselves off to India without punishment. He had left Chamdo with a force ample enough to wipe them out, had spent long weeks in frustrating and exhausting pursuit, had almost been humiliated by them on several occasions – indeed, *had* been humiliated! – and was now offering them freedom. Why?

He thought back over all he had seen of the country, and the small number of its inhabitants he'd come to know. No revelations there – except that there were times when the people seemed almost part of the rocks, of the landscape. The little party in his charge, the old Abbot and his retinue, the woman and child, had a way of rejoicing in the bleakest surroundings that at times made Duan want to shout an obscenity at them. On the coldest, darkest morning, when the camp was breaking up to move off into storms and weariness, he'd see the captive Tibetans standing at the perimeter, gazing at the hills all around. They'd do and say not a thing: they merely stood and stared at the glacial mountains, the barren, wind-scoured plains, the rubble and the mud and the snow ... and drank it in, as though it were a piping hot comfort to them.

And so it might be that he had realised what exile would do to them. Possibly, there was no punishment as great as that they would inflict on themselves by going to India.

Or had he gone soft? Had two decades of the harshest military conditioning fallen away? The woman's touch, was it, or her curious joined brows, maybe? Was he sparing the miserable Khampas for her sake? Silently, with his face set tingling by the fire, Duan scoffed at himself. A pitiful irony there, for she seemed to bear her compatriots little enough love. She piqued him unbearably. She had not surrendered to him. Not finally, not ultimately. She had made a choice to save her little girl: no more than that. There was no other pressure that Duan could put on her that would induce any more meaningful submission. He wondered, uncomfortably, if she had defeated him after all. Her unresisting compliance appalled him: she had the frigid civility of a slave. She said hardly a word to him. He was damned if he knew why he should care so.

But the villagers. Back to the villagers: think! Stare into the low flames that throw weak multiple shadows about this horrid little stone room, and *think*! What were they about? Why were they surrendering? Was it that they also knew that exile was intolerable? What did they expect at his hands? Summary execution, surely, the whole lot of them – unless, that was, that they'd heard of the liberty, fraternity and amnesty that Peking had ordained. Perhaps, in every way, Duan was too late. As he sat on into the night, he searched in himself for the fury that had sent him out from General Wang's headquarters on this pursuit – and he knew that it was fading. So: what exactly would he do with them in the morning? He would be harsh. Annoyance with his own vacillation hardened him: he would not be a soft touch.

Duan sighed, and was about to bestir himself and call for

his bedding to be prepared when he became aware of voices in the passageway outside. He looked up as an officer of the watch appeared in the doorway.

'Well?'

'Sir, there is a request.'

'Then it can wait.'

'Yes, sir, but ... the Tibetan Abbot is very sick, sir. He has asked that the woman be allowed to attend him.'

Duan raised an eyebrow imperceptibly. It must be serious now. The monks had kept Puton at a chilly distance from the Abbot throughout the journey. He nodded.

'Very well. Tell her to go to him.'

'Also, sir, there is a Tibetan who wishes to speak with you.'

'Really?' retorted Duan witheringly.

'I'm sorry, sir, but you'll want to hear what he has to say. He's a newcomer, a senior monk, and he has news.'

*

The village men approached Khenpo Nima's valley of the poppies well after midnight. It was curiously still, the wind that had earlier threatened them with renewed gales having petered out. It was, however, intensely cold, and a glacial moon shone on the column that picked its way above the scree slopes. The air itself seemed to glitter all around the men, while the shadows between the rocks were a profound blue-black. After climbing steadily up and across the eastern face, they reached a place where some ancient geological cataclysm had cut a deep notch across the ridge through which the head of a high valley might be gained. Along this valley, a frozen stream descended gently to a sudden steep drop over the ridge's western flank, above the castle that crouched on the lower slopes. The secret valley was not large, not wide. After no more than a mile and a half, the almost level floor reached an edge and tumbled away. Down through the mountain debris dropped the thread-like path they were seeking, to emerge upon the rear walls of Kantu-Dzong.

The column of men crossed the upper lip of the gorge, moved beside the stream of ice and among a stone herd of colossal boulders. The high-altitude winds had contrived to keep the valley relatively free of snow even so late in the year. Wangdu led the men alongside the silent stream dropping gradually towards the farther edge. They marched in silence, looking around them at the vast stones. Something of Khenpo Nima's regard for this place had infected the men, though it would be many months before the sun would induce any poppies to show their heads. Indeed, this was near the extreme altitude for flowering plants. Any higher, and the ground would be too hard over too much of the year for roots to function.

Halfway down the valley, they stopped to rest. Only for a few minutes, because the night was passing rapidly. Although the moon still shone brilliantly, dawn threatened.

'We mustn't stop,' said Jamie, urgent and anxious. 'Wangdu, we're late.'

'Just a moment to take breath and a mouthful of food.'

They were nervous: the heights, the silence, the intense still cold touched them all.

'Move on!' ordered Wangdu, with a hint of shrillness.

Down the valley they crept, and approached the open lower end. Across that shelf, as hints of light seeped into the sky, an astonishing panorama of Tibet came into view. Awe came upon Jamie all over again, even as his stomach quivered with nerves, even as he stumbled through the rubble after his friends.

'Faster,' called someone anxiously. 'We're late ...' And they began to jog along the valley floor, weaving between the boulders in single file, their rifles jigging up and down on their backs.

Just before the ground fell away suddenly, there was a cluster of a dozen or more massive rocks the size of temples. Between these lay an open space at most thirty or forty paces wide. Into this space, the Jyeko men trotted. They slowed towards the lip of the valley, about to begin the steep descent. One last time, Jamie paused, raised his eyes from the stony ground and took in the vastness of the country ...

He saw the lead man, just in front of Wangdu, go between two well-defined rocks that stood like a great portal. As he passed through, a shadow moved out from behind a boulder and came in among the column of men. It was at once followed by another, more, a score and more of dark shapes emerging silently, coming swiftly from the pockets of deep darkness on both sides of the path, across the snow and closing on the column, like flitting spirits. For a moment, in front of and behind Jamie, the Khampas hesitated and looked around ...

Then a whistle blew. Suddenly, the narrow passageway was cut about by a score of shafts of light as Chinese officers shone powerful torches at the leading Tibetans. Bewildered, the Jyeko men stood like rabbits transfixed, as rifles with bayonets glittering came up at their faces. Towards the rear of the column, a few of the Khampas began to bring their weapons off their shoulders. But what should they shoot at? There was an absurd confusion of shapes on all sides. Jamie swung round to look behind in disbelief, tugging at his carbine, swearing as it snagged in the webbing of his knapsack, stumbling as he wrenched at it, gagging with rage – and falling, as a rifle butt struck his shoulder with paralysing force.

The Chinese were among them, everywhere, front and rear, with orders snapped and quick arms seizing the dazed men. There was nothing to be done.

Not a single shot was fired. It was the queerest of routs.

*

The notion that they had been betrayed did not occur to the men of Jyeko. It was far too gross an idea. The prisoners whispered among themselves, speculated as to their fate and that of the novices and lamas, wondered anxiously about their families, concluded that Chinese spies must have watched their every move from the pass – but they never thought of treachery. Then the guards ordered them to be silent.

They were corralled in the open yard of the fortress of Kantu-Dzong, as though in a pit. The high walls of mottled grey stone lowered over them. There they stayed all morning, forcibly seated in six rows of a dozen or so, cross-legged. Soldiers remained on guard all around them, waving the bayonets on their rifles near to the prisoners' faces. The Khampas did not need telling that Major Duan was not to be trifled with. They all recalled a young shepherd in Jyeko market.

They were in shade, and without movement they became very cold. They were not permitted to speak a word and were given neither food nor water. A few of the men looked about them at the Chinese on the far side of the yard who were busily removing all clips of ammunition from the heap of rifles. But most of the captives hung their heads and studied the dirt in dejection. All spirit, and most bodily warmth, seeped from them into the ground.

'I'm still alive,' thought Jamie. He thought it over and over, because he badly needed convincing. 'I will not give up, not while I am alive and draw breath, I will not ...' Repetitive mantras of debilitated hope filled his head. He shivered, with increasing force. Try as he might, he could not prevent the shivers bashing about in every muscle.

Soldiers and officers came and went busily, strutting through the castle, disappearing through one doorway and reappearing from another. Above one long side of the yard hung a decrepit balcony of wood so weathered as to resemble pale grey bone. It seemed that the commanders were up there; he could see NCOs and junior officers clumping noisily along the old boards, saluting and entering through a door at the far end where two sentries stood. Jamie wondered if Duan was inside. And ... who else?

He glanced at the Chinese guards. It was puzzling: why were they removing every bullet so scrupulously, stacking the rifles neatly against the wall? Why not simply take the whole collection away? He noticed them indicating their prisoners, discussing some immediate practical issue. An NCO was pointing to a space below the wall opposite where a puny hint of sunlight touched the ground. Feeling dully sick, Jamie concluded that this was where they were to be lined up and shot.

He saw a soldier emerge from a doorway lugging two poles around which was wound a length of dirty off-white cloth. A screen of some sort, maybe. Two of his comrades followed, calling jokes to their friends, and now Jamie began to pay closer attention. One soldier carried a tripod, the other a black box with brass catches. A moment later, Jamie saw a cine camera fixed to the tripod and pointed in the direction of the sunlit wall.

Suddenly the Chinese soldiers began waving and gesticulating at the Tibetans, signing them to get to their feet. Glad to relieve their cold and stiffness, the Khampas rose, glancing warily at one another. As they did so, two soldiers went to the stack of rifles from which they had stripped all ammunition. They picked up two apiece and stepped smartly up to Agon, Dawa, Yonten and Tsering Norbu, handed over the weapons and pushed the recipients past the camera towards the wall.

'Go along now, warriors!' The soldiers laughed. 'The rest of you as well, move!'

Uncertain, the Khampas dithered in the centre of the yard, until the soldiers laughed again and beckoned impatiently to them. Jamie had stood up also but the soldiers waved him aside. More rifles were handed out, and the men were chivvied across to stand in front of the camera. There they stood, blinking into the cold sun.

A large group of Chinese had gathered to watch. Now there came a shouted order and these soldiers also picked up their rifles and came towards the Jyeko men. Yonten and Karjen hefted their guns in reflex, then blushed in frustrated shame at their helplessness. But the Chinese were not menacing them. The soldiers went among the Khampas, standing between them, smiling and laughing: 'Movie, movie! Tell the world!' A lieutenant stepped up to the camera and prepared to operate it, crouching and peering through the viewfinder at the fraternal gathering by the wall. Finally, two Chinese picked up the rolled cloth. They opened it out at the rear of the party, hoisting the banner above the heads:

REUNIFICATION WITH OUR BRAVE TIBETAN BROTHERS!

It was proclaimed in bold crude characters, English and Chinese.

Jamie saw the watching soldiers around the yard begin to applaud mockingly as the camera rolled. He saw the bemused Khampas frown and shrink as the soldiers among them placed arms about their shoulders, beaming at the camera. He saw Agon turn and peer uncomprehendingly at the banner over his head.

Suddenly, there was a shout of fury. The gathering of film stars swayed, staggered and broke apart. Jamie glimpsed an elbow sink into the stomach of a soldier who groaned and doubled. Arms reached, pushed, grabbed – and then Karjen burst from the cluster. Something in his hand flashed. His old legs boiled over with the last of their strength and he rushed at the lieutenant behind the camera who only then began to lift his head in surprise. He was just yards away – even old Karjen required only a second to reach and disembowel him with the bayonet he'd seized.

But he did not cross those few yards. A rifle shot crashed through the yard: a sergeant had fired from the hip. The bullet took Karjen full in the chest, knocking him down in a heap. His face crashed onto the stony floor of the yard, grazing and scraping. The sergeant fired a second time, more deliberately; Karjen kicked, then lay still. The bayonet clattered against the foot of the tripod where the lieutenant stood immobile.

For two seconds, no one moved. The gun's report sped echoing round the hills. The lieutenant gabbled a furious order; his men broke out of the group and moved away, turning to face the Tibetans with their rifles brought up in readiness. Nothing more happened. Karjen's friends and neighbours stared at him as he lay face down. A moment later, the Chinese propelled them at bayonet point back into the shade.

*

Karjen's corpse was taken outside; Jamie did not see how it was finally disposed of. But the two Khampas who were ordered to drag it out through the gate came back in great excitement. They had glimpsed the hamlet below the fortress and had seen the Jyeko caravan, all the non-combatants and the animals, halted just outside the cluster of houses.

A long, tedious time later, the Chinese soldiers called Jamie for interrogation.

'Wi-lih-soh! Wi-lih-soh!'

He stood wearily, two soldiers beckoning to him from a stone doorway. It occurred to him that he might feel frightened now: he hadn't forgotten the Jyeko crucifixion either. But increasingly a feeling had come upon him that was almost disembodiment: such was the cumulative effect of months of living so far beyond what he'd been born to. He had reached some sort of experiential saturation. It was a great mercy.

He walked stiffly to the archway through which the soldiers waved him towards a flight of stone stairs. Hands pushed at his shoulder and he went up the dark, dank steps, then out onto the wooden balcony. He was propelled quickly past an entrance covered by a rough woollen curtain, towards a second door at the far end. Momentarily, his way was blocked by the sentry's rifle across the door. He had a sudden recollection of a similar moment in Jyeko monastery, when delivering an invitation to ping-pong.

As he paused there, Jamie's eye was caught by someone emerging through the curtain that he had just passed. He looked round. Khenpo Nima had stepped out onto the balcony, going to the wooden rail to look down into the yard at the village men. Jamie heard a few puzzled calls from below: 'Reverence? Reverence?' At that moment, Khenpo Nima glanced aside and saw Jamie. Though their eyes met, neither spoke. Jamie had time only to register that Nima looked exhausted, haggard and grey.

A low voice spoke from the room before him, and Jamie was shoved inside.

*

'Really, Mr Wilson, you should have waited to hear our original instructions on your departure from Jyeko. It would have been a lot less trouble, don't you think?'

A month or two previously, Jamie would have wondered at Duan's ponderous sarcasm, at what it meant for him. Now he felt nothing more than dumb insolence.

'Aren't you talking to me today?' enquired the Major. 'Your position is hardly an enviable one, after all. I'd say you have good reason to be down on your knees.'

Jamie regarded him without expression.

'The beginning and end of it is, you are a spy.' Major Duan, seated on his folding canvas stool behind an ancient wooden chest, picked up a cardboard file and drew out a thick sheaf of papers. He flicked through them: 'But, really, a curiously incompetent spy.'

He tossed down onto the chest, one after another, Jamie's watercolour sketches and pen drawings of Jyeko: the market, yaks, temples ...

'I have to conclude, Mr Wilson, that you were never a terribly serious threat to the peaceful liberation of this country.'

'What will you do with the men outside?' said Jamie suddenly. 'And all the people?'

The Major frowned, as though giving the matter its first consideration. 'I expect that we shall send them back to their village,' he replied. 'This resistance has all been so futile. Why *did* they ever begin it? There was no call.'

'You can't send them back to their village,' said Jamie, 'because you've burned – '

'The future of those people, Mr Wilson, is none of your business,' snapped Duan, suddenly terse. Jamie fell silent. The Major continued: 'You will be leaving at once. My men will escort you to the border and hand you over there. You will be in India in a week.'

'What if I ask to stay?' began Jamie. 'I've a part in all this too – '

'Don't be absurd, Mr Wilson. Just go home. You are of no significance here.'

Duan swept up the pictures, tapped the pile straight and held them out. 'I expect you'd like to keep these as a souvenir of Tibet.'

Jamie took them. Then he said: 'May I ask for one other souvenir?'

Duan regarded him in surprise. 'What would that be?'

'That. The flower there, by your briefcase.' He pointed. It lay by the Major's papers: a single dried flower, a thin, desiccated stick with small spines on which a few petals hung, quite brown and crisp. The sort of stuff that, in armfuls, you might use as kindling for a fire.

Duan frowned slightly. 'Do you know what that is?' he asked.

'It was a poppy,' said Jamie. 'A blue poppy. They grow near here.'

'And why should you want it?'

'As I said: a souvenir.'

The Major picked up the flower and examined it, twiddling it between his fingers in such a manner that it might disintegrate at any moment. Then he presented it to Jamie. 'It's of no interest to me now. Farewell, Mr Wilson.'

*

On the balcony outside, Jamie was about to pass the middle door when he suddenly stopped, evaded his escort and pulled the curtain brusquely aside.

Within, the room was golden warm, lit by half a dozen butter-oil lamps, more like a shrine-room than a bedchamber. Four monks were seated on the floor in a semi-circle, spinning little prayer wheels and murmuring more prayers as fast as they could, so that the close air hummed as though with a swarm of bees. By the far wall was a couch covered with deep furs among which Jamie glimpsed the wasted face of the Abbot. At the head of the bed knelt Khenpo Nima, urging his master to drink a little from a wooden bowl. On a stool at the foot of the bed, another figure waited. As Jamie pulled the curtain aside, the head turned to see – and it was Puton.

For a split second, Jamie and Puton stared at each other. As though, once more, her reflexes raised her up to confront her fate, Puton began to stand. But there was no chance to speak. Jamie was seized by his guards and propelled along the balcony to the staircase before he could make a sound.

Dazed, he stumbled in the dark stairwell and slithered awkwardly against the wall, earning the guards' curses. The soldiers took his arm, marched him out into the light and across the yard. He was dimly aware of the Jyeko men who half stood to greet him, 'Mr Jemmy!' before their captors snarled at them to sit and shut up.

Jamie raised a trembling hand towards them, with a semblance of a grin on his numbed face. Then he was steered past.

He was taken through the gate, out into the cold bright day and onto the steep, pebble-strewn path that wound down to the village. If he'd not been held by both elbows, he would certainly have fallen. He was stunned, his eyes would not focus, and though his look passed over a brilliant winter spectacle, nothing of it reached his mind. It seemed to him that he had been taken by the throat and was being garrotted, the oxygen cut off. His head felt as though it would swell and burst. He staggered and stumbled, and was dragged. In this fashion, they reached the encampment below, where the rest of Jyeko sat in miserable apprehension.

The soldiers attempted to make him identify his belongings, to pick them up and strap them to a pony once again. But Jamie only sat on the ground with his legs sprawled askew, staring into some vacuum in front of his face. He was in the grip of something like apoplexy; mental and muscular control had fled from him. The Chinese gestured angrily to villagers nearby, and so the work of making Jamie ready for departure was done by others. The Chinese set about preparing their own mounts and pack animals. A group of six soldiers and two enforced guides from Kantu-Dzong village would be riding with him.

'One bag!' the guards shouted at Jamie. 'One bag only!' He barely registered that they were speaking to him, and he raised his head as slowly as if it were a hundredweight of lead.

'You hear me, Wi-lih-soh?' the sergeant shrieked, 'One bag!'

He turned to repeat the instruction to the cowed villagers who were bundling up Jamie's clothes. As the sergeant made to kick at the small heap, there came an electrifying snarl followed by furious baying. Hector leaped to his feet. The colossal dog, who had lain half hidden by the packsaddle, hurled imprecations at the Chinese NCO who stepped backwards in surprise and tumbled over a rolled saddlecloth on the ground. As the man sprawled among the pebbles in absurd indignity, a wave of grateful laughter swept over the crouching people.

'Shut up at once! Shut up!' roared the guards, flourishing their rifles impotently as their sergeant scrambled upright. Hector lay down by the saddle once more, mollified by this victory. Though the overt laughter subsided, the grins lingered on the Jyeko faces, some small fire restored. Through his misery, Jamie heard a murmur close by: 'Mr Jemmy, the Khampas are not afraid ...'

The preparations took no more than twenty minutes. Throughout this period, Jamie sat quite still and silent. Shortly before departure, he seemed to come to himself and stood up. The soldiers of the escort, busily lashing their own bedding rolls, gave him a suspicious glance but soon concluded that he was not going to run away. A few yards off, the nearest of the Jyeko villagers regarded him with more concern. Jamie did not return their mute enquiry. He looked up at the fort – and was jolted into wakefulness.

On the steep triple bend of the pathway, two figures were making their way downhill. They were coming as quickly as they could; for the child and the woman with her stick, there were many obstacles and difficulties. Still they came on, foolish in their haste, risking a tumble, almost down now.

'Wi-lih-soh!' called the sergeant of the escort. Jamie threw a quick look at him. The man waved towards the pony he was to ride. Jamie half raised his hand in vague acknowledgement. The two figures had reached the foot of the castle path. Jamie saw the wind catching the hair of both, tossing and tugging it across their faces. He saw the woman gripping the child's hand, the stick bouncing clumsily among the stones.

'Hey, Wi-lih-soh!' called the sergeant again, sharper,

pointing emphatically at the pony.

'Yes, yes,' replied Jamie, dithering, reaching for a bag on the ground by him, taking his coat off, pointlessly fiddling with a button, putting it on, taking it off again for no reason, prevaricating, buying time. He saw several of the villagers look past him: they had seen Puton, were watching the mother and child.

'Right, almost ready ... ' sang out Jamie, his attempt at fake cheery bustle sounding fragile. He picked up the bag and went to the pony ... but left the coat where he must return for it ...

'Come now!' ordered the sergeant.

'At once!' said Jamie, but he turned back yet again, leaving the sergeant speechless at his insolence.

She was standing twenty yards from him, holding Dechen by the hand. She did not speak, and he could not have answered. For a moment they only regarded each other in stillness, with the wind nudging them together. Then Puton freed her hand from her daughter's, and Jamie saw that together they had been holding something. Puton opened her fingers – and there was the little blue lacquered box from Bhutan. He had given it to Dechen; Karjen had chased her for it. There it sat in Puton's hand; she raised the box a fraction before him. In its tiny way it was the proudest clarion to memory. It was the only gesture left to her.

Jamie's reply came quite easily. He raised his two hands to his throat and unwound and rewrapped, slowly and ostentatiously, the embroidered red scarf that was tied there. The two ends, covered with their intricacies, he laid out on his chest so that she could see them: *T4JW*. Only when he saw the saddest trace of a smile from her did he fasten his coat over the scarf.

'All right, going to India,' said the sergeant, gripping his upper arm and pulling at him. Jamie backed towards the ponies.

'Mr Jemmy!' came a young woman's voice.

He'd heard no movement behind him – but when he looked, Jyeko was on its feet there. Drolma the young widow stood forward, holding up her smallest child. Jamie peered at her in surprise.

'Lord Buddha bless your journey,' said Drolma.

And behind her, they called out: 'Bless you, Mr Jemmy! Thank you! Remember us at your home!'

He went to his pony, nodding to them in tearful eagerness. But by nightfall he was gone into exile.

Already available from bookshops and the 11:9 website: www.11:9.co.uk

Hi Bonnybrig 1-903238-16-1
Shug Hanlan
'Imagine Kurt Vonnegut after one too many vodka and Irn Brus and you're halfway there.'
Sunday Herald

Rousseau Moon 1-903238-15-3
David Cameron
'The most interesting and promising debut for many years. [The prose has] a quality of verbal alchemy by which it transmutes the base matter of common experience into something like gold.'
Robert Nye, *The Scotsman*

The Tin Man 1-903238-11-0
Martin Shannon
'Funny and heartfelt, Shannon's is an uncommonly authentic voice that suggests an engaging new talent.'
The Guardian and *Guardian Unlimited*

Life Drawing 1-903238-13-7
Linda Cracknell
'*Life Drawing* brilliantly illuminates the contradictions of its narrator's self image ... Linda Cracknell brings female experience hauntingly to life.'
The Scotsman

Occasional Demons 1-903238-12-9
Raymond Soltysek
'a bruising collection ... Potent, seductive, darkly amusing tales that leave you exhausted by their very intensity.'
Sunday Herald

The Wolfclaw Chronicles 1-903238-10-2
Tom Bryan
'Tom Bryan's pedigree as a poet and all round littérateur shines through in *The Wolfclaw Chronicles* – while reading this his first novel you constantly sense a steady hand on the tiller ... a playful and empassioned novel.'
The Scotsman

The Dark Ship
Anne MacLeod
This vast literary saga celebrates love, music and poetry in a finely woven s
that reflects the complex past of a community on a Scottish island.
1-903238-27-7
£9.99

Dead Letter House
Drew Campbell
Suspend your disbelief for a bizarre trip into the surreal. On a twenty mile walk
home a young man explores time and space and discovers his own heaven and hell.
1-903238-29-3
£7.99

The Gravy Star
Hamish MacDonald
One man's hike from post-industrial urban sprawl to lost love and a burnt-out
rural idyll.
'A moving and often funny portrait ... of the profound relationship between
Glasgow and the wild land to its north.' James Robertson, author of *The Fanatic*.
1-903238-26-9
£9.99

Strange Faith
Graeme Williamson
This haunting novel tells the story of a young man torn between past allegiances
and the promise of a new life.
'Calmly compelling, strangely engaging.' Dilys Rose
1-903238-28-5
£9.99

About 11:9

Supported by the Scottish Arts Council National Lottery Fund and partnership
funding, 11:9 publish the work of writers both unknown and established, living and
working in Scotland or from a Scottish background.
11:9's brief is to publish contemporary literary novels, and is actively searching for
new talent. If you wish to submit work send an introductory letter, a brief synopsis
of your novel, a biographical note about yourself and two typed sample chapters to:
Editorial Administrator, 11:9, Neil Wilson Publishing Ltd, Suite 303a, The Pentagon
Centre, 36 Washington Street, Glasgow, G3 8AZ. Details are also available from our
website at **www.11-9.co.uk.**

If you would like to be added to a mailing list about future publications, either
register on our website or send your name and address to 11:9, Neil Wilson
Publishing Ltd, Suite 303a, The Pentagon Centre, 36 Washington Street, Glasgow, G3
8AZ.